A N‌⋯ of Red

Jennie Alexander

www.JennieAlexander.biz

JennieAlexander@hotmail.co.uk

For Dad, I miss sharing a glass of red with you…..

Chapter 1

Winnifred Mayhew clicked off her phone and returned to the living room, smiling to herself and shaking her head as she sank back down onto the over-sized squashy sofa.

Doug looked up from where he was crouching at the wood-burning stove.

'Thought I'd get the fire going, there's a bitter wind out there this evening.'

'Yes, good idea.'

'And I poured you a nice glass of red – thought you might need it.'

'Mm, lovely.' Winnifred took a sip and replaced the glass on the table, recognising immediately the full-bodied Cabernet Sauvignon, savouring its dark fruit flavours and herbal notes.

Doug looked over at his wife as she leant back, eyes closed, contented, still smiling.

'I take it, it was a good call? And what are you grinning at?' He sat down heavily in his armchair right next to the fireplace, pleased with his efforts to get the fire going, and cradled his whisky glass in both hands, full attention now on his wife.

'Oh, they just make me laugh that's all. I've been meeting up with my friends from work every six months, for what is it, over twenty years? And, I swear, for the last ten we've done exactly the same thing. It's so frustrating.'

'And why's that a problem now? I'd say it's amazing you agree on doing something you all enjoy.'

'Well, that's just it; it would be nice to do something different for a change. I think it's got to the point where no-one likes to suggest anything new. We're probably all sitting there hating pizza and pasta with a passion!'

'Why don't you suggest something?'

'I did. I was talking with Esther just then – it's her turn to organise the evening. I recommended the new Thai restaurant in town, but after a few seconds of stunned silence, I backed down and suggested a good old Chinese meal. Thought we could share a buffet and all use chopsticks – it would be fun. My god, you'd think I'd suggested a strip club in Vegas!'

Doug laughed, the last of his whisky sloshing in the glass held close to his slightly rounded belly.

'But actually, it is quite ridiculous. It'll be exactly the same as ever. We'll go to the same place, meet at the same time, eat, drink and even leave at the same time. Sue will go on about calories and carbohydrates, Fran will take fifteen minutes to decide and then end up with the same pasta dish she always has. Mary, bless her, will do the same and then drink a few too many glasses of wine and end up getting tearful.'

Doug smiled and without comment got up to replenish his glass then sat down next to Winnifred on the sofa and placed his hand over hers in her lap.

'What's this all about? Really? Why is all this silliness suddenly bothering you? I mean, take poor Mary - how often does she get to go out? That bugger of a husband never takes her anywhere, he's too busy drinking the house dry. Can you honestly blame her for making the most of it when she gets a chance?'

'Oh god, yes, poor Mary; she looked awful last time. Not well at all.'

'Honestly Love, a night out with you lot once every six months is probably the extent of her social life. And you begrudge her always choosing her favourite meal of spaghetti carbonara?'

'How do you know she always has spaghetti carbonara?'

Doug shook his head, the sofa jiggling with his heavy laughter.

'I didn't know. It was just a lucky guess.'

Winnifred freed her hand from his and reached over for her glass of wine, giving him a sideways look, one of her mock-disapproving frowns, trying not to laugh herself.

'Ah, come on Winnie, you'll still have a good time. And that's what it's all about. Sometimes it's the routine and the sameness of things – familiarity I suppose that bring us comfort – security.'

'Hm, maybe. Don't mind me, I love them all really.' Winnie gazed into the wood-burning stove at the flames flickering inside. Doug usually had a good way of summing things up.

Since their two daughters had left home quite a few years ago now, their lives had fallen into a very solid routine which seldom varied. And although they enjoyed their comfortable life, in this instant, it irked her to realise that perhaps she wasn't so different from her friends after all.

'I was looking at online courses today, in my lunch hour.'

'Hm.' Doug had returned to his chair by the fire.

'Oenology – the study of wine. The advanced course. I'm going to register for it.'

'You've been saying that for ages.'

'Yes, I know. But finally, I'm really going to do it.'

'Good. About time. Go for it.'

It was a little white lie; Winnie hadn't been looking at online courses in her lunch hour at all. She intended to, almost every day, but once inside the work canteen she usually got chatting with someone over a quick bite to eat and the time just disappeared.

But by saying it out loud to Doug, it felt just that little bit closer to reality. And predictably, she felt guilty for lying to him, knowing it would spur her on to make it the truth – tomorrow. Having already completed the basic oenology course a couple of years ago, she would enrol for the advanced course tomorrow for definite.

And maybe in a few weeks' time when she met up with her friends again, she'd be able to offer expert advice on their choice of wine – even if it was at the same old Italian restaurant.

Chapter 2

December

'Hellooo, I'm home - early for a change.' Doug called out as he banged the back door shut, bolting it against the gusting wind of a dark autumn evening.

'Winnie? Only me, Love.' He hung up his coat and flipped off his shoes. The compact boot room was warm and snug with its tiny radiator providing the first defence against the elements. Beyond this point it was a constant battle to heat the big, old, draughty house.

Doug stepped into his slippers, warming underneath the radiator. This is where the dog basket would go one day – he and Winnie had talked about it often. Doug smiled; if the pooch had any sense, they'd have a difficult job ever getting him to leave this cosy little spot.

Through into the hallway, Doug immediately registered the drop in temperature, and it was always worse when the wind was howling like tonight.

His meeting with a new client had finished early and with the forecast of heavy rain and possible sleet, he'd decided to get off home and miss the worst of the rush hour traffic.

He was sure Winnie was starting a new shift at the hospital today, meaning she should have been home since mid-afternoon.

'Freddie? Where are you, Love?'

Freddie was Doug's pet name for his wife of over thirty years. When he'd first met her as a petite twenty-year-old studying to be a midwife, he thought her so unlike a 'Winnifred', he'd immediately come up with something cuter that suited his young love much better.

But she was Winnie to just about everyone else. And now, at the age of fifty-eight, she was a confident and stylish woman, a senior midwife with a long and successful career behind her, as well as mother to their two wonderful daughters. She wasn't 'Freddie' in public anymore, it was just between the two of them, and he loved that she never attempted to correct him or make him use her proper name.

'Doug? Is that you?'

'Yes. Why, were you expecting someone else?'

He glanced up from the hallway to see Winnie peering down from the landing. She grinned at him.

'Well, actually, Bob was going to nip over and give me a cranial massage.'

'I bet he was!' They laughed out loud.

'I'm just finishing my studying; I'll be down in a sec and make some tea.'

'Sod the tea! I need something stronger than that – it's horrid out there.'

Doug took two heavy crystal glasses from the kitchen display cabinet and went through to the living room. He poured a generous measure of whisky into each and placed the glasses on their respective coasters on the coffee table and immediately set to, building a fire in the wood-burner. This was his job.

As he waited for the flames to catch, he looked up and noticed the box of Christmas decorations in the corner of the room, and then Winnie appeared with a huge, tangled mess of fairy lights in her arms and plonked them on top of the box. 'I was in the attic earlier; thought I'd bring this lot down.'

'I'd have got them down for you.'

'I don't think you'd fit through the hatch, with that belly!'

Doug cringed. 'Hm, I know. After Christmas, I'll do something about it.'

'Ah, I love you, just the way you are.' She placed her hands on her husband's shoulders as he crouched, carefully selecting logs, and planted a kiss on the crown of his head.

'It's torrential rain out there, sounds like a hailstorm now,' she said.

'Tell me about it. It's a ghastly evening.'

'You got away early?'

'Yeah, was a good meeting, wrapped up quicker than I thought. Nice bloke, knows what he wants – makes my job a lot easier. We'll get some preliminary drawings out to him and hopefully go from there. Thought I'd miss the worst of the traffic and get home early for a change.'

'What does he want you to do?'

'A luxury family home.' Doug raised his eyebrows. 'Architectural services and project manage the whole lot. Could be good.'

Doug headed up a small architectural practice. He had a good loyal staff with a wealth of experience, but the size of the company often prevented them from getting a look in at the bigger projects even though he knew they were capable.

He'd designed dozens of houses over the past few decades, and he often commented on how times and people's tastes had changed. Now they all wanted eco-friendly, everything sustainable, luxury bespoke design but the sticking point was always the cost of the invisible services behind the scenes that made all these things possible.

'Anyway, how was your day? All OK?' he asked as he plonked himself down in his chair. He was weary, sighed deeply, and rubbed the back of his neck, and then glanced across to Winnie who was staring absently into the fire.

'Yeah, you know, fine really.'

'You're miles away. Everything alright?'

'Well, actually I'm not sure. I was looking through our pension paperwork earlier. It's not great, is it?'

Winnie looked up at her husband, a concerned look on her face.

Doug was visibly taken aback; this was completely out of the blue. 'Oh, well, I think we're OK. But, yes actually, it's something I've been meaning to do for ages; you know, go over everything and review exactly where we are. Hey, don't look so worried, we're doing alright, both got solid jobs. And anyway, we've got a while yet to work on things if we need to.'

He pulled a mock grimace to make her laugh, but it didn't quite do the trick. Winnie gave a little smile instead and decided not to mention the rumours at the hospital about impending redundancies.

'I don't want us to work forever Doug. I like my job, you know I do, but I'm looking forward to a time when things are different. I'm looking forward to the next chapter in our lives and I don't want to think it's too far off.'

She reached over for the glass of whisky and took an over-large gulp that caught in her throat and made her cough. She shuddered and replaced the glass. She'd tried to get to like whisky for Doug's sake, to share his pleasure, but she'd only just about managed to get used to it, just.

Now it was Doug's turn to stare into the fire, his brow furrowed. 'You've got me thinking now.'

'I know what you're going to say; I'm probably just worrying about nothing. It's just that a statement came in the post this morning for my pension plan and then I started looking at the rest of things.'

'No, no, it's not nothing. You're absolutely right, we do need to keep on top – this is important. At the weekend, I'll go over all the paperwork. I promise.'

Winnie physically relaxed and felt her shoulders loosen, all helped by the growing warmth of the fire. They simultaneously reached for their glasses, chinking them together gently before taking a sip, their smiling eyes locked together, all tension immediately dissipated.

'Anyway, when we are finally retired, do you know what I'm looking forward to the most?'

'Go on, tell me.'

'More than anything, I'm looking forward to us heading off to the vineyards in the south of France, doing the wine tours, tasting all the wines of the region – becoming experts.'

Doug laughed out loud. 'Count me out!'

'What do you mean? It'll be lovely; touring around from one pretty village to the next. We can take the car, bring back some cases of our favourites.'

'No way, not for me.'

'You're joking me. This is something I've always wanted to do; wanted *us* to do. You know that. What do you think I'm doing the oenology course for?'

'I think it's always been more your dream than mine. OK, well maybe we could, we'll see, but then you've got to take me on a tour of the distilleries – all over Scotland!'

Winnie smiled but Doug looked thoughtful.

'Seriously though Love, you'll be retired a good few years before me. You need to think about what you want to do – for yourself.'

'Well, I'm not going around France on my own, that's for sure. And anyway, it won't be that much longer. I'm looking forward to us doing things together, that's what we've been working for isn't it? Winnie laughed; a small nervous-sounding laugh.

'Well, yes, of course. But if you think about it, we've both worked full time all these years, that and bringing up the girls. It wouldn't suddenly suit us to be joined at the hip 24/7.

Winnie was momentarily flummoxed. For a second, she didn't know what to say. Doug quickly filled the silence.

'All I mean is, it's still a while off before I retire, so don't wait for me. None of us know what's around the corner; I could get run over by a bus next week!'

'Oh Doug, don't say things like that.'

'Listen, you know exactly what I mean. Just give it some thought, make some plans otherwise, well, I'm just saying, there's more to life than having a clean and tidy house. You don't want to spend all your time doing that. You could meet up with your friends more often, stay out late, go clubbing, knowing you haven't got to get up at the crack of dawn for work.'

'Clubbing! Don't be ridiculous. I've still got to coax them away from the Italian restaurant. Anyway, I've got things I want to do.'

'Good. Do them. I tell ya, when I'm retired there'll be no stopping me. I'm going to pursue my passion for fly-fishing for one thing.'

'I didn't know you had a passion for fly-fishing.'

'Exactly. I don't – yet. But I want one. And then I'm going to learn to sail – a life-time's ambition that is.'

'You might want to learn to swim first!' she said sardonically, one eyebrow raised, a little uncomfortable at the direction of this conversation.

'Yes, maybe that too.'

'And I'm going to take my bike for one of those famous rides across Europe – maybe the Danube bike trail.'

'But I don't like cycling.'

Doug didn't answer. He looked down into the dregs at the bottom of his glass, as if he'd suddenly run out of steam.

11

'Drink up, I'll pour us another.'

'Not for me. I'll have a nice glass of red instead. There's an opened bottle on the side.'

Doug disappeared into the kitchen leaving Winnie thinking about what he'd been saying. Maybe he had a point, although it was a slightly unsettling thought. They'd been a couple for so long, and in snatches of spare time they'd always done everything together. When she retired in a few years, it would feel very odd to suddenly have so much time to herself – alone. And she couldn't even begin to think what she would do with herself. Not without Doug anyway, it was almost unimaginable.

She fidgeted on the sofa trying to get comfortable and suddenly had the inspired idea of delaying her retirement and staying on at work for a few more years. Then they could retire together - that would work out much better.

And she was sure that by then she would have managed to warm him to the whole idea of touring the vineyards. Maybe they'd even be able to afford a little holiday place in the south of France, so they could visit more often.

Anyway, it was much more plausible than her husband ever getting into a sailing boat. Winnie smiled to herself, feeling suitably reassured. They'd work it out, they always did. She snuggled into the sofa, tucking a cushion behind her back and a throw over her legs. The growing flames flickered in the wood-burner giving off more heat now as she waited for Doug to come back with her glass of wine.

Chapter 3

January

Winnifred unlocked the back door and stepped into the boot room, it was dark and cold. She switched on the light and then the central heating, hung her coat on the hook next to Doug's, eased her boots off, and momentarily gazed at the allotted space where the dog basket was supposed to go one day.

In the icy cold living room, she switched on a single lamp and sat down in Doug's chair next to the wood-burner, staring into its emptiness.

The plan was to stay here a while. This had become her daily ritual.

It was eight-thirty and although she'd finished her shift at the hospital two hours ago, the additional couple of hours overtime meant a little extra to put away for 'one day'. And working was mildly better than coming home to a cold and empty house.

Her phone beeped from inside her handbag to signal she had another message. She fished it out, knowing already what she would find, and she was right. There were two missed calls - one from each of her daughters. They phoned every day, both meaning well even though they had very opposing tactics for keeping their mum from going under.

Winnie placed her phone on the coffee table planning to call them back in a while, or maybe she'd just send them a text message. She was struggling tonight to psyche up for the 'brave face' performance.

They were probably each going to invite her over for the weekend, and she needed to concoct an answer that would decline without causing them to worry. She just didn't have the energy for family company this weekend.

Sighing deeply, she shivered and pulled a throw from the back of the chair, draping it over her knees and hooking it under her feet on the floor. She closed her eyes, dropping her chin to her chest, hoping sleep would come and take care of another couple of hours – a couple of hours when she didn't have to think.

It was only thirty minutes later when her phone rang again, waking her with a jolt. She glanced at the screen to see it was Gloria on the other end.

Winnie smiled, lovely Gloria. She phoned often – not predictably, not every day, but reliably enough to make her comforting presence felt.

Winnie took the call, knowing she wouldn't need to bother with her 'brave face' – Gloria had been widowed before, she knew exactly where Winnie was right now.

'Hello Gloria. How are you?'

'I'm good. Just been chopping some logs. Wow, it's bitter out there. Good way to warm up though! How's your Friday evening?'

Winnie smiled. She didn't know many women in their seventies who went out on a bleak winter's evening to chop wood.

'Oh, you know, it's fine. I only got in from work a little while ago. There's a lot of sickness; very short staffed.'

Gloria knew her friend was working extra hours, as much as anything, to avoid going home. 'And otherwise, everything OK?'

'Yeah, well, you know. Not a great evening tonight.'

'One of those?'

'Mm, I'm afraid so.'

'It's still early days Wynne.'

'Yep, six weeks, five days. And it still doesn't seem real. I still can't believe he's gone.'

'Shall I come over?' Gloria asked gently.

It took Winnie a second or two to realise she was nodding into the phone, unable to speak.

'Wynne, are you there?'

Gloria could hear Winnie sniffing and trying to speak, unable to clear her throat.

'OK, don't worry, just hang up. I'm on my way. I'll be there as soon as I can.'

Winnie remained where she was in Doug's favourite armchair, the phone in her lap and tears free flowing until they pooled into a wet patch on the blanket. For over twenty years she'd been intimately involved in bringing new lives into the world – but she couldn't deal with the other side of the coin.

She stayed there until she heard Gloria rapping on the back door, getting up quickly having managed to compose herself slightly. She'd stopped crying and was dabbing her face dry as she unlocked the door. Gloria stepped inside and rubbed Winnie's shoulder – a simple gesture that didn't need any accompanying words.

She followed Winnie through to the kitchen; a huge family room that seemed bigger every time she visited lately – it seemed to expand with emptiness.

Winnie made coffee and placed the mugs on the big round table in the middle of the room - the scene of many family dinners past. Still in silence, they scraped their chairs back over the flagstone floor and sat down.

Winnie sighed, shuddering slightly as she sat. Gloria placed her hand over her friend's and gave a brief squeeze, waiting patiently for her to speak whenever she was ready.

Finally, Winnie looked up into her friend's kind face, a sad, resigned smile on her own.

'You'll never guess what's happened now. I've been made redundant. Brilliant timing, eh?'

'Oh Winnie, no.' Gloria couldn't keep the shock from her voice. The consequences of Winnie losing her job right now were too cruel to even think about.

'I can believe they've done that to you. You've only just returned to work. The bastards!'

Winnie smiled feebly, grateful for the support.

'It's not personal, is it? That's what I keep trying to tell myself.'

'Even so. They could have given you a bit more time.'

'It wasn't a complete shock; there have been rumours for ages. But then, there are always rumours.'

Winnie stared down at her hands resting on the table, she fiddled with her wedding ring, the look on her face confirming her sense of absolute defeat.

Gloria sat calmly, hoping to be inspired with something useful to say. The obvious suggestion was to start looking for other jobs, but Winnie was a senior midwife, she was at the top of her profession, and more importantly she'd worked at the same hospital for over twenty years. She had dozens of friends there, had accumulated respect on all levels, and lately she'd been spending almost more time there than at home. To pull Winnie away from all that would be an unbearable wrench right now.

The silence between them was almost tangible. Winnie raised her face and met Gloria's, her look saying it all.

'Is it definite?' Gloria clung to the smallest of hope.

Winnie nodded. I've known for a little while the announcements were coming. I tried to ignore it. They call it being in denial, don't they? That was me; in absolute denial.'

'When does it happen?'

'I leave at the end of next month. They like to wrap these things up pretty quickly.'

Gloria looked shocked, and suddenly shivered. 'Crikey, it's cold in here Winnie.' But Winnie was already miles away.

'Winnie, come on, let's go through to the living room and we'll get a fire going.'

Gloria could hear the hum of the central heating, but the house had that bitter chill to it, typical of a big old place that's been empty all day. She'd have to encourage Winnie to use the timing facility to take the edge off and start warming the place before she got in from work. At least for the few weeks she had left at work.

She led the way out of the kitchen and across the hallway, the wind gusting and whistling, shaking the front door.

'It's a wicked night out there,' she said as they entered the living room, closing the door on the penetrating drafts.

'OK, you sort the fire out Wynne, and I'll have a look at what we've got over here.'

Gloria was at the drinks cabinet. She took two glasses and a half bottle of what she knew to be an expensive bottle of brandy.

'Mm, this will do perfectly I think.'

Winnie was standing looking helpless next to the wood burner. She'd managed to do without so far.

'I don't know how to light the fire. Doug always did it.'

'Of course you do. You must have watched him hundreds of times. Come on Wynne, have a go. It's freezing in here.'

Gloria could see the sentimental look on her friend's face, as if to take over Doug's job of lighting the fire would be something of disrespect to him and of course further acknowledgement that she had to find ways to manage without him.

More gently now, Gloria offered a little encouragement. 'That's it, you do the fire and I'll pour us a couple of these. We could do with a little heat on the inside too.'

Winnie crouched down on her knees and opened the door of the stove, peering inside its emptiness. She used to sweep it out every evening when she got in from work on the shifts when she was home first, ready for Doug to build a fire as soon as he arrived home.

She used to like watching him and the methodical way he worked. She would laugh as he explained to her many times what he was doing and why – as if he were presenting a fire-building training course.

She hadn't been able to bring herself to take over his job before now. But she had to admit this evening had to be the coldest this winter and it would take an age for the heating to truly begin warming the place. The house was icy cold, uncomfortable and unwelcoming, and she wanted Gloria to stay.

Automatically, she stacked some kindling and then placed some logs on top, exactly how Doug used to. She lit the match and popped in some firelighters, and within seconds the golden flames were dancing brightly, heat radiating immediately.

Winnie sat in Doug's chair and looked across at Gloria, a slight almost imperceptible smile seemed to say that she was pleased with herself and maybe it wasn't so painful doing one of Doug's little jobs after all. He'd taught her well.

Gloria gave a little nod – an intuitive acknowledgement of all that.

She'd poured a generous measure of brandy for each of them, picked up her glass and nodded at Winnie to do the same.

Gloria took a tentative sip, gin being her usual tipple of choice.

'Ooh, that's nice. Your Doug, he knew how to pick good spirits, didn't he?'

Winnie smiled, remembering. 'Yes, he knew what he liked.'

A few moments silence while they both sipped. A companionable quietness during which Gloria deduced she'd very likely be staying the night.

Winnie gazed into the fire for some time.

'What do you see in the flames there?' Gloria asked gently, almost whispering.

Winnie smiled at her old friend who knew exactly how to read her. Whatever look was on her face, her tone of voice, laughing eyes or sad smiles – she couldn't hide anything from Gloria. Not that she ever wanted to; there never was such a non-judgemental, affectionate, life-loving soul as Gloria.

Winnie shook her head, almost unable to speak. 'I don't know,' she whispered. 'A lifetime of memories, wonderful memories, our hopes and dreams. And dreams we had, that won't come true now.'

Winnie took a slug of brandy, tossing it down her throat, gulping it and her tears deep down inside.

Gloria sipped her drink and let the moment pass.

'Don't be too hard on yourself Wynne. It will take time. It's such a cliché but you know yourself, how Doug would have wanted you to get on with your life.'

Winnie gazed down into her drink. 'He was my life,' she whispered. 'I miss him so much.'

'I know Dear.'

'I know I'm lucky; the girls have been great. And you've been great. I've got lots of good friends – from work mostly. Lots of people to do things with. But, you know, it's the odd times that catch me out, when I feel so lonely. The evenings, like now, if you weren't here, I wouldn't want to go to bed, that big so empty bed on my own. And I just sit here. It might sound silly but it's all very well keeping busy - I know how to keep myself busy, but I miss having him here, just around, you know. He was my someone to do nothing with.'

'Yes, I do know.'

Winnie nodded. Of course Gloria knew.

'How long have you been on your own now?'

'Four years almost.'

'And how have you managed? You've been through this three times. And you're still so full of life. And positive about life.'

'Oh, I don't know Wynne. I'm not always Mrs Chirpy! There's no manual, no one-size-fits-all instruction sheet. Everyone just has to find their own way. You get up in the morning, you make your bed, and you put one foot in front of the other. And gradually it gets easier.'

Winnie gave her a doubtful look.

'Yes, it does. It gets easier. I promise you.'

Winnie suddenly moved to the edge of her seat, put her glass on the table and put her head in her hands. 'Oh god, it's all so confusing. Sometimes I even feel angry with him. How awful is that?'

Gloria got up and squeezed in close next to Winnie on the armchair. She placed an arm gently around her shoulders, feeling the quiet sobs underneath her touch.

'He's left everything in such a mess,' she whispered, so quietly it was as if she hardly dared say the words out loud.

'How do you mean? Winnie?'

'We'd been talking about sorting our finances, looking at our pension plans and everything. I knew it didn't look good. I couldn't believe at the time that Doug could have let things slip to such an extent. He always looked after things like that. He said he'd take a look at it. But, as I know now, it was too late.'

Winnie met Gloria's eyes, ashamed of the bitterness in her voice. 'I can't help it Glo. I get so angry with him sometimes. I don't know how I'm going to manage. And now I'm without a job, I don't know what I'm going to do. I get angry and I blame Doug for everything, and then I feel just awful.'

'It's OK to feel angry. It's OK to feel whatever it is you're feeling. There's no right or wrong.'

'But it feels so wrong.' Winnie looked up, retrieving a tissue from her sleeve and wiping her eyes, an automatic movement.

Gloria held her dear friend as she sobbed, shaking wretchedly in her arms. They sat in silence, Winnie leaning into Gloria's shoulder absorbing the love and comfort there. Gloria gazed past her into the fire which was flaming furiously now as she wondered what on earth she could do to help her friend.

Chapter 4

Zoe Thomas wandered into her kitchen. It was modern, minimalist, with black granite worktops and lots of white space, almost stark except for the strategically placed pot-plants, interior designer chosen for their luminescent lime green foliage.

She ran her hand along the smooth cool surface of the worktop, often a little lost at this time of day. She frowned at the idea that the kitchen is traditionally supposed to be the heart of the home. That had never been the case in her childhood home. The kitchen there had mostly been the setting for endless arguments between her mum and dad, one or other of them threatening to leave and never come back.

She smiled wryly at the irony, and then glanced around her own kitchen – had she, with the help of a very expensive designer, managed to make this the heart of their home? She had no idea.

Zoe glanced up at the oversized wall clock which brought a much happier smile to her face. The huge clock took up a whole wall with its six-inch roman numerals and three-foot-long hands – seven o'clock. Wine o'clock.

But where the hell was Lawrence?

Her mobile rang.

'Hi Hon, it's me.'

'Where are you?'

'I'm stuck. Still at King's Cross. My train's delayed.'

'Honestly? Again? How long until you're home?'

'I know, it's a pain in the ass. Should be home within the hour.'

'OK, I'll get the glasses ready.' Zoe laughed, but it didn't ease the tension she felt.

'Yeah OK. Wait for me, eh?'

'Yes, of course. See you soon. Hurry home.'

Fine crystal glasses were already placed on the worktop waiting in anticipation. For no good reason, Zoe opened the wine fridge and stood gazing at the multitude of bottles; whites, rosés, and champagnes of various vintages.

Lawrence was the wine buff; he knew what he liked but he liked trying new things too. Zoe never quite understood that. Stick to what you like was her motto. Minimise the risk of disappointment. But then again, she couldn't actually recall having a wine she didn't like.

She giggled aloud, thinking - perhaps I'm just a wine tart. I'm easy, me – I'll drink anything.

She tried to remember what Lawrence said about different vintages, and grape varieties and the terroir – whatever that was. She tried to remember to swish the glass and have a good sniff before she drank but really, it didn't make any difference to her. It all tasted good. Very good. And that was good enough for her.

So, Lawrence should be home within the hour although she knew from experience it could be a lot longer. At this moment an hour felt like a very long time, and now as her phone beeped through a text message, she knew even before she read it, that it would confirm he hadn't even boarded his train for home yet. She read the message. She was right.

With a big, bored sigh, Zoe lifted out a bottle from the top shelf of the fridge – these were Lawrence's favourites. She read the label – Grüner Veltliner – Austrian. She put the bottle back for now, but as Lawrence could sometimes be a little grumpy when he got in late from work, she decided to open it for him as a treat but not until she heard the automatic garage door open, signalling Lawrence was home and putting his motorbike away.

She then lifted out a bottle of supermarket standard Pinot Grigio and placed it on the worktop and without giving herself time to think otherwise, she broke the seal on the screw top and poured herself a glass. Just one, she promised, to keep her going until Lawrence got home.

That one glass lasted well as she tried to busy herself around the house, trying on the new shoes she'd bought last week, flicking through magazines and making a mental note to empty the dishwasher – she always forgot to do that, and it drove Lawrence mad, she knew, even though he never said anything.

The second glass of Pinot quickly became the third and then with over half the bottle gone, and Lawrence still not home, she felt perfectly justified in finishing the bottle. She alternated between feeling totally irritated with him for being so late, and an affectionate longing for him just to walk in the door.

She picked up the bottle to pour another glass, and was irritated with that too, for being empty. Looking up at the clock, she wondered, with a slightly wobbly head, why wine never seemed to last as long these days. Perhaps those sneaky winemakers were producing bottles with thicker glass so they could put less wine in each one. That was definitely it, she reasoned. Money. Everything was always about money.

'But money doesn't make you happy' she said aloud, surprised at the sound of her own voice, and wondering, not for the first time, if she was going mad.

'Talking to yourself is the first sign of madness,' she whispered.

With the empty bottle still in her hand, she debated going outside to put it in the already jangling recycling bin. But that ever-growing stash of bottles was so accusatory. She could just imagine Lawrence's disapproving look.

And anyway, she had a clever little trick up her sleeve - she simply placed it in the kitchen bin, tucking it under some paper towel and then placing the local newspaper on top. No-one ever read it anyway. She returned to it a third time to ensure it was well hidden, out of sight.

Finally, Zoe heard her phone beep with a text from Lawrence saying he'd arrived at their local train station, and just a few minutes later she heard the garage door open, her husband's pride and joy purring gently, powerfully, in the background.

She sucked the last drops of wine from her glass and dashed to the kitchen, uncorking the bottle she'd chosen earlier and pouring two glasses full – even though she knew Lawrence preferred just a small taster at a time.

As he turned his key in the lock, she was already in the hallway, her cheeks rosy and eyes ever so bright but also slightly glazed over.

'Hey! Home at last – that's good timing, I just poured these. Here you go,' she said indicating his glass in her hand as she sashayed into the living room back to her place on the sofa.

Lawrence closed the front door gently, as yet unspoken, but his eyes watching, knowing. He dropped his heavy backpack to the floor and followed her slightly unsteady gait and sat down next to her, slowly lowering himself down, tired and weary.

'This is very nice,' Zoe chirped. Her glass hadn't yet left her hand. 'It's the, let me think, the Grüner Veltliner – if that's how you pronounce it. From, where was it? Oh yes, Austria. That's the one. Go on try some.'

'I will. Give me a minute.' Lawrence groaned inwardly. This bottle had been a present from his boss as appreciation for him bringing a particularly important project in on time. They'd worked together for many years and were good friends; it was a heartfelt gift, and that bottle would have cost in the region of thirty pounds. He'd been saving it for something special.

'Go on, try some,' Zoe insisted.

Lawrence looked across at her, scorning her for not appreciating the difference between it and the cheapest plonk, and then immediately hating himself for the thought. He dutifully took a sip and replaced his glass back on the table and then put his hand on Zoe's knee, squeezing affectionately, smiling at her flushed face, wondering, not for the first time, what was really going on behind those bleary eyes of hers.

She attempted to smile back but it was more of a silly grin, too many teeth on show, too much effort to bely the fact she couldn't think of anything to say.

Which was unfortunate as Lawrence would have liked to talk, just about general stuff, about his day which had been particularly challenging even before the nightmare journey to get home.

He picked up his glass again and took a larger sip, nodding at this wife who was still grinning into her glass – there'd be no meaningful conversation tonight – about work or anything else.

Lawrence was about to ask if she'd organised anything for dinner, but the absence of any cooking smells told him what he needed to know and from a strange sense of loyalty he didn't want to make her feel bad, so he said nothing. He went through to the kitchen and pulled open the fridge door.

The pack of raw jumbo prawns had defrosted and if he'd been home on time, he'd have made a Thai coconut curry for dinner.

Zoe didn't really cook these days; she wasn't that particular about what or when she ate and at times wouldn't even bother to.

Lawrence took a lump of cheese and a jar of pickle to make himself a sandwich. He made to return to the living room but changed his mind and sat at the kitchen island to eat instead, preferring to be alone. Again. He noticed the dishwasher still full and wondered why the hell she never thought to unload it. He'd see to it in a minute; he hated rummaging around for a clean mug first thing in the morning.

His sandwich was tasteless, and he didn't have much of an appetite anyway. He threw the remains in the bin, noticing the strategically placed local newspaper on top, knowing full well there was an empty wine bottle hidden away underneath. It was an old trick by now.

It was 6:30am and Lawrence was already in the shower. His morning routine was a well-practiced precision timetable of habits he followed on autopilot, no need to even think about it.

It got him out the door by 6:55 am precisely and off on his motorbike in time to catch the 7:15 to London. He'd be in work, cool and relaxed well before 8:30, settled at his desk, enjoying a coffee as he watched his colleagues arriving – at two minutes to nine, two minutes past nine, ten minutes past – red-faced, flustered, already wrong-footed even before the long day had begun.

Lawrence came out of their ensuite bathroom, a short towel around his waist, his wet hair still sticking up in a spikey do.

He looked over at the bed where Zoe was still sleeping. He wasn't sure if she'd moved at all, all night.

He opened the top drawer of the large chest and took out shorts and socks, and for some reason, before he could stop himself, he slammed it shut, shaking the collection of glass bottles and even the mirror on top.

Instinctively he looked over at Zoe who was finally stirring. She twisted around and poked her head from the duvet, her hair tousled, her eyes barely able to focus.

'What was that? That noise?'

Lawrence busied himself, towelling himself dry and flattening his hair, ignoring her question.

Zoe disappeared under the covers again while Lawrence dressed and went downstairs.

It was already 7:00, he was running late, and he needed to go. He stood at the bottom of the stairs and shouted 'Bye' up to Zoe but there was no answer.

He sighed and headed for the front door, but at the last second changed his mind and bounded up the stairs two at a time. He peered around the bedroom door.

'I'm off Babe. See you later.'

'Mm, OK,' was all he got.

Lawrence plodded back down the stairs, suddenly feeling very weary, aware of another long day stretching out before him. He wondered what time in the day Zoe would actually crawl out of bed and the thought suddenly irritated him.

As he climbed onto his bike and started it up, he noticed it had just begun to rain and he needed to put his foot down to get to the station on time. He had a morning full of meetings, but the afternoon was relatively clear – god, the weather, and public transport permitting, he'd be home on time tonight.

Chapter 5

Gloria had laid awake in Winnie's now familiar spare bedroom for a while, reluctant to leave the cosy warmth of her bed. Badly fitting windows had allowed the cold winter air to sneak in throughout the night and now the room had an icy feel.

She and Winnie had talked into the early hours; grief, tiredness and anxiety together with a mixture of brandy and wine had Winnie pouring out her heart.

Suddenly she could hear Winnie descend the creaky stairs and then she heard the murmur of the central heating chug into action and then finally the kettle being filled. She pulled back the duvet, quickly showered and dressed in warm clothes, pleased with her decision a few weeks ago to leave a selection of toiletries in the ensuite bathroom which was beginning to feel as familiar as her own. The chest of drawers was already stocked with her clean underwear, extra jumpers, thermal vests and socks for impromptu sleepovers.

She went downstairs to the kitchen, following her senses towards the smell of bacon cooking.

Winnie was attempting to organise breakfast, but with a fuzzy head and clumsy brain-to-hand co-ordination, it was proving to be a task almost beyond her.

'Good morning. Wow, that smells good.'

Winnie turned and gave a weak smile. 'How come you're so chirpy? I feel terrible.'

Gloria smiled to herself as she scraped back a chair, noticing in her peripheral vision how Winnie physically cringed at the noise.

'I can see you grinning there. It's not funny. You're a bad influence on me.'

'I certainly hope so!' said Gloria, turning in her seat to face the rather delicate looking Winnie.

'Shall I make coffee?'

'Oh yes please.' Winnie came to the table and plonked herself down.

Gloria got up and put the coffee machine to work.

She looked amazing; in her mid-seventies with a trim but full figure and looking simply stunning in purple velvet jeans and a silvery grey fluffy sweater which matched her silvery grey wispy hair which she'd scooped up into a casual knot.

Winnie watched her as she stretched up for the coffee mugs and bent down low to unload the dishwasher – not a creak or a groan from her nimble self.

In the past, Winnie had envied her friend's sensual figure, and her style too. But even though she'd lost at least fifteen pounds over the last few weeks, and they were now of comparable size, the likeness ended there. She used to take care of how she dressed, longed to get out of her hospital uniform at the end of the day but now as she looked down at her most unflattering faded baggy jeans and orange sweatshirt, she tried to remember how many days she'd been wearing them.

Gloria made the coffee and glanced over at the frying pan, giving it a tentative shake, the bacon already slightly burnt.

'You're sure a fry-up is a good idea Wynne?'

'Oh, I don't know, it seemed to be at the time. What do you think?'

Winnie looked up at Gloria's doubtful face, they shook heads in agreement, and Gloria turned off the gas, pushing the frying pan to the back of the hob.

She brought the coffee over and sat back down at the table placing a mug in front of each of them.

'Thanks,' said Winnie, inhaling the invigorating yet soothing aroma of strong, fresh coffee.

'And thanks for staying over. Again. And for listening. I know I rambled on rather a lot last night. You're so good to put up with me.'

'Don't be daft; I'm not putting up with you. I'm just glad to be able to help in anyway.'

Winnie put her hand over her friend's and gave a squeeze. She blew on her hot coffee, blinking the steam from her eyes which were already watery with tears.

Gloria sipped her coffee and realised she was, in fact, extremely hungry. Neither of them had eaten much last night. It was obvious Winnie had lost her appetite from the way her clothes were hanging off her, but Gloria had managed to find a lone pizza lurking in the depths of the freezer last night and encouraged her to have some. She noticed the pizza box on the floor, tucked behind the overfull bin.

She didn't fancy a greasy fry-up, but her mouth watered at the thought of a soft, fresh croissant with a spoonful of apricot jam. She wondered if she could get Winnie to come out for a bit of breakfast.

'Are you hungry Wynne? Do you fancy popping out? We could find a nice teashop nearby?'

Winnie shook her head and wrinkled her nose. 'Not really. But help yourself Glo. I've got cereals and eggs, not sure if there's any bread for toast though.'

'OK, not to worry. I'll find myself something in a minute.'

Winnie fell silent again, as if it took all her concentration to drink her coffee, both hands cupping the mug, as she sipped repeatedly.

While Winnie was distracted, Gloria quickly swept her gaze discreetly over the kitchen. Despite years of working full time, Winnie had always kept her home spotlessly clean, but now little tell-tale signs were appearing, showing she wasn't quite on top of it all. The bin needed emptying and the floor needed a good mop or at least a sweep. But who could blame her?

Gloria returned her gaze to Winnie who was still staring into her coffee. She looked totally lost. Gloria leaned in and turned towards her. She rubbed her back firmly and affectionately, in a gentle attempt to bring her back to the moment.

'OK, you have me at your disposal all day. What shall we do? Shall I help with a bit of cleaning?'

'No. Doug told me not to spend my life cleaning,' said Winnie wearily.

'Well, yes, there are more important things than just a clean and tidy house.'

Winnie looked up into her friend's face questioningly. 'That's exactly what he said.'

'Wise words indeed. But what he might have meant is that there are more important things to do *as well as* a bit of cleaning. Maybe?' Gloria gave a cheeky smile, but it wasn't reciprocated.

She inhaled deeply but silently, feeling at a loss. She was worried for her friend who seemed to be sliding away into an unreachable distance.

'And it's too cold to go out anyway,' said Winnie, re-joining the conversation of a few minutes ago. 'They're saying more snow on the way.' She sighed long and heavy.

'We can get togged up. How about we do some shopping? Get some extra supplies before the snow comes?'

'Oh gosh no, we never go food shopping on Saturdays. We always go on Thursdays – make sure we're all stocked up for the weekend.'

'OK.' Gloria stood up. 'In that case, if you don't want to go out for breakfast or for shopping, I suggest we get warm and hunker down in the living room for the day. You go and light another fire – and make it a good one. I'll make more coffee and seek out the biscuit tin.'

Finally, Winnie smiled, seemingly content with the prospect of staying home for the day. 'Yes, you know where the tin is, in the top cupboard there.'

Winnie left the room, and while the coffee was brewing, Gloria found the biscuit tin, noticing a couple of Christmas gifts of luxury biscuits, probably given as presents, but still unopened.

By the time she went through to the living room, the fire was burning nicely, and Winnie was ensconced in her chair, Doug's chair, by the fire. She had a fleece throw tucked over her knees and had placed another one ready for Gloria.

'I think the wind's changed direction. It feels like it's coming in at all angles now, it makes the house bitter. Do you want to borrow some slippers Glo?'

Winnie looked down at Gloria's feet, warm and cosy in chunky cashmere socks.

'No, I'm fine. These will keep my toes toasty.'

Gloria sat down and placed the tray on the table. 'I found these, very posh biscuits. Shall we start on them? Or were you saving them until next year?'

Winnie was used to Gloria's cheeky sarcasm, but she gave her a reprimanding look anyway. 'Hannah bought them for me. They were Doug's Christmas favourite, especially the shortbread.'

'Ah, I see.' They shared a look of mutual understanding. 'But it's OK to eat them?'

'Yes, come on, open them.'

Gloria took a chocolate one out of its gold wrapping and dunked it in her coffee, sucking the chocolate off before biting into the slightly soggy biscuit.

'Crikey, that's good. These aren't just M & S biscuits, are they?' She smiled over towards Winnie but noticed again the distant look glaze over her face, as if she was only half present.

Gloria ate the rest of her biscuit, took a sip of her coffee and settled back, pulling the throw over her lap. She took a deep breath and then said.

36

'Did I tell you what I did when my Bill died?'

'No.' Winnie shook her head, seemingly disinterested, her expression dull.

'Bill. He was my husband number two. You never met him.'

Gloria paused, looked intently into Winnie's face to ensure she was paying attention. Winnie needed a temporary distraction from her tangled thoughts, but Gloria didn't often talk about Bill, and if she were to now, it wasn't going to go unheard.

'Bill, William Woodward. My darling Bill. Well, I kind of had a meltdown when he died.'

Winnie looked up immediately. She was listening now.

'He had a heart-attack too, just like your Doug; out of the blue. It was such a terrible shock.'

Winnie nodded in agreement. 'I never gave things like that a thought. Doug was healthy, hardly ever a sick day off work.'

Gloria smiled. 'Ah yes, the curse of the self-employed.'

Winnie knew exactly what she meant. 'He was always talking about taking up cycling and things like that. There was some famous bike-ride he wanted to do in Europe somewhere.'

'It's all very well talking, but it's not enough. He needed to be doing that stuff, not just talking about it.' Gloria stopped abruptly. This was hardly the time to be reprimanding Doug. She looked across to her friend who was staring into the fire.

Winnie grimaced, remembering how she used to tease Doug and his rounded tummy, gradually expanding a little each year. If only she'd realised the seriousness of the consequences of being that bit overweight. Her eyes slid discreetly over Gloria's amazingly svelte figure. She was in great shape, and Winnie knew she worked hard to keep herself busy and active. It certainly paid off.

'Anyway, where was I? Yes, my Bill – he had a massive heart attack, just the same, a few weeks before Christmas. He was never big on Christmas. In fact, he was a bit of a humbug on that front.'

'Oh, was he?' Winnie was dismayed, knowing how Gloria was totally smitten by the festive season, her own home decorated like Santa's grotto on the first of December every year since she'd known her.

'Yes, he was, so I always use to play all of that down, kept it all quite minimal.'

'But why? You love Christmas.'

'Well yes. But I loved Bill too.' Gloria smiled, a wide happy, twinkly eyed smile.

Winnie's glance flicked over to the corner of the room and the boxes of unopened decorations still there.

'Anyway, on this particular year, out of the blue, he gave me free rein to decorate and do whatever I wanted. I didn't hold back.' Gloria chuckled lightly, remembering. And then her face darkened.

'It was less than a week later when I got a call from his friend saying he'd been rushed to hospital.' She paused for several seconds, gently pushing her glasses back up her nose with her finger, taking a moment.

'So anyway, I couldn't bear to be in the house. Couldn't bear the sight of all those blasted Christmas decorations.' She looked up at Winnie who was staring hard back at her, expectantly.

'And so, I smashed the lot to pieces! Every last bauble!'

'Gloria! Did you really?'

'Yep. And then got the hell out of there.'

'What do you mean? Where did you go?'

'Well, I had to go somewhere. As much as anything to avoid being taken in by Bill's children. He has three from his previous marriage and they're all great, and I love them dearly, but of course they were concerned about me being on my own over Christmas.'

Winnie's thoughts wandered off to the previous few weeks, her first Christmas ever without Doug and how she'd been shepherded back and forth between her daughters, as if they were scared to leave her alone for even a second when in fact that was exactly what she craved.

It was difficult at first to refuse their offers of kindness; the look of rejection on their faces was almost too much to bear. She understood that by having their mother close to them, it was in some small way a means of having their father too. But she'd spent most of the Christmas holidays with one or other of them, and finally she insisted, gently, that she needed some time alone.

She couldn't imagine completely upping and leaving them at this time.

'Where did you go?'

Gloria was now the one gazing into the fire, her thoughts years away in the past.

'Somewhere cold. I wanted to go somewhere bitterly cold – to match my bitterly cold heart.' She snorted, as if laughing at her own silliness.

Winnie gave a questioning look.

'Bill was a sun worshiper. We always holidayed in the Med; southern Spain, Greece, the hotter the better for him. I would have liked for us to have had some different kinds of holidays, but he was never really interested, and so it was always the heat and the sunshine that we followed.'

Winnie couldn't help thinking that Gloria's second husband came across as a little selfish in her eyes, but then again, she'd never met the man so perhaps it wasn't fair to judge. Gloria certainly had happy memories of him.

'So, I packed a great big suitcase and got myself off to Iceland – open ticket. No plans of when to return.'

'How long were you gone?'

'Eight weeks. A beautiful place, Iceland. Hauntingly beautiful.'

Gloria took a sip of her coffee, a simple smile lighting her face by the flickering firelight.

'And what about when you came back? How did you manage then?'

'A little easier by then I think. Being away acted as a kind of buffer, if you see what I mean. Being away somewhere completely new to me and so very different from anything me and Bill had shared, I think it helped. Stopped me from getting drawn into clinging to the same old routines, and you know, getting stuck in the past.'

They sipped their drinks, comfortable in the silence that enveloped them, their respective thoughts and memories swirling around like a snowstorm.

Winnie looked up first. And they smiled. Winnie was getting the not-so-subtle message that Gloria was offering – the danger of not allowing herself to move on by sticking too close to old traditions and rituals. But it had only been six weeks.

'Anyway, I don't need to go to Iceland – we have our very own Iceland here.'

'Yes, good point. And very neatly side-stepped. But you know what I'm saying. Might not be the worst thing, to take yourself off somewhere for a while. Take yourself away from the shock of it all. I'll come with you if you want.'

'Hm, I'll give it some thought. But I like being here, in my own home, in our home.

Gloria smiled. 'OK, I won't go on about it, but the offer's there.'

'I know. Thanks, Glo.'

'Now, of course, it was a very different thing when George died. There was no shock there. We both knew he was ill. That's why we got married. He insisted.'

'Ah, lovely George. He was a romantic.'

'Yes, partly that, but he was practical too. He wanted to be sure I was properly looked after as he put it, that I was all set financially. Even though I insisted I didn't need anything from him in that way.' Gloria stopped abruptly, realising too late she was being insensitive.

'I wish Doug had organised things so that I was set financially. It's such a mess. I don't know where to start sorting everything out.' Winnie got up and put a few more logs on the fire.

The large wood-burner certainly did its job, Gloria thought, it positively gobbled wood. The obvious thing to suggest would be to sell this enormous house, but Gloria sensed the time wasn't right. Winnie was nowhere near ready to consider such a thing, although she may have to at some point.

Chapter 6

Lawrence was taking his usual morning shower, but today he was singing – loudly. As he towelled himself dry, he smiled at the thought of Zoe downstairs making coffee.

Yesterday, Valentine's Day, had been their second wedding anniversary, and Lawrence had managed to get home a little early. He'd sent Zoe a stunning bouquet of soft pinks and blues offset with delicate feathery foliage. And for a special present he'd bought her a gold necklace - a tiny solid gold heart on the daintiest of chains.

He wanted the evening to be perfect and rather than spend time cooking, he ordered a Chinese takeaway for their candlelit dinner. Zoe laughed out loud when the massive amount of food arrived and she watched as Lawrence unpacked the bags, placing tubs and pots and sauces on the coffee table, almost covering it completely. They used chopsticks and Lawrence relentlessly encouraged her to try every single one of the dishes, even the dubious chicken and jellyfish noodle salad.

His plan had been successful; they both ate a lot of food which helped alleviate the effects of several glasses of wine. Lawrence kept a close eye and made sure he matched her, glass for glass, teasing her playfully when her sipping turned to gulping.

The occasion had been a success and finally they took their glasses up to bed to complete their evening of celebrations.

Lawrence came into the kitchen now, clean and fresh, and smelling of expensive aftershave. He nuzzled into Zoe's neck, kissing her gently.

They sat at the island, facing each other, drinking coffee. It was a very ordinary morning ritual, but it felt very special to him in that moment. Just normal, but wonderful.

Perhaps they'd turned a corner, he thought – but not for the first time.

Suddenly Zoe looked distracted.

'Everything OK Zo?'

'Yeah, I was just thinking.'

Lawrence was shocked to realise he'd almost laughed out loud. But it was true; the odd look on his wife's face was that of her seriously deep in thought and it was a look he wasn't used to.

He simply looked at her, eyebrows raised questioningly.

'I'm meeting my friend Nicky for lunch.' It was an announcement, like a proud achievement, and in a way it was. Zoe had lost touch with most of her friends.

'Nicky? Remind me, where's she from?'

'We were actually at school together, we were really good friends – thick as thieves in Environmental Studies, but you know how it is, we didn't keep in touch. And then we met up years later when we were both working at Towergate Insurance. Remember? I'm sure I told you before – she interviewed me for the job. It was so funny.'

'Ah yeah, I think I remember.'

'We haven't seen each other for ages, not since we got married anyway. We keep trying to set a date, but I think she's really busy – she works full time and she's got kids, so anyway, we're meeting today for lunch. At The Coach.

'Hm, ladies who lunch eh?'

Zoe gave a small laugh. 'Yeah, who'd have thought it? Me? Actually, I'm a bit nervous.'

Lawrence glanced at his watch – he needed to get going. He slid from the stool and kissed Zoe on the top of her head, smiling and laughing.

'What are you nervous about, silly thing? It's only lunch. You'll have fun.'

He left the room, left Zoe sitting there, unable to put into words, even to herself, why she felt so anxious at something so seemingly ordinary as meeting up with an old friend for lunch.

She'd left Towergate Insurance a few months before she and Lawrence were married. She hated her office job with a vengeance and Lawrence had told her to jack it – concentrate on overseeing the wedding arrangements instead. She remembered being over the moon to be able to leave – and vaguely recalled her managers weren't that sorry to see her go either.

She and Lawrence were living together in his flat at the time. His job in IT logistics earnt well, they wouldn't miss her admin salary.

He'd assumed she'd find something else, long before now, get into something she'd enjoy, something she had a passion for – but two years into their marriage and neither of them seemed to know what that was.

Lawrence dashed back into the kitchen, motorbike leathers on and helmet in hand. He took his keys from the hook on the wall and pointed at the little pile of papers on the worktop.

'Don't forget my passport, will you Hon? I can't believe I forgot about renewing it – good thing Greg just happened to mention the Hamburg trip – I'd be in serious crap if I couldn't make it. Application's all filled out, just hand it in at the post office for them to check or whatever they do. It should be OK. We've got plenty of time. The trip's not until end of April. It You don't mind, do you?'

'No, of course I don't mind. Don't worry, I won't forget.'

'Great stuff. See you later - and have a great day.' Lawrence kissed her on the top of her head and was gone.

Zoe stood in the bedroom and vaguely registered the sound of Lawrence's motorbike riding out into the distance. Fitted wardrobes spanned an entire wall of their bedroom, and she opened all the doors and drawers in an effort to choose the perfect out-to-lunch outfit.

Her friend was doing well in the world, still at Towergate but now in a senior management role. She'd be here to pick her up at midday and even though Zoe had plenty of time, she wanted to be absolutely ready and waiting.

In a red ditsy print tea dress, and ridiculously high strappy sandals, she was finally ready even though the bedroom was almost entirely buried under the contents of the wardrobe, and she could hardly believe she'd ended up wearing virtually the first thing she'd tried on. It didn't matter, she'd tidy up when she got back.

Keeping a keen eye on the clock, she paced between the kitchen and the living room window, looking out for Nicky's car. She'd been to the loo a number of times and checked her handbag yet again for keys, money and phone. Nicky was just over five minutes late and Zoe's heart was pounding with anxiety.

Drumming her fingernails on the kitchen worktop, she heard her phone ring and grabbed it from her bag. It was Nicky apologising for running late, and confirming she'd be there in another ten minutes.

Zoe sighed - she couldn't bear this for another ten minutes. She glanced down at the wine fridge and quickly snatched open the door and grabbed a bottle, unscrewed it and poured a little measure into a mug. She'd already decided not to have a drink over lunch, but just a little one now would help settle her nerves, that's all.

She finished it quickly, and then realised she needn't have. Nicky wouldn't arrive for at least another ten minutes. She poured a little more wine and resolved to make it last until she arrived, and then she continued to pace from room to room, mug in hand, but calmer now, and looking forward to their date.

Peering through the bay window, she saw a massive Mercedes pull up and wondered if it was

Nicky. It was. She downed the last of the wine, rinsed the mug and dashed out the front door.

Zoe had never been to The Coach Inn before but knew it to be a particularly swish place to dine. She and Nicky were ensconced at a cosy corner table in front of a large window overlooking the restaurant gardens.

A waiter appeared almost immediately with menus and enquired about drinks. Zoe paused, ready to go with whatever Nicky wanted.

'Shall we have tea?' she asked, and Zoe nodded with what she hoped came across as enthusiasm.

'A pot of tea for two, and I think it will take a while for us to order something from this gorgeous menu. I could eat it all.'

Zoe glanced over the menu, dismayed to realise she wasn't very hungry. She'd be happy with a sausage sandwich, and maybe a little glass of something.

Finally, Nicky, snapped the menu shut. 'Yep, I've decided, I'm going for the salmon and dill quiche, sounds divine. How about you?'

'Yes, that sounds good, I'll have the same. And shall we have a small glass of white to go with it? Do you think?'

'Oh, lovely idea, but I'd better not. I'm picking the kids up later, plus just one glass and I'll be wanting to snooze all afternoon. But you go ahead, I'm dropping you off anyway.'

'Oh no, that's fine. If you're not drinking, I won't.'

When the waiter returned, Nicky placed their order and at the same time ordered a bottle of sparkling mineral water. He turned to Zoe and asked if she wanted anything else to drink.

Her head was just about to affirm the negative but before she knew it her mouth had opened, and a small voice had asked for a small glass of dry white wine.

'I'll just have the one,' she confirmed to Nicky.

'Yes, why not? I would if I could,' she smiled. Zoe felt much better already.

'So, you're a senior manager now?'

'Yes, it's all very exciting. I've had my eye on this position for a while. It all became official a couple of month ago. How about you? Have you found anything? Your last email said you were half looking.'

'Well, no, nothing yet. Just waiting for the right thing.'

'Lucky you. Lady of leisure.'

'Yes, I am. Very lucky.'

'Sometimes, my life is just crazy mad, but I do actually enjoy it all really.'

Zoe finished her glass of wine – much sooner than anticipated. And she needed another.

Nicky sipped her sparkling water. 'I keep meaning to ask – how are things between you and your mum, are you talking these days?'

'Oh god no. Still haven't spoken to her for years. And I don't want to.'

'It's a shame,' said Nicky, tucking into her salmon quiche.

'It's a shame for her. We don't miss her. She's the one who buggered off and left us. Poor Dad, he didn't know how to handle us, two teenage girls, he suddenly had to be mum and dad. He was clueless.'

'And he's OK, is he? Do you see much of him?'

'No, haven't seen him for years either. We do the Christmas card thing, and I phone him occasionally. As soon as me and Tina were off his hands, he went up to Scotland. I think he's got a fancy bit up there.'

Nicky laughed. 'Fancy bit? That's an old-fashioned expression, isn't it?'

Zoe smiled but suddenly felt very self-conscious and uncomfortable. Was she letting herself down? Was Nicky laughing at her? She felt suddenly irritated, and turned in her seat, catching the attention of the waiter as he immediately attended the table.

'Can you bring another glass of wine please? Actually, can you bring the bottle?'

She turned back in her seat just in time to catch Nicky's raised eyebrow, which irritated her further.

Nicky continued to sip her sparkling water, and Zoe wondered now if she was trying to make a point. Or was she just being paranoid?

'We're so lucky to have my parents close by. They're a great help with the kids and everything. Honestly, I couldn't manage without them.'

Zoe's wine arrived and the waiter poured a small glass. As he left, Zoe picked up the bottle and filled her glass to the brim.

It was mid-afternoon when Zoe turned at the front door to wave to Nicky, but her car was already at the end of the road. She fiddled with her key, muttering to herself and wondering what was wrong with the stupid lock.

In the hallway she stopped and turned to face the large full-length mirror. She smiled at herself and then noticed a greasy stain on her dress in her reflection. She grimaced but was embarrassed to wonder how long it had been there.

She went through to the kitchen to get a wet cloth, plonked her handbag onto the worktop, and then froze. Lawrence's passport – she'd forgotten all about it. She looked at the clock, it was almost three o'clock. What time did the local post office shut? She had no idea. She grabbed her handbag and the paperwork, her heart beating terrifically fast. Horribly aware that she'd had a few glasses of wine, she convinced herself she'd be OK, the post office was only a couple of minutes away in the next street. If it was already closed, then she'd be stuffed; she couldn't risk driving into town to the main one.

Zoe half ran, half shuffled in her stupid high heels, and threw herself into the car, starting it up and feeling distinctly uncomfortable trying to feel the pedals beneath her silly shoes. In desperation she hit the accelerator, but the car was still in reverse gear and went shooting back, hitting the double-sized garage door bang in the middle. The sound of crunching metal on metal hit Zoe's brain like a hammer as she closed her eyes, unwilling to look or get out of the car or even think about what she'd just done. She managed to convince herself it probably sounded worse than it actually was, and finally she climbed out, looking around tentatively to see if any of her neighbours had come to investigate. Fortunately, no-one had.

Before she'd got to the back of the car, she could already see that not only had she smashed into the automatic garage door but had also caught the brickwork to the side of the door, totally wrecking the back lights and cracking the rear offside panel.

'Oh god, no.' Zoe stood frozen to the spot for a few moments. She felt sick but was unable to move even though she thought a couple of times she was about to throw up there and then. She took a few deep breaths, willing herself to stay calm. Slowly she got back into the car, and drove it forward, very carefully, just enough to look as though it was properly parked but hopefully hiding most of the worst of the damage. Lawrence wouldn't be able to open the garage door to put his bike away but perhaps he would just park on the drive tonight, allowing her to think of some way of explaining this.

Back in the kitchen, with her handbag and the passport application back on the worktop, Zoe stood at the sink willing herself to be sick, in the hope she might feel better. She was terrified and could hardly believe what she'd just done. She was a good driver, had passed her test at eighteen, had never had so much as a prang, but she felt the full force of guilt knowing what had just happened was nothing to do with her driving skills. And it could have been so much more serious. She took a mug and filled it with water, shocked to notice how her hands were shaking. She obviously needed something stronger, she reasoned. After all, she'd just had a nasty shock.

Zoe took the bottle of wine from earlier and half-filled the mug, but just as she was about to drink, she stopped. What the hell was she doing? It was this stuff that had got her into this mess. Why hadn't she stuck to mineral water like her friend?

'What am I doing?' she yelled into the silence.

She threw the wine down the sink, and banged the mug on the side, still shaking and unable to calm her breathing.

She switched on the kettle, picked up the mug again to make some strong, sweet coffee. She would take a bath, change into something nice, find something in the fridge or freezer to cook something good for dinner. Lawrence would come home to something delicious smelling in the oven. And they would have a lovely evening together. Just like last night. It would be as if this never happened.

But there was still the problem of the passport application. She held the paperwork in her hands, pondering the best thing to do. She opened the bottom drawer that held all sorts of unidentifiable gadgets they never used, and slipped the papers inside, carefully, neatly, respectfully, so as not to crease them. Tomorrow, first thing in the morning, she would walk to the post office and get them sent off, and no-one would be any the wiser and everything would be OK.

Chapter 7

The gravel crunched and swished aside in deep grooves as Cathy drove the hefty 4 x 4 onto the drive. Winnifred jerked back in her seat as they came to a final stop, relieved to have arrived, but wishing her daughter didn't drive quite so fast.

It was simply the way things were, she supposed. Everyone seemed to live ever busier lives, time was at a premium and everything simply had to be done quicker.

And to prove the point, Cathy was already out of the vehicle. She'd thrown her voluminous black shawl back in place around her shoulders and was at the boot unloading the shopping she'd bought between dropping the kids off at school and collecting her mum.

Winnie opened the car door and carefully descended the substantial drop to the ground. She went to help but Cathy had already thumped the tailgate shut and had two heavy shopping bags in each hand. Winnie looked a little lost. It still felt so odd being at her daughter's home without Doug by her side.

'Come on Mum, let's get inside out of the cold, and get the kettle on.'

Winnie had to walk quickly to keep up and as soon as she stepped inside the big hallway, she was completely enveloped in warmth. She closed the front door, a firm seal keeping the inside in and the outside out. She was struck immediately by the silence; no traffic noise and no wind blowing through rattly doors in this modern house and was somewhat surprised to realise she hadn't noticed before.

She wondered, not for the first time lately, whether it was a physiological fact that while in the midst of grieving, all your senses became more acutely tuned. Sights and sounds had a heightened intensity and an often-profound impact – just to add to the agony of feelings she was already struggling to process.

Cathy was already in the kitchen and called out as she unpacked the shopping.

'Honestly Mum, I thought spring had arrived last week and now look at it. It's cold and windy, big black clouds, looks like it's going to pour down. I hosed the patio down; thought we'd be able to sit outside over the weekend. I'm beginning to think we'll be lighting a fire instead.

'Yes, I know. It's been a long wait for the warmer weather.' Winnie answered quietly, almost to herself.

Cathy hadn't heard and popped her head round the kitchen door.

'OK Mum?' Cathy smiled at Winnie who appeared to be just standing there, as if waiting for something.

'Yes, I'm fine. It's lovely and warm in here.' Winnie took off her coat and placed it on the settle and then followed Cathy into the kitchen.

'Really Mum, it's at times like these, I can understand people upping and offing to warmer climes. For good I mean. You know, like on those TV programs where they pack up and go off for a completely different life – in the south of France, or Spain. Or Australia even.'

'On no, not Australia dear, that's much too far.'

'No, not us Mum. We couldn't go anywhere – not with Tom's business based here. You know that.'

'No, of course not. And I can't deny I'm pleased about that.' Winnie smiled at her daughter who finally paused to take a breath.

'Don't worry Mum, we're not going anywhere.' Cathy continued to pack away the shopping and then she suddenly stopped, grabbed her handbag from the floor and checked her phone.

'I was worried the school was going to call. Hugo wasn't too well this morning, just a bit sniffly but I thought he might turn it on a bit so he can come home. But that's good, they haven't called.'

Cathy looked up to see Winnie staring through the window into the garden, but not at anything in particular.

'Mum?'

'Yes dear, sorry, I was miles away. What were you saying? You've got to call the school? Poor Hugo, is he OK?'

'Yes, he's fine Mum. All fine. Now, how about you make us a cup of tea?'

'Good idea. Let me do that.'

They continued with their respective tasks in silence while Cathy kept a watchful eye on her mother as she filled the kettle and set out two mugs.

'Shall I take it through to the conservatory?' asked Winnie.

'Yes, we can watch the rain when it comes. I'll be there in a sec; I'm just going to put a wash on.'

Winnie carried the mugs of tea out to the conservatory and settled herself in a large wicker armchair.

From her vantage point, she could see back through the kitchen into the utility room where Cathy was loading the washing machine, simultaneously tidying various things away and then quickly watering some plants on the windowsill. She was a whirlwind of activity.

Winnie sat and observed; her eldest daughter – hard-working, capable and efficient, tirelessly busy. Nobody would know it to look at her that only a few months ago, she had lost her adoring dad. Inside, her heart would be breaking. But, as they say, life goes on. Especially if you have a job, a young family and a workaholic husband. If anything, Cathy seemed busier than ever today.'

Cathy returned to the kitchen. 'Be there in a sec, Mum. I'm just going to give the school a ring, see if Hugo's alright.'

'OK, no rush, I'm fine here.' It occurred to Winnie that maybe this non-stop frenzy of activity was Cathy's way of coping. Maybe she was afraid to be still with her own thoughts.

Winnie could definitely relate to that. She understood the well-meaning advice of keeping busy, and she followed it as best she could. But it was at odd times like this, now, sitting in Cathy's conservatory with nothing to immediately occupy her that her thoughts started to take hold.

She reached over for her mug of tea, quickly blinking away the prickling in her eyes. She was here to stay for the weekend and of course they would talk about Doug and there would be more tears, but she didn't want to give Cathy cause to worry about her any more than she already did.

Cathy had invited her a number of times over the last few weeks, and in the end, Winnie had agreed to come and stay, as much as anything, to show that she was OK. It wouldn't help her case if she was found to be crying into her teacup five minutes after arriving.

She took a deep breath and sat up straighter in the chair, cleared her throat and composed herself. She looked out onto the large garden, slightly greener after the recent sunshine. And now dark heavy clouds were gathering low.

It made her smile to notice the contrast – professional gardeners pruned and sculpted the mature shrubs, trimmed the lawn edges and kept the flower beds pristinely neat and tidy. And in the middle of all this was a huge, netted trampoline, a climbing frame and a slide and swing set, all with their respective bald patches on the lawn.

It summed up Cathy precisely. She had a demanding job and was unrelentingly busy, but her family, and especially her two young children, were everything to her.

At last Cathy came in, breathless, and plonked herself down in an opposite chair.

'Ah, lovely. A hot cup of tea. Look at it out there, it's getting darker by the second. We're in for a mighty storm I think.'

Winnie nodded, remembering how she and Doug had loved a good storm, provided of course, they were holed up at home, with the smell of a beef casserole cooking and plenty of logs brought in for the wood-burner.

'Are you OK Mum?'

'Yes, I'm fine Love.' Winnie answered dutifully, but it didn't go amiss with her daughter.

Cathy paused, allowing the automation of her mum's response to resound in the big open conservatory.

'No, really, I mean. Are you OK?'

Winnifred looked directly at her daughter, eye to eye, for what seemed like the first time in – a long time. She was tempted to let it all out, her worries and fears, her anger and frustration. How had everything so safe and secure, solid and loving, so totally disappeared in the blink of an eye?

'Yes, of course I am. I'm OK. Really, I'm absolutely fine. No need for you to worry.'

Cathy sighed and rubbed the back of her aching neck. She followed her mother's gaze out onto the garden, understanding that of course she wasn't fine. She was simply doing her best to cope and all they could do was to be there for each other. As she stared outside, the rain began; heavy drops bounced and slid off the shiny leaves of the holly bush just outside the window.

'Here it comes,' said Winnie, bringing Cathy's attention back to the moment.

Cathy got up and switched the light on; a cosy golden glow warmed the room.

'It's your leaving do next week, isn't it? How do you feel about it?'

Winnie grimaced. 'I'd avoid it, if I possibly could,'

'It'll be good to get out for a change, won't it? You'll be with all your friends.'

'Oh yes, they'll be fine – it's just all the other pomp of the evening. It's not just me, there's a number of us leaving.'

Cathy was aware that apart from work, her mother was spending every evening at home, mostly alone apart from the occasional evening when she had Gloria for company.

She'd spotted Gloria at the petrol station recently and went over for a chat. Gloria mentioned she'd tried getting Winnie to come away with her for a weekend break, but without success. Her suggestions of going to the cinema or out for a meal had met with the same weary resignation that she wasn't yet up to anything like that.

Cathy herself had asked her mother over for the weekend a number of times. Finally, she'd been forced to make something up – asking her mother if she'd babysit. And then she had the tricky task of trying to persuade Tom to take her out somewhere fancy.

'And you're OK with babysitting tonight?'

'Yes, of course I am. And it'll be good for you both to get out too. It's been ages since I've babysat for you.'

'Yes, I suppose so. Tom could do with a night out; he's been putting in extra hours at work lately. And he's been so great over the last few months. I'm lucky to have him.'

Cathy stopped dead.

Winnie smiled. 'It's OK. Yes, you are very lucky to have each other. Make the most of every moment.'

Cathy smiled back, just as a low rumble of thunder sounded, way off in the distance.

Later that evening, Cathy appeared in the living room, fiddling with an earring, having difficulty putting it in. She smiled at the sight of Winnie on the sofa; six-year-old Hugo tucked under one arm, and eight-year-old Tilly clutching the other. Both children couldn't get any closer to their gran. They were watching 'Finding Nemo', both kids totally entranced but her mother seemed to be staring straight through the TV screen.

'We're off in a few minutes Mum.'

'OK, love. You look nice. That colour suits you. Silver grey, very nice.'

'Thanks. I bought it especially, but I wasn't totally sure of the colour. But you like it?'

'Yes, it's very flattering on you. You have to go careful as you get older; you can't get away with wearing black all the time. Apparently, it's not so kind on older skin.'

'Mum! I'm only 34!'

Winnie grinned. 'It's just a silly something I read somewhere. I'm only telling you for your own good.'

Cathy laughed, feeling a sudden rush of abundant love for her mum. It was so good to see her joking and smiling. She'd forgotten what a good sense of humour she had and was a little ashamed to realise she hadn't noticed it missing until just now.

'OK, enough fashionista tips from you thank-you. I *think* there was a compliment in there somewhere.'

Winnie just smiled and kissed the top of Tilly's unruly curls.

'OK, Mum, there's a bottle of that cherry liquor you like out in the larder – help yourself. Although, I don't want to come home to you slurring your words! And then,' Cathy lowered her voice slightly, 'there are treats and snacks in the top cupboard – in the usual place.' She deliberately avoided using the words crisps and chocolate and in return Winnie nodded with a knowing smile.

Finally, Cathy quickly kissed everyone good-bye, insisting Winnie stay in her comfy spot as much as anything to allow her to slip out the door without too much fuss from the children. Tom called out a quick 'see you later' from the hallway, reminding Cathy they were running late.

As the back door was locked, Hugo and Tilly competed for who could shout 'Byeee' the loudest and then Tilly swung her attention to more important matters. She turned away from the television and sat on Winnie's lap.

'Grannie? Can we have treats now?'

Winnie chuckled; they didn't miss a thing.

In the kitchen she put a selection of bowls on a tray and filled them each with a small amount of crisps, cheese biscuits and various other goodies. She'd have to watch they didn't scoff everything too quickly otherwise she'd be dealing with a couple of hyperactive little imps who'd never get off to sleep.

And she had the whole evening to entertain them yet. It felt very odd; to be here with the children on her own. She and Doug used to babysit together. Sometimes Hugo and Tilly would stay at their home but mostly they used to come here where the children had their own beds and she and Doug would go home when Cathy and Tom returned. This was a first, spending the evening with the little ones completely on her own. She wasn't sure she even had the energy for it. They could be a handful when they got excited.

And as much as she was happy to be here, she was already getting used to the quiet and solitude of her own company and home, this weekend was definitely going to be change of pace for her. She suddenly realised everything was disturbingly quiet and she grabbed the tray and returned to the living room where, surprisingly, she found Tilly and Hugo exactly where she'd left them, sitting as still as statues, totally absorbed in the film.

They quickly moved aside to make room for Winnie to place the tray on the coffee table, and in barely a second, they'd slid to sitting on the floor, tucking into the snacks without hardly taking their eyes off the tele.

'Now, don't eat everything too quickly,' said Winnie, pleased she'd only half filled each of the bowls and noticing that her words had fallen on little deaf ears.

'Come on Gran, eat some things,' said Hugo. 'Mummy said we've got to look especially after you. And make you prickly happy.'

'Prickly?'

'He means particularly,' joined in Tilly. 'Mummy says we've got to make you busy and play games all together and not just watch the tele - so that you don't get sad.'

'And we're going to give you lots of cuddles because they always help.'

Winnie swallowed hard. 'Pass me one of those tissues, will you Tilly?'

'You're not being sad are you Grannie?' asked Hugo, suddenly looking very serious.

'No, no. I think I've got a bit of biscuit crumb in my eye, that's all. Silly me.' Winnie dabbed gently at her eyes. 'There, that's it, it's gone now.'

Instinctively, Tilly got up and plonked herself astride Winnie's lap, leaning in close and then very gently she placed her cheek against her Gran's while stretching her arms around her shoulders and holding her tight. Winnie could feel the strength and tension in her small form.

'Granny?'

'Yes, darling?'

'You know - I really miss Grandad.'

Winnie held on to her little granddaughter, patting her back and blinking the tears away. She didn't want the children to see her upset.

'Hey Tilly, we need to tuck in otherwise Hugo is going to be full of all those cheesy puffs – how about you pass me a couple.'

Tilly immediately returned to the floor and quickly collected two little handfuls of snacks and deposited them onto Winnie's lap.

Happy to see Grannie was OK again, Hugo and Tilly quickly returned their attention back to their own snacks and the tele.

After a comfortable while with the children happily engrossed, and Winnie finally relaxing into her thoughts, there was a sudden brief flash of light which floodlit the entire room for just a second. A deep growl of thunder followed.

Hugo and Tilly simultaneously swung their heads around to their gran.

'Well, it sounds as if we have a bit of a storm nearby. It's nothing to worry about – just a little thunder and lightning. We're perfectly safe in here.'

'It sounded like a dragon!' shouted Hugo, not sure whether he was excited or scared.

'No. Aunty Hannah is the dragon,' Tilly replied, very matter-of-factly. They giggled in conspiracy, but Winnie had heard the comment and needed to know where it came from.

'Why is Aunty Hannah a dragon?' she asked gently.

'I don't know!' said Tilly, absorbed in collecting the last crumbs of crisps with her tiny fingertip, and licking them off. And then she suddenly laughed. 'That's what Daddy's always calling her – The Dragon Lady.'

Hugo joined in shouting, 'The Dragon Lady!' Again, they grinned, obviously this was a well-known joke.

Winnie didn't see the funny side at all but left it there for now.

But she intended to find out why her son-in-law was making her youngest daughter out to be such a joke in this household.

With that, there was another flash of lightning, even more intense this time, followed by an enormous clap of thunder which vibrated the house.

The children leapt from the floor onto the settee in an instant – one on either side of their gran, clinging to her arms. 'Oh Grannie, save us' said Hugo dramatically. Winnie freed her trapped arms.

'Now, come on, you're too old to behave like babies. You know it's only a storm and nothing to be frightened of.' Winnie noticed it was almost time for them to go to bed, but she knew it would be impossible while the thunder and lightning kept up.

The film ended and as the credits rolled, another crash of thunder had the children yelping in unison.

Winnie needed to calm them down otherwise they'd never get to bed.

'OK, you two. One more short cartoon DVD and then we're all off to bed. This storm will be well and truly over by then, I'm sure.'

By the end of the film, with the thunder and lightning still at full pelt, Winnie managed to coax the kids up to bed with the promise of stories – she even agreed to them both getting into bed with her so they could all cuddle up together.

It was a little before midnight that the storm finally drifted off, and Winnie led each tired child into their own bed.

As she lay alone in hers, with her mind too busy for sleep; her thoughts turned to her financial worries.

What if she couldn't support herself and keep her home? What would happen to her?

After a while, she heard a key in the lock as Cathy and Tom returned home. She heard Cathy's light footsteps up the stairs and Winnie knew she'd be checking on the children.

Tom's heavier steps followed up. 'They're both fast asleep, thank goodness,' whispered Cathy. 'I thought the storm might have kept them up – well done Mum for getting them off.'

Winnie couldn't hear Tom's response and within a few more minutes had fallen asleep herself.

The following morning Cathy knocked gently on the bedroom door, and then let herself in.

'Morning Mum. Cup of tea for you.'

'Morning Love. That's lovely, thank you.'

'I know it's horrendously early, but the kids were up, and I thought they're bound to have woken you so I thought you might like to enjoy a quiet cuppa in bed first while they're distracted with breakfast.'

'Yes, very civilised. Thank-you'

'Everything alright last night?'

'Oh yes, we had a great time. How was your evening?'

'It was good actually. I enjoyed it more than I expected. I'll tell you about it later, I'd better get back. Tom's cooking pancakes – god help us!'

Winnie smiled as Cathy disappeared back downstairs.

Tom was swirling batter in a frying pan as the children decided on their concoction of toppings.

'So, you had a nice evening with Granny, did you?'

'Yes', shouted Hugh. 'We watched lots of cartoons, but then she got a biscuit in her eye.'

'A biscuit?'

'Yes, and she had to wipe it out with a tissue.'

Instinctively, Cathy glanced over at Tilly for clarification, who picked up on the importance of her contribution and said very matter-of-factly, 'It was a biscuit crumb actually, and it made her eyes water, so she needed a tissue.'

Cathy smiled and nodded, understanding immediately.

'But she was OK, was she?'

'Oh yes, she was fine,' said Tilly with authority.

'And then we made her laugh, didn't we?' said Hugo, dipping his finger into the jar of chocolate spread.

'Did you? What did you do?'

'We told her that Daddy calls Aunty Hannah The Dragon Lady. She thought it was really funny,' concluded Hugo, getting carried away with his story telling.

Tom turned from the cooker to catch Cathy's disapproving look. She knew Hugo was telling the truth; she'd heard Tom say it many times. But despite her son's conviction, she knew for sure her mother would not have found it at all funny.

Chapter 8

Winnie had mooched idly around the house for the last few days. She'd fidgeted from one place to the other, totally unproductive and fed up with herself.

The weather was foul, arctic again. Winter had returned with a vengeance. Gone were the teasing signs of spring; short spells of bone-warming sunshine followed by mid-season storms, promising to clear the air. Now there was four inches of snow on the ground; a good excuse for Winnie to keep herself to herself, and others away. Until now.

Gloria had just phoned. She'd dug her car out of the snow and braved the weather for some supplies and had decided to drop some things around to Winnie. She'd cheekily placed her order for lunch - anything piping hot in a soup bowl with something doughy to dunk in it. And she'd be there in ten minutes.

Winnie dashed around the kitchen, stashing numerous coffee mugs in the dishwasher together with a pile of side plates from days of snacking. The bin was full to brimming again, but it would have to wait; the heavy layer of new snow outside the back door made it a trek too far to the wheelie bin in the garage.

From the window she caught site of Gloria's bright red mini as she drove carefully onto the snow-covered drive. She opened the back door just as Gloria tentatively made her way towards the house, crunching the fresh snow with her flat rubber soled boots, a carrier bag of shopping in each hand.

'Hello there, well this is fun, isn't it?' Shouted Gloria, carefully watching where her feet were landing.

Winnie just smiled, realising that in fact she hadn't been outside at all over the whole of the last week of bad weather.

'Come on in Glo,' said Winnie taking one of the bags. 'You do know, you are slightly mad coming out in this weather.'

'I ran out of loo rolls – I had no choice.' Gloria looked up and grinned. 'And gin, I ran out of gin too!'

Gloria stamped her snow caked boots on the mat inside the boot room and allowed Winnie to help her off with her boots and huge padded coat, woolly hat and scarf. She followed her through to the kitchen, plonked her bag on the worktop and began to unload it.

'I thought you might need some things too.' A quick glance around the kitchen told Gloria that despite Winnie's frantic spit and polish, her visit had caught her by surprise.

Winnie picked up a packet of fig rolls. 'Fig rolls? I hate fig rolls! They're *your* favourite.'

'Well, who knows, I might get snowed in, and have to stay the night. And then I'll be very glad I've got my fig rolls.' Gloria grinned and continued to unpack.

'It's two weeks into my redundancy, I haven't suddenly lost the ability to feed myself you know.'

'You've lost the ability to tidy up though; that bin needs emptying for a start. It stinks.'

70

Winnie glanced sheepishly at the bin; the lid didn't quite close properly and there were crisp packets and chocolate wrappers guiltily peeking out. She lifted the other carrier bag and piled all the goodies on the worktop – tins of beans, ham, cheese, and biscuits.

Teasing aside, Gloria was seriously concerned as to how Winnie would manage her time now that she had so much of it to herself.

'I got some delicious fresh bread too. Lucky to get that, there was hardly any left. A few inches of snow and everyone's panic buying.'

'A few inches? It's virtually the north pole out there.'

'Hm, it's been a bloody long winter, hasn't it?'

Winnie just nodded as she thought back over the last few months. Time had passed surprisingly quickly enough, but winter had been long and dark and cold, not only because of the weather.

'So, I have the bread, but I can't smell any soup cooking. Winnifred?'

'What?'

'Soup!'

'Oh yes.' Winnie turned and grabbed a couple of tins from the cupboard. 'You have a choice – tomato or spring vegetable?'

'Oh, go on, spring vegetable. Let's kid ourselves it's just around the corner.'

They ate their lunch at the kitchen table, dunking thick slices of buttered bread into creamy soup. Gloria noticed again how chilly it was in the house. If it wasn't for the low murmur of the boiler, she wouldn't have known the heating was on. She guessed Winnie was economising and concentrated on finishing her soup while it was still hot.

Winnie finished and pushed her bowl away from her. She sighed, head in her hands. Gloria gently rubbed her back.

'Sometimes, it all just seems too much, doesn't it?'

Winnie nodded her head and closed her eyes, overwhelmingly thankful to hear a comforting word.

They watched through the window in silence as delicate lacey snowflakes floated down light as air. They were hypnotised by the continuous movement of never-ending snow falling and falling.

'So, tell me, how's it been? Your first weeks of freedom, and not having to get up for work. Have you been staying in bed until midday and watching rubbish daytime TV?'

Winnie smiled. 'No, none of that. Although it's tempting to stay in bed, it might be the best way of keeping warm.'

'Yes, it's a big house to heat Wynne.'

Winnie gazed around the kitchen, her expression thoughtful as if she was trying to find the right words, but in the end, she said nothing except to offer Gloria some coffee.

'Yes, I'd love some, but first of all we're going to empty that bin before I puke!'

Winnifred couldn't help laughing out loud. 'Is it that bad?'

'Yes, it is! You must have got used to the smell. Let's get it out of here. Get your wellies on, we'll haul it out together.'

Winnie lifted the over heavy sack from the bin and just about managed to tie it without everything spilling onto the kitchen floor. She lifted the garage door keys from the hook and then heaved the sack outside through the kitchen door that led direct onto the garden and waddled along under its weight, taking care not to slip.

Gloria grabbed her mittens and put them on and then led the way along the narrow path that skirted the lawn, feeling carefully for hidden steps and guiding Winnie behind her.

The garage extended far back into the garden providing ample room for storage. Winnie unlocked the door and Gloria opened it and then opened the wheelie bin lid just as Winnie hauled the sack up and over, hurling it inside.

They laughed at their team effort and then both glanced over at Doug's black BMW at the far end of the garage. There was a heap of cash sitting right there, thought Gloria.

'Have you thought what you're going to do about the car? If you're going to sell, you'd be better doing it sooner rather than later. It won't do it any good just sitting there unused.'

Winnie pretended to tidy already tidy shelves, stacked with all sorts of bottles and tubs of car cleaning stuff – the car was Doug's pride and joy. 'Hm, I'm not sure yet.'

'You could learn to drive?'

'Yeah, maybe.'

'You should.'

'Driving lessons are expensive, Glo. I have to think about these things carefully, I can't just do whatever I want anymore.

'Yes, I know. Things are different now. I know that.'

Gloria paused. Winnie's intense focus on her changed financial status was perfectly understandable, but Gloria was picking up on how she was increasingly sliding into a dogged pessimism.

'Everything's different. Everything's changed; nothing will ever be the same. All the plans we had, all my dreams – they're never going to happen now.'

'Don't say that Wynne. Yes, things have changed, and no, they won't ever be the same, but you can still make your dreams come true. Doug wouldn't want you to give up pursuing all the things you want to do.'

'Apart from the fact there's no money to do these things with. Come on, let's get back inside.'

Gloria knew it was time to let the subject drop. She followed Winnie out of the garage and waited while she fiddled with the tricky lock.

As she waited, she kicked gently at the fluffy snow on the pathway, perfect snowball snow. She bent and scooped a handful in her red woolly mitten, patting it into a neat ball. She was grinning as she strolled casually a little further up the garden and then turned to face Winnie who was still struggling at the garage door. She took aim and hurled the snowball at Winnie's back, who just at that precise second turned and caught the snowball, full thwack, in the chest. Her fleecy zip top was open, and the loose snow covered her neck and was already falling into her jumper and cleavage.

Poor Winnie, she looked up, open mouthed. 'I can't believe you just did that!'

'Woops, sorry, that was a pretty rotten shot. Anyway, it was your fault; you weren't supposed to turn around.'

Winnie stuffed the keys into her fleece pocket and quickly bent to grab some snow. It was biting cold in her bare hands, but she didn't care.

Gloria turned to get away. Not daring to run, she walked quickly, gingerly, but even then, she got caught out by a hidden step – her heel caught it and she stumbled landing on her bottom in the snow.

'Oh my god! Gloria, are you OK?' Winnie was at her side in an instant.

'I think so. Apart from the fact I've now got a soggy bottom!'

Winnie's sympathy was short-lived.

'You're gonna have a soggy top too. Take that Madam!' Winnie pulled at the back of Gloria's jumper and thrust a handful of snow down her back, quickly patting the jumper back in place for good measure.

Gloria arched her back but there was no escape from the icy sludge slipping down her back. She looked up to see Winnie doubled over, hands on her knees, she was laughing, red in the face and eyes watering, hardly able to catch her breath.

Gloria held out her arm. 'Help me up you beast! Is that any way to treat an old lady?'

Winnie helped haul her friend out of the snow. 'Ah, you're not an old lady. You're an old tyrant. And anyway, you started it!'

Gloria got to her feet and shook out her jumper at the back, but most of the snow had already melted against her warm skin. 'Urgh, it's all wet. You rotter.'

'Come on, let's get inside, I'll find you something dry.'

They quickly retraced their steps across the garden, back into the kitchen where Winnie shut the door, bolted it and pulled the curtain across to keep out the draughts. Gloria marvelled at how it now felt delightfully warm inside.

They grinned at each other, both out of breath, but invigorated, and warmer.

Winnie took a hand towel and mopped the melted snow from her chest as Gloria grimaced at the feel of her cold, soggy jumper against her back.

'I have another jumper in your spare room, I left it here last time – I'm going to pop up and change.'

They both changed into dry clothes and met back in the kitchen.

'Shall we have that coffee?' Gloria asked, taking down mugs and setting up the coffee machine while Winnie put a new liner in the bin, noting it needed a good wash inside and out.

'Remember my offer of getting away for a few days, if you fancy it.'

Winnie shook her head. 'I just like being in the house. I feel comfortable here and comfort from it, do you know what I mean?'

'Yes, of course.' A few moments silence had Gloria choosing her words carefully but determined to say something.

'How long is it, that you've lived in this house?'

'We moved in just before Hannah was born. We managed fine in the one-bedroom place, just us and Cathy but when we knew another one was on the way, we had to get somewhere bigger. This felt like a palace at the time – so huge we didn't think we'd ever know what to do with all the rooms.' Winnie looked up and smiled, and then continued.

'We were so used to living in that small space, just a few boxy rooms in a new build. Doug hated it. Right from the beginning he wanted to design our own home, but I always found the idea much too daunting. When we saw this place, it was a wreck but even I could see the potential, and of course because it needed so much doing to it, we got it at a great price.

'And now it's rather a big house just to have me rattling around inside it, but it holds so many memories. I'm glad the girls live nearby and of course Cathy's two will start to come to stay again occasionally.'

Winnie was making all the right observations, Gloria noticed, but still not quite joining the dots. The house was an enormous place for one person, but instinctively she could tell Winnie was nowhere near even considering leaving it.

'So, come on, I interrupted you earlier. How's it been? Your first weeks as a lady of leisure?'

'That only applies to rich women, doesn't it?'

77

Gloria stared at her for a good few seconds and then sighed. 'OK, so you need to make some money. What do you intend to do about it?'

Winnie looked momentarily shocked. 'I don't know. What can I do about it?'

Gloria held the silence, willing Winnie to answer her own question, but she looked so tired and weary, and defeated.

'I've no idea where to start. I try to work out my options but half the time I just can't think straight.'

'What's the situation with Doug's business?'

'It's in the red. Seriously. I had no idea. Another pleasant little surprise for me.'

'Oh god, Wynne.'

'One of his partners is interested in taking it on. But it's all legal stuff now. Cathy's husband said he'd go over it with me, which is good of him, but I don't know what's going to happen.'

'Expensive?'

'Oh, I'm sure it will be.'

Gloria grabbed a stray envelope on the table. 'Can I scribble on this?'

Winnie nodded and got up to get a pen from the dresser. 'What are you doing?'

'We're making a plan.'

Winnie sat back down, not looking particularly enthusiastic.

'OK, you could get a job. But you're not looking to go back into midwifery, are you?'

Winnie shook her head. No explanations were needed.

'And I'm guessing you don't fancy being a checkout girl?'

Winnie gave her a look.

'Don't dismiss the idea. Lots of the bigger stores favour mature women for these responsible roles – you'd be in good company.'

'I'm not sure. I don't think I could handle that beeping all day long.'

'What about a boutique? No beeping in a boutique. And maybe good discount.'

'You think people would come to me for fashion advice?'

Gloria glanced at her orange sweatshirt and gave a disparaging frown.

'OK, moving on. Now what we need to do is to establish exactly what it is you want to do – right now or at least in the near future. With yourself, I mean. Does that make any sense?'

'No.'

'You're not being very constructive Wynne.'

Winnie sighed, hopelessly.

'All the things I want to do? I want to do them with Doug.'

'OK, things like what?'

'Oh, you know, I've told you before.'

'Tell me again.' Gloria listened; pen poised ready to take notes.

'Well, for one thing, I wanted us to go to the south of France, tour the vineyards, become wine tasting experts.' Winnie suddenly smiled. 'Doug wasn't at all keen at first, but he'd have come around. That's why I started the oenology course – it was kind of the first step, or at least a step in the right direction. I don't suppose I'll ever be able to afford it now. I may treat myself to the odd bottle of wine, but that'll be it.'

'OK, we need to think laterally. Out of the box. There's got to be something here. Did you finish the course?'

'No, unfortunately not. I was doing well with it too, flying through the modules and getting the assignments done quite a bit quicker than the suggested pace. It was easy, I was enjoying it so much.'

Gloria looked at her expectantly.

'I haven't touched it since Doug died.'

'OK that's totally understandable. So, is the course fully paid for?'

'Yes, they offered a monthly payment scheme, but I just paid it in full. Stupid really, I might have been able to cancel and get some of my money back.'

'No, this is good. You need to finish the course. I have an idea.' She grinned.

'Gloria, what are you plotting?'

'Look, you need to find a way of earning some money, if you want to stay in this house.'

'Of course I want to stay in this house. It's my home.'

'OK then. And you also need extra funds so that, one day when you're ready, you can continue to follow your dreams.'

Winnie cut in. 'Don't be ridiculous. I can't travel around France on my own, not at my age anyway.'

'Now who's being ridiculous? I'm thinking about taking up belly dancing.'

'That is totally ridiculous.'

They stared at each other for a few seconds, Winnie taking in the fact that even though Gloria was in her seventies, her age wouldn't stop her from doing something if she wanted it enough.

Gloria continued, knowing Winnie was lost for something to say.

'The situation is, you have all this time on your hands. You're a bright, confident, intelligent woman with…. skills.'

They looked at each other and laughed.

'You haven't actually written anything down yet,' said Winnie. 'Not much of a plan, is it?' she teased.

'I'm getting there,' replied Gloria, deadpan serious and ignoring Winnie's flippant comments. 'I'm thinking,' she said as she gazed out the window, deep in concentration as she watched the pretty snowflakes glide to the ground. 'I'm thinking you should finish the oenology course and then teach people about wine.'

She looked at Winnie who stared back somewhat dumbstruck. She watched as Gloria finally jotted down some notes.

'Or something like that. Along those lines. What do you think?'

Instinctively, Winnie felt compelled to object, but a little something about it was causing the tiniest tingle of excitement. She paused for a few seconds, but then the objection took hold.

'It's a crazy idea. I can't teach.'

'Why not? You taught at the hospital, didn't you? All those young student midwives working under you – they'd have learnt a thing or two from you.'

'That was different.'

'I knew you was going to say that. A different subject and a different audience that's all.'

Gloria paused her scribbling and looked up into Winnie's baffled face.

'The more you think about it, the more it makes sense. You have a big welcoming house, a passion for learning about wine, and lots of experience in ……..drinking it!'

Gloria snorted, and in spite of herself, Winnie started to laugh too.

'Well, when you put it like that.'

'Exactly.'

'But it is still a totally crazy idea.'

'Worth some thought though eh?' Gloria continued to make notes.

'Hang on Glo, I need time to think about this.'

'It's OK, we're only playing with ideas at this point, we're not signing anything in blood.' Gloria patted Winnie's hand. 'We're just having fun at this stage. All the hard work, angst and regret comes later.'

'Oh whoop! You're really selling this to me.' Despite her lack of enthusiasm, Winnie couldn't help denying Gloria might just have hit something good here.

Gloria was also thinking this would be the ideal project to occupy Winnie's time and give her a worthwhile focus that could end up being her saviour over the coming months.

'What are you writing now?'

'Just some prompts; things to think about. How many people? How often you should meet – weekly or fortnightly? Wine supplier, glasses, structure of course.'

'Crikey. There'll be one hundred and one things to think about.'

'Just for starters.'

'I'll probably have to get some sort of insurance, won't I? If I'm to have members of the general public in the house.'

'Very likely. Just in case someone slips on some Chablis or impales their finger on a corkscrew!'

'Hm, yes exactly.'

'The first thing you need to do is finish your study course. Good thing you paid up front after all, eh?'

'Yes, wasn't it?' agreed Winnie, unable to find anything negative in that although she was still struggling with how the whole idea would work.

'I'm not sure how I feel about charging people.'

'Winnifred! That's the whole idea.'

'Yes, but it's essentially a hobby.'

'Only at the moment. Soon you'll be a qualified wineologist, or whatever it is. And the idea is to provide a unique experience – your gorgeous home, the opportunity to discuss wine with like-minded others, and of course a couple of glasses of the actual tipple itself. I mean, how much does a glass of wine cost in a pub, and people are quite happy to pay that.'

'Yes, but it wouldn't cost me that would it? I'd buy it in bulk.'

'Ta-daa! Exactly! We'll make a businesswoman of you yet Winnifred Mayhew.'

Chapter 9

Zoe didn't know what to do for the best. Everything seemed to be going from bad to worse. She was humble. Truly. But even this seemed to irritate Lawrence all the more. What was beyond humble? She had no idea.

She had tried to blag it about crashing the car, implying there was something wrong with the gears, but Lawrence knew when she was trying to cover something up. Eventually she'd broken down in tears and confessed it all, promising to never let anything like that happen again. But Lawrence had heard it all before, and his patience was running out.

Things were still strained between them, and she was resigned to feeling completely lost, not knowing what to do or say. And it went on like that for a few days until the atmosphere between them finally, but very gradually, started to lighten.

Lawrence came home from work one evening, via a shopping expedition for ingredients for a meal he was planning. He immediately began cooking, and feeling completely uplifted, Zoe put on some jazz music. Lawrence was whistling away while he chopped and crushed and sliced things. She felt as if her smile had never been so happy.

She didn't even dare glance at the wine fridge but eventually Lawrence opened a bottle and poured them each a small glass which she sipped furtively. This was going to be a perfect evening, she decided. Lawrence had forgiven her, and this was to be a new start. She would be a different person. A better one.

She began setting the small table over by the French doors overlooking the garden. They would dine by candlelight and even make use of those fancy linen napkins they'd been given as a wedding present but had never used.

Zoe hummed as she found the napkins in a drawer – pleased with herself, and slightly stunned too, that she'd remembered where she'd put them. She nudged up close to Lawrence, carefully as he was slicing onions dangerously fast.

'Mm, that looks interesting. What are those?' She pointed at some very unappetising looking brown wrinkly sort of vegetable.

'Dried mushrooms. Full of flavour. I'm doing a very light garlic mushrooms on toast thing to start, which I've prepared and can now leave until we're ready. And then, my dear, we have duck with a red wine and cherry sauce, which I am just about to get going. Couldn't get fresh cherries, they'd sold out, but I'll give it a go with a tin – I'm sure it'll be fine.'

Zoe smiled as she wandered back to the table with the napkins. How lucky was she to have a culinary wizard for a husband? Even if he did insist on wearing a jokey apron that made him look like a lady in her undies.

'Ah, that's a bummer!' said Lawrence, studying the tin of cherries.

'What's up?'

'These have still got the stones in. It's going to take me ages to chop them up. Haven't we got one of those cherry de-stoning things?'

'Oh god, I don't know. I don't think so.'

'I thought we got one as a wedding present. Didn't someone buy us a load of kitchen gadgets, you know, the sort of things no-one ever uses – the sort of things that get thrown in the bottom drawer, never to see daylight ever again.'

Lawrence glanced around the kitchen, deep in thought.

'So, if we had such a thing where would it be?'

Zoe looked over her shoulder towards Lawrence with a cheeky grin on her face. 'In the bottom drawer?'

He grinned back and disappeared immediately below the island, opening and shutting a couple of drawers.

Zoe fiddled about arranging cutlery and wine glasses and candles. It was a few moments before she realised Lawrence hadn't reappeared. The music had stopped, and the kitchen suddenly seemed very quiet. She walked over to where he was still crouched down in front of the very bottom drawer. He was holding his passport application in his hand and looked up at Zoe as she approached.

She was shocked at the ash white pallor on his face and at the same time she felt the blood drain from her own.

'Oh my god,' her voice was barely audible. She had no breath to speak. 'Oh god Lawrence, I'm so sorry.'

Lawrence stood and slapped the bundle of papers on the worktop. He tore off the jokey apron and threw it on top, and then gave his wife a look, a look warning her not to say another word.

Zoe stood there with her face in her hands, hardly able to believe she'd messed up yet again. She only looked up when she heard the front door slam.

Turning around, she leant back against the island, not trusting her legs to keep her upright. Her half empty glass was right beside her and she picked it up and drank the contents in one. She grabbed the bottle from the fridge and filled her glass to the top, leaving the bottle on the side – she'd made the decision it wasn't worth putting it back.

Zoe took her glass and headed for the living room and an evening of looking at someone else's pretty pictures on Instagram. As she left the kitchen, she looked at the expensive bottle of red Lawrence had opened allowing it to breathe. She knew exactly what she was going to do, and that it would hardly help her case, but knew she couldn't stop herself. Not tonight.

She smiled even as the tears filled her eyes, and said quietly, 'I'll be back for you later!'

Chapter 10

The kitchen table was a productive place, strewn with books and pages of information Winnie had printed from the internet. She was deep into her studies, peering at the laptop screen trying to learn about the tank method of sparkling winemaking.

Pages of her notes covered the table as she continued to write about the three primary grapes used in making cava. She copied the names carefully, not sure she could pronounce them, let alone spell them.

She looked up and took a deep breath, wondering if perhaps she was going into too much detail for an informal wine-tasting club, and promptly crossed out the last few paragraphs, feeling relieved in reminding herself to stick to the basics.

Since the day Gloria had suggested she teach people about wine, she'd been unable to think of anything else. Her entire days had been filled with thoughts about whether or not she should go for it. She then started thinking about the structure of the course and started scribbling little notes on scraps of paper as ideas came to her. And when she started to wake in the middle of the night wondering how many people might be interested in such a thing, if anyone at all, she knew she needed to make a decision.

A huge electric bill followed by a gas bill a couple of days later helped her make the decision. She needed an income, anything, and soon.

She was completely shocked at the size of the bills, convinced there'd been a mistake. It took her some time to find previous bills filed away by Doug in the upstairs study, but she had to concede they were both about average for the time of year. Doug had always dealt with the bill paying. She'd had no idea.

'The price of living in a big, old house – literally,' she muttered to herself.

Since committing to the idea, she had spent several weeks working very hard, spending hours every day studying and planning.

Winnie clicked to a different web page on basic wine characteristics; reminding herself of the five basic traits of wine: alcohol, acidity, tannin, sweetness and body. This was a fascinating subject, and she was deeply engrossed.

A powerful speeding car pulled up and parked nearby, coming to an abrupt stop. Winnie heard it on the periphery of her consciousness but didn't actually acknowledge it until there was a sudden loud knock at the back door.

She looked up and through the kitchen window saw Cathy's monster of a car on the drive. Hurrying to open the door, she didn't have time to clear the table and wondered if this was maybe the right time to tell Cathy about her project.

'Hello Love, this is a nice surprise.'

Cathy kissed her mum and swept past her into the kitchen, pulling off her shawl and aiming it towards the worktop but missing it, leaving the shawl to fall to the floor.

'God, Mum, I've had a morning of it! I need a strong coffee; I hope you've got some on the go.'

Winnie picked up her shawl from the floor, placing it carefully on the worktop. Her daughter was already busy with filter papers and opening a new pack of coffee.

'Honestly Mum, sometimes, just sometimes!' Cathy was shaking her head, banging mugs down onto the worktop, getting milk from the fridge and slamming the door shut.

Winnie had no idea what she was going on about, but knew, no doubt, she was just about to find out.

She casually closed the laptop, her mind still busy with the fundamentals of wine bottle labelling. Reluctantly, she moved some books and her pages of notes out of the way onto the dresser. She smoothed her fingers over the glossy pages of the huge volume of Wines Around the World, vaguely aware of Cathy muttering to herself at the far end of the kitchen.

'A girl in Tilly's class is in hospital with a broken leg and now Tilly's convinced every ache and twitch she has is a broken bone. Apparently, it was a bad break, poor thing, and there are complications. And now that's the in-word. Everything has *complications*. Honestly, tell me about it.

'And now Hugo is jumping on the band wagon. He noticed a bruise on his knee this morning and warned me he might need counselling. Where on earth do they get this stuff? It feels like I'm raising a couple of hypochondriacs! I can't believe me and Hannah were ever like this.'

It was a rhetorical question, of course, and Winnie simply smiled, remembering many occasions when her young daughters had argued over who had the worst cough or cold.

Finally, Cathy stopped talking, and Winnie enjoyed the moment of silence. Cathy had days like these, when she was completely overwhelmed by her responsibilities.

'Go and sit down, I'll finish the coffee.'

Cathy pulled out a chair and sat, still thinking about her children's current obsession with bruises and breaking bones. She noticed the pile of books and papers on the dresser.

'You look busy, Mum.'

Winnie brought the coffee mugs over. 'Yes, just sorting some paperwork and things like that. Getting back into my studies.'

'Oh OK. But don't feel you have to rush into sorting everything out all at once, or throwing things out, will you?'

Poor Cathy; she didn't like change. 'No, don't worry, I won't.'

'And I can give you a hand with all that – at some point.'

'Thanks, Dear, I know. Actually, I took matters into my own hands a few days ago and spent the whole evening going over finances. It was a dreadful job, but I think things might not be as totally awful as I thought at first.'

'Oh, right.' Cathy tousled with the knowledge that her mother had been worried about her financial situation. She didn't remember them discussing it at any point. Perhaps she hadn't been listening – her mind had a tendency to wander these days - even during sometimes important conversations. She felt terribly guilty now.

'Well, that's good to know, isn't it? You must be relieved.'

'Yes, I am, somewhat. I still need to find a way of earning to help ease the way, things are still very tight, but I think I might just be OK.'

'You're thinking of finding something else at the hospital?' Cathy's phone beeped, and she bent down to dig it out of her handbag, completely missing the answer to her question.

'Everything OK?' asked Winnie after a few seconds of watching Cathy's frowning face.

'Oh yeah, it's just Tom, letting me know he'll be home late – again.' Cathy threw her phone back into her bag. She sighed deeply and took a long sip of her coffee. 'Mm, that's good.'

Winnie sipped her coffee, observing her daughter over the top of her steaming mug. She was slightly bemused by these impromptu visits. She knew what her daughter was doing – seemingly popping by on her way to or from somewhere just for a quick coffee and a chat. She was checking up on her, making sure she was coping, which was all very sweet but not really necessary. Winnie suspected the visits were more to do with Cathy's needs than her own. Something was telling her that her daughter needed to feel she was being useful.

Winnie couldn't decide on the kindest option – to let Cathy know she didn't need to call round all the time alongside all her other duties, or whether to simply let her continue if that's what she needed to do.

And judging by the absent look on her daughter's face right now, she'd be better off reserving some quiet time for herself. This brought Winnie back to thinking about what she'd rather be doing right now – working her way around the world in wine.

A sudden knock on the kitchen window had Cathy and Winnie jumping in their seats. They looked up to see Hannah grinning in at them. Winnie laughed but Cathy frowned.

'Why can't she just knock at the door, like normal people?'

Winnie got up to unlock the back door again. 'What are you up to? You scared the life out of us.'

'Oh sorry. Couldn't resist.' Hannah hugged her mother and kissed her cheek. 'Hi Sis.'

'Hi Hannah,' Cathy sighed, wondering how quickly she could get away.

'This is a nice surprise, continued Winnie. 'To what do we owe this pleasure?'

Cathy pursed her lips, ruminating on how her younger sister seemed to simply breeze in and out on a whim, never for any useful purpose and yet everyone was always so pleased to see her.

Hannah, in turn, noticed the look on Cathy's face – it was a familiar sight – the sucking on a lemon screwed up face. And she knew it was aimed at her for something or other.

Hannah turned her full attention to her mother, and said, as if it were an announcement, 'I've come to congratulate you!'

'Oh, what for?' Winnie laughed; this was bound to be some silly joke. 'Have I won something?'

'No. I'm talking about your wine tasting club. What a fantastic idea.'

Cathy suddenly looked up; her attention caught. 'What's this? What wine tasting?'

'Ah, yes, thank-you.' Winnie flapped her hands about – a gesture most unlike her but somehow, she was hoping to convey to Hannah this wasn't the best time. Largely because she hadn't mentioned anything about it to Cathy yet.

'How do you know about it, anyway?' asked Winnie, trying desperately to sound casual.

'The woman in the little Tesco – can never remember her name. She lives just down from Gloria. I get all my gossip from her.' Hannah looked over at Cathy who was staring back, totally bewildered. 'I know ev-ery-thing,' she said cheekily, just to wind her sister up. Which it did.

Cathy was up out of her chair. 'Mum? What's she talking about? And when do I get to know what's going on?'

'Oh dear. Now really, there's nothing much to know. And anyway, actually, nothing's *going on* as you put it. This is my way of trying to earn a little money and at the same time, hopefully, enjoy myself.'

'Bravo!' cheered Hannah.

Winnie glared at her. She was being deliberately provocative, and it wasn't helping. She hoped Hannah would leave now so that she could talk to Cathy – her daughters each needed a different style of communication and the two didn't overlap very well.

But unfortunately, still with a stupid grin on her face, Hannah pulled out a chair and plonked herself down, for all the world, like she was enjoying the show. 'Is there any coffee left?'

'No, but you could make some fresh, make yourself useful,' Winnie snapped.

Hannah huffed and puffed dramatically like a petulant child as she rinsed the coffee jug, but finally she saw sense to calm down a little, realising she had actually put her mum in a bit of a pickle.

With Hannah at least at the far end of the kitchen, Winnie took Cathy aside over by the dresser.

'I've been continuing with my wine studies – remember I started them a time ago?'

'Yes, I remember, last year, before...before Dad...'

'Yes, that's right. And the idea is, to get some people together, every fortnight and I'll give a little presentation on a country's wine with some examples to try, of course.'

'What, here in the house?'

'Yes, of course.'

'Oh.'

Winnie could see the cogs turning in Cathy's mind at the prospect of strangers filing into her old family home. She was the sentimental one in the family. But she didn't say anything, for which Winnie was grateful. This was difficult and enough of a challenge for her already without any objections from her family.

'But don't you need proper qualifications to do that sort of thing?'

'Well, I've done the basic and advanced courses in oenology and I'm still studying the subject, so I'll know what I'm talking about. And it's just going to be a casual get-together with like-minded people who want to chat about wine – I'm not passing myself off as an expert or anything. What you see is what you get. I've designed a eight-session course that I'll set out at the beginning, people can pay each time they come and if they don't like it, they don't come back.'

'You can't say fairer than that!' piped up Hannah as she brought two mugs of coffee to the table, going back for her own. 'Sounds like Mum's got it all sorted.'

Cathy was visibly struggling to take it all in. 'Why can't you just get a proper job?'

'It is a proper job!' continued Hannah, taking up the argument on behalf of her mother. 'And anyway, what's your definition of a proper job then? Something in an office, like you?'

Cathy ignored her. 'I thought you were going to look for something at the hospital.' Cathy couldn't actually remember if her mother had said that or not. She hadn't been paying attention earlier.

Winnie confirmed. 'No, I didn't say that.'

Again, Cathy struggled to find the right words. 'But surely it would be better to do something – I don't know – more professional?'

Hannah nearly choked on her coffee. 'Better for who?' She banged her mug down, sloping it onto the tabletop.

Cathy was simply too confused to react.

Winnie sensed a sisterly spat on the horizon, and stepped in to finally calm things down.

'Now come on, you two, I don't need this right now.'

Both women remained quiet, hanging their heads like scolded children, causing Winnie to suddenly laugh out loud.

'For goodness' sake – you look like I'm about to send you to the naughty step!' Winnie took a deep sigh. 'Now, I've put a lot of effort into this project so far, and I'm going to give it my best shot. I'm very nervous about it, of course I am. I don't know, maybe it's a huge mistake and I'll make an absolute fool of myself but I'm going to give it a go. And it'll be a lot easier if you're both pleased for me.'

She could hear Hannah mumbling something incoherent, but she ignored it.

'I hope to start the classes towards the end of June, and we'll go from there. If it all ends up a disaster – really, there's nothing lost. Except perhaps, a bit of my pride.' Winnie smiled.

'June?' Cathy asked, obviously trying to recall something significant. 'Tom's cousin is getting married sometime then, and we'll probably be away for the weekend. You'll still be able to babysit, won't you? I'm sure I asked you before.'

'I'm sure we'll work something out,' confirmed Winnie, not recalling any such conversation.

Hannah was less accommodating. Banging her coffee mug down again, and scraping her chair back, she made to leave. 'I'm out of here! You're unbelievable.' She stabbed a finger in the air, pointing at her sister, who was open-mouthed, oblivious to her insensitivity.

Hannah was at the back door in an instant with Winnie close behind almost acting as a human barrier between the two young women.

'Well, Mum, I'd better go. I only called around to congratulate you; I think it's a terrific thing you're doing, a brilliant idea.' And to particularly emphasise her point, she stood on tip toes peering over her mum's shoulder aiming her words at Cathy. 'It's an absolutely brilliant idea, and you have my full support.'

Chapter 11

The atmosphere between Zoe and Lawrence was bringing her to screaming point. She wanted to shout at him, ask him what he wanted her to do. She'd even be happy if he shouted at her, but this interminable seething politeness from him was unbearable.

After finding his passport application in the kitchen drawer, he'd gone for a drink with a friend. He returned late to find Zoe passed out on the sofa and left her there for the night. He took the next day off work and headed for the nearest passport office to submit an emergency application.

She was terrified their marriage would end. She would do anything to save it, provided Lawrence didn't suggest she have counselling or anything like that. That was the one thing she knew she couldn't handle.

Tonight, they were attending an award evening at Lawrence's offices. It was an important annual event and at first Zoe had tried to excuse herself. She couldn't bear the thought of spending an evening with him at something like this if they were hardly talking to each other – it was painful enough at home.

Lawrence had made a point of telling her he would like her to be there with him, the strong implication being, as long as she behaved herself.

Zoe had resigned herself to simply getting through the evening. She would stay in the shadows or at least stay in Lawrence's shadow, let him do the talking and schmoosing or whatever it was they were all there for. She was absolutely determined to be the perfect, well-behaved wife.

She'd bought a new outfit for the occasion; very expensive but very sombre, almost bland, and even Lawrence noticed. As she stepped into the beige shapeless dress, he did a double take. She had a great figure and usually favoured bright reds or dramatic black evening dresses.

'Do you like it? She asked, worried.

'Yeah, it's OK. Not your usual style though. Maybe a bit old for you?'

'Well, I was going for an understated look. I just wanted to look classy and restrained.' Zoe smiled up at him hopefully.

'You will be classy and restrained. Provided you don't drink too much.'

It was a cutting comment. But obviously heartfelt. Lawrence grabbed his cufflinks from the top of the chest and went downstairs. Zoe sighed and plonked herself down on the edge of the bed, closing her eyes, her head in her hands, overwhelmingly weary. This was going to be a very long evening.

The taxi ride into London had taken forever, not helped by Lawrence's reluctance to chat. She understood why he was angry with her, but for goodness' sake, she was trying to make things better. She was making an effort tonight so they could both enjoy the evening. He could at least meet her halfway.

The taxi pulled up right outside the hotel entrance and they easily found their way to the function room.

It was a huge hall with a grand stage set for various speeches and awards. Round tables with black linen tablecloths and huge silver candelabra formally lined the floorspace. Zoe could feel her chest tighten. She was hoping for something much more informal; a disco ball and a large dance area would have made her feel more comfortable.

She stuck to Lawrence's side as he spotted people he knew at the seemingly never-ending bar which appeared to stretch the entire length of the hall. He ordered drinks and for the first time in what felt like days, he looked directly into her eyes as he asked what she'd like to drink.

'An orange juice,' she said, quietly, but defiantly.

A couple of Lawrence's mates started making jokes about her not drinking, how they were all staying at the hotel, and no-one had to drive, and anyway it was all free.

She smiled sweetly, took her drink and looked around wondering how on earth she was going to get through the evening sober, especially with all these idiots for company.

Later into the evening, the noise levels had risen considerably, and Zoe's head was banging. Everyone appeared to be having a great time – except her.

Lawrence had gone to the bar for more drinks, but that was a while ago, and to be honest, she didn't think she could face yet another fizzy orange. She might have to step it up to a caffeine ridden coke. She looked over to the bar and saw Lawrence centre stage with a group of colleagues, she recognised a couple of them.

She was bored sitting on her own, she'd been here for ages, but worse than that, she spotted a familiar face in the near distance - a well-known flirt from Lawrence's office – he was always at these dos, and he was heading straight for her. She got up and walked in the opposite direction, avoiding his gaze, and then detoured back to the bar. She tried to capture Lawrence's attention, but he was deep in conversation and hadn't even noticed her standing there.

Zoe felt awkward, like a spare part. She was just about to nudge herself into the group when the lecherous flirt appeared at her side.

'I saw you trying to avoid me, young lady. Now, I know we've met before, but remind me of your name.'

'It's Zoe,' she mumbled, not having the slightest interest in having a conversation with him. She couldn't remember his name either and she didn't care.

'Well let's get you a drink, Zoe.'

Good luck with that, she thought. The bar was crowded, people were queuing for drinks and the bar staff were struggling to keep up.

'Stanley, my man, a drink for this young lady please. You're a wine-drinker, aren't you? I seem to remember. A large glass of something white, is it?'

Zoe looked up into his flushed round face. Maybe he wasn't so irritating after all. She quickly glanced over at Lawrence who was still completely distracted.

'Yes please, a large glass of something white and dry. Thank you very much.'

Zoe took the glass and just as she took a first sip, suddenly her eyes met with Lawrence who was glaring accusingly at her. She glared back, and without a word returned to their table, making a quick exit as the letch was mercifully distracted by another poor woman trying to get the barman's attention.

She sat at their table all alone, sipping her wine slowly, feeling slightly more content with each sip. It was fine, she told herself. She wasn't going to overdo things. She could make this large glass of wine last for the rest of the entire evening. Maybe.

She was having fun, observing the guests at this lavish event, particularly the women in their party outfits. She was scoring them, points out of ten for design, style, and suitability – there were a lot of women of a certain age wearing certain things they shouldn't. She was beginning to wish she'd chosen something bolder instead of this awful beige. Her intentions had been well meant but really, she could have worn a sherbet lemon jumpsuit this evening and it would have mingled in perfectly. There were representatives of every kind of style and taste including no style and no taste.

And there at last, she spotted what she'd been looking for. A ten out of ten on all accounts. This woman, only a little older than herself, had style as well as that elusive special something else. Long thick curly hair with a tinge of coppery red, her perfect pale complexion and that clever kind of makeup that takes a heck of a lot of it, to make it look like you've hardly got any on.

Her red silk dress with a shimmer of gold thread, skimmed her petite but curvy figure and she walked demurely despite the daringly high spikey heels. Zoe was enraptured. Occasionally she was taken like this, totally smitten not just by a woman's appearance but by her whole sense of being. She wondered, not for the first time, if it meant anything more. Was it normal to be interested in a woman in this way? She tested herself with a few questions. Did she fancy this woman? No. Did she want to kiss her? Date her? Anything else? No, no, no, definitely not. She just liked the look of her. She was talking animatedly to someone at her side, and it was only now that Zoe realised it was Lawrence. And they were both heading in her direction.

Lawrence looked very happy. He sat next to his wife and the redhead sat next to him. It was the first time Lawrence had spoken to her all evening and the irony wasn't lost on her that it was to introduce this gorgeous woman. But despite all that, Zoe wasn't worried. Funny, even though they had tensions enough in their relationship, she never once doubted Lawrence's love for her and never worried that he might be disloyal, not even with this beautiful woman.

'Claudette, this is my wife, Zoe. Zo, this is Claudette St Paul from work. We were on the project team for the Hamburg trip.'

'Lovely to meet you,' said Claudette reaching over to shake Zoe's hand.

'And you,' mumbled Zoe.

'Lawrence was just telling me he nearly didn't make it. Forgot to get his passport renewed.'

Zoe froze, she could feel her face getting hot and she knew was going red.

Claudette continued, laughing. 'Told me he'd stuffed it in a drawer out of the way and forgot all about it. Silly twit.'

Zoe smiled, relief flooding through her. She looked across to Lawrence, but he was looking down, refusing to meet her gaze. She wasn't entirely forgiven yet then.

Claudette continued. 'Your husband had just been telling me about his interest in wine, well it seems we have a shared interest but apparently, he's quite the expert. He's been impressing me with his knowledge. Are you an aficionado too?'

'Well, I like drinking it, if that's what you mean.' Zoe giggled, and immediately noticed out of the corner of her vision Lawrence's head snap up, as if in warning. She ignored it. As if to illustrate her point, she finished her wine and placed the empty glass back on the table gently. Oh, how she so wanted to wipe her mouth with her sleeve, just to wind him up. But she resisted and simply smiled sweetly at Lawrence.

'I'll have another whenever you're ready Darling.' She noticed the slight flare of his nostrils and got the teeniest amount of pleasure from knowing she was rattling him. For Christ's sake, she'd only had one glass.

Maybe Claudette picked up on the tension, but anyway she continued the conversation very diplomatically steering it back to what she thought was a safe subject.

'I was just telling Lawrence that me and my husband often go to wine tasting events – all over Europe mainly. It's a great way to try new flavours and styles, and a fun way to meet other likeminded people.'

Zoe was tempted to say that she had a wine tasting event right at home every single night, but it wasn't always fun, and she didn't often feel that she was with a likeminded person. But she managed to keep her mouth shut. In fact, she found she was actually interested in what Claudette was saying. She seemed genuinely passionate, not just sounding off and trying to impress.

'Whereabouts have you been? What countries I mean?'

'Well, we've just come back from Italy. I've been before, you know, Venice, Milan - the usual spots. But on this occasion, we went to a far-flung little village right down south, a few hours out of Rome. We stayed on a vineyard, in this gorgeous farmhouse, and tried all of the local wines, at least I think we did. Had a fantastic time, met great people. Brilliant.'

'Oh wow, that's very interesting. I really never knew there was so much to it. I just tend to stick to the one same dry white wine every night.'

Zoe noticed, out of the corner of her vision, Lawrence looking at her. She glanced across, annoyed to see his questioning look. She got it; he thought she was taking the mickey, being sarcastic towards his work colleague. How dare he?

'As you've already gathered, Lawrence is the wine expert in our house. He's always trying to get me to try something new – I see now, he's got the right idea. I need to be braver.'

'Yes, you should just give it a go. I tell you what, let's try something now. I noticed they have a very good selection at the bar. Lawrence, would you mind being the gentleman. I propose the Californian Pinot Noir they have. I had it the other night, it was featuring at a wine bar near our offices – it was gorgeous. Not too heavy, just right.'

Zoe could see Lawrence was reluctant. She looked him direct in the eye. 'Go on, be the gentleman.' She was amused to see he just didn't know what to make of her. And in all honesty, neither did she. She wasn't drunk, she was enjoying the company of whoever Claudette St Paul was, and irony of ironies, she was totally enthused by her passion for wine.

Lawrence returned from the bar a few minutes later, and plonked himself back down, in somewhat of a huff. 'They're going to bring the drinks over – they said they'd bring the bottle.'

'Great idea,' said Claudette. Lawrence smiled over at her, obviously pleased to have pleased her. Zoe knew she wouldn't have got away with the same sentiment.

The bottle of red wine arrived on a tray with three bulbous glasses, and Claudette poured them each a small measure. They sipped, Claudette and Lawrence exclaimed over its attributes and aromas, while Zoe listened intently.

The rest of the evening passed off uneventfully. The three of them remained sitting together while various speeches were made, and awards given. The rest of the wine was shared between them, enjoying small measures at a time, savouring the rich flavour, and the slow, gentle intoxication – an altogether new experience for Zoe.

As the event wound down, and the guests began leaving, or making their way up to their rooms, Lawrence and Zoe followed Claudette out to the hotel lobby where she was getting a taxi home.

'I'll see you in the office on Monday Lawrence. It was great to meet you, Zoe.'

'Yes, and you too. I really enjoyed meeting you, and I enjoyed your company, and everything you know about wine. It was fascinating.'

Claudette gave a little laugh, slightly embarrassed to have gained such an enthusiastic fan.

Lawrence was silent as they took the lift up to their room, but as soon as they were inside, he let it out.

'What was that all about? I enjoyed your company and everything you know about wine?'

'I know. I was a bit gushing, wasn't I?'

'Just a bit,' he snapped.

'Well, I like her. There's nothing wrong with that, is there? She's nice. Really nice.'

'Yes, she is.'

'Well then.'

'You didn't need to paw all over her. It's like you're...'

'Like what?' She dared him to say it. Like she was drunk? He didn't dare say it. Because she wasn't.

'Like what then?' She raised her voice now, frustrated, what had she done wrong now?

'I don't know. It's just weird. You've only just met her – you can't know what she's like.'

'I know enough to have an opinion. And you like her too, admit it, you're practically smitten.'

'Don't go there Zo.'

'Oh, what's the matter? Have I hit on something? You were all over her before I was! Admit it, you like her.'

'Yes, I like her. But not like that.'

'And I wish I was like her. OK? And I bet you wish I was like her.' They were both shouting now.

'No, I don't wish you were like her! I wish you were like you!'

A few seconds past while they each caught their breath and calmed down. And now Lawrence spoke quietly.

'At least, I wish you were like the old you. Before…before, all this. It's only you who doesn't like you, Zo.'

Chapter 12

'Winnifred Mayhew, what on earth are you doing?' Winnie mumbled to herself as she looked hard at her reflection in the bedroom mirror. Her worried face stared back at her, eyes wide as if in shock, her hands gently together in prayer resting just under her chin.

She was contemplating what suddenly seemed such a foolish thing to be doing. Tomorrow would be the first of her wine-tasting evenings, but she couldn't help wondering if there was time enough to call the whole thing off.

She'd lost some considerable weight over the last few months, and even though she was eating better now, the weight was still staying off. She wasn't sure whether that was a good thing or not. Her face was gaunt, and she didn't look overly healthy.

'I'll scare them off before they even get in the door!' she mumbled.

The shrill ring of her mobile phone made her jump. She'd finally learnt to take her phone everywhere with her – ready to answer it in a business-like manner in relation to queries about the wine club and the myriad of other details she'd been dealing with.

'Hello?'

'Hi Mum, only me, it's Hannah. Just wanted to wish you luck for tomorrow evening – won't be able to phone tomorrow because I'm scooting up to Scotland for a festival. You know, I might forget or worse still interrupt you all, just as you're about to spit some Beaujolais or something. Are you really going to do the spitting thing?'

'Well, no, that's not really the idea. Hopefully we're going to enjoy a couple of glasses of very nice wine – I sincerely hope no-one will want to spit anything out.'

'OK, well, have fun with it all. Look forward to hearing all about it. Gotta go though – I'm already late for Mick, and he won't be happy.'

'OK love, off you go then, and thanks for phoning.'

Winnie was relieved Hannah was in a hurry - she wasn't in the mood for a lengthy chat. She clicked the phone off and tossed it onto the bed where it immediately rang again. She sighed, disingenuously hoping the whole of her evening wouldn't be filled with well-meaning calls. She saw it was Gloria calling – good, she wanted a word with her.

'Hello Winnie-Love, just wanted to check what time you want me over tomorrow. I can come as early as you like – you know, if you need me to help with anything.'

'Yes! I'd very much like some help in cancelling this whole thing! I can't believe what I've got myself into. I can't believe I let you talk me into it.'

'Oh, don't be daft. I didn't need to talk you into it – you knew it was a winner of an idea.'

'Well, it doesn't feel like that now. I think I must be mad, trying something like this at my age.'

'At your age? What a ridiculous way to talk is that? Honestly Wynne, you're just having some folks over for a few glasses of wine. You're not going bungee jumping.'

'My hands are sweating; my heart is thumping – it feels like I'm going bungee jumping. And I've got another twenty-four hours to go yet.'

'Look, what's the worst that can happen? If you sense it all going belly-up, just chuck some more plonk down them, they'll all get slightly piddled, and probably won't even pay attention to what you're saying.'

'Well thanks, that's completely reassuring.'

'You're very welcome. And so, do you want me to come over in the morning? Or the afternoon? Or shall I just turn up a bit before everyone else?'

'Well, there's nothing much else to do – come over whenever you want.'

'OK, and how many have you got coming?'

'I've got twelve confirmations. And a couple of my friends from the hospital are coming by, mostly for moral support – I don't think this is really their thing.'

'Twelve. That's a good number for your first week. Once word of mouth gets around, you'll need a marquee in the back garden. And how wonderful that your friends are coming too, just what you need to settle your nerves; some familiar faces, perfect.'

'Yes, they're a good bunch.'

'OK, I'll come over a little earlier and help you set up or whatever. Oh yes, I wanted to ask – would it be OK if I smuggled in a bottle of gin, much prefer it to that grape juice, and no-one will notice if I'm not drinking wine, will they?'

'Of course, they will. And no, you can't bring gin. You'll enjoy the wine – like everyone else.'

Winnie went downstairs, noticing how clean and tidy the place was. All her recent hard work had paid off. After months of alternating between getting away with doing as little as possible, and then finding a sudden burst of energy leading to fitful bursts of crazy cleaning sprees, it was very calming to finally feel she had some semblance of control over the old house.

It was late June but a blustery evening with warnings of heavy rain on the way. Heavy black clouds were already hovering overhead making the living room dark, and it was chilly in there as always.

She switched on a couple of small table lamps, and then decided to build a fire, just a small one to take the chill off. She was an expert at building log fires now, and the skill was still there even though she hadn't used it for a few weeks. The dry logs soon lit, and flames crackled in the stove. She sat in what she still thought of as Doug's chair and gazed into the fire.

She felt completely lost. Tomorrow was such a big day for her. In less than twenty-four hours her home would be full of strangers all expecting her to keep them entertained for the evening. What on earth was she thinking?

Reaching over to the coffee table she picked up a simple white candle in a brass candle stick. After Doug died, she used to light it every night for him. Now she would only light it occasionally, when she was in a particularly thoughtful or melancholy mood, like tonight. She struck a match and lit the candle, took a deep breath and gazed into the flame.

'Am I doing the right thing Love?' she whispered. Winnie often spoke to her husband in her head, throughout the day. She wondered fleetingly, if she was completely losing the plot now.

'Or am I totally crazy? Having all these strangers in our home – how do you feel about that?'

Suddenly, the table lamps flickered, and a couple of seconds later there was a low rumble of thunder. Winnie laughed nervously. 'Was that a yes, or a no?'

The thunder continued to roll, a little louder and more persistent now.

'OK, I'm taking that as a yes, on the basis that you've always encouraged me to do my own thing and would never try holding me back if I wanted to do something.' She laughed at her silliness, but she could feel the tears coming, and continued her conversation.

'It feels so weird to be doing this, and you not knowing anything about it. I wish you were here.' Her immediate thought was that if Doug were here, she wouldn't be doing this at all. Despite her nervousness about tomorrow evening, deep down, a small part of her was looking forward to it.

But did this mean she was moving on? And what did that mean anyway? Did it mean she didn't need Doug anymore? Tears trickled down her cheeks. She wanted him to be a part of her, always, to know what she was doing in her life, and to be a part of it. It felt disloyal to be starting something new without him.

Thoughts like these had been building up over the last few months and now they escaped, rambling, in between her heaving sobs.

'Maybe I'm crazy starting something like this at my age. But please let it work, I need it to work. It'll mean I get to stay in this house, our home. And then I won't ask for anything else. I'm not bothered about going to France, and all of that silliness about touring the vineyards. I know that won't happen now. All I ask is to be able to stay here.

'Oh Doug. Help me Love. Am I doing the right thing? Do you give me your blessing? Please help me.'

Winnie held her face in her hands and after a while she wiped the tears from her face with her fingertips. As she looked up, she saw the candle flame dancing to and fro, and then a fluttering of pretty sparks flew from the flame and disappeared upwards.

She stared, blinking the last of her tears from her eyes but laughing at the same time. She watched as the candle flame calmed and remained upright once again, suddenly feeling inexplicably calm herself, and comforted.

Chapter 13

Zoe lay in bed and heard the front door close. A few seconds later the mechanics of the garage door whirred as it opened, and again when it closed automatically as Lawrence roared away on his bike. Even his motorbike sounded angry.

She'd purposely waited until he'd gone before getting out of bed. He hadn't called out 'good-bye' over the last few days, and actually it was easier just to stay out of the way rather than encounter his too quiet moods and the silence that screamed between them.

They were at rock bottom. Zoe knew it was all her fault, but she didn't know how to put things back together again.

They managed to avoid each other for the majority of the evening; Lawrence staying in the living room watching sport while Zoe remained in their bedroom watching TV there, just popping downstairs at intervals to refill her glass with wine.

She came into the kitchen now and flicked on the kettle. There were two empty wine bottles next to the sink from last night. It didn't take much working out who'd drunk the most of them. There was no point pretending otherwise. She didn't even bother to hide the empty bottle she'd already drunk on the evenings Lawrence was late home from work, which seemed to be almost every night lately, and he was stressed and tetchy when he got home too.

The empty bottles were making her feel guilty and she took them and placed them in the bin. The local paper was still lying on the kitchen island, its usefulness totally superfluous now.

'I don't care,' she said out loud. But her words were feeble, and the sound of her voice sounded strange to her, as if she weren't used to hearing it.

Zoe made a large mug of strong coffee and took it through to the little snug room at the front of the house, putting the TV on for company as she did every morning. She sighed and sipped her coffee. Her head was foggy, and she was tempted to take a nap, noting the ridiculousness of it bearing in mind she'd only just got out of bed.

As she settled herself on the sofa half laying, half sitting, propped up with a number of cushions, her mobile phone rang. She reached over to the coffee table, saw it was her younger sister, Tina, and ignored it.

She just didn't have the energy for her today. She was probably phoning to have a moan about her boyfriend, or about her terrible job or that her Facebook account wasn't working properly and could Zoe pop over to sort it out. And to get over all her woes, Tina would want to go out one evening for a session in the local pub – and honestly, even she could see, that was the last thing she needed to do right now.

Zoe flopped back down among the cushions. She'd hoped it was Nicky phoning, to say she'd enjoyed herself the other day and they must meet up again soon. In fact, any contact from Nicky would be good - it would be confirmation that she hadn't behaved as badly as she believed, from the little she could remember about the day. It would be good to know they were still friends.

Zoe closed her eyes and thoughts of Claudette came to mind. Now, she would really like to be her friend. It was difficult to put into words, but Zoe was thinking how she'd like some of Claudette's vibrancy and confidence to rub off on her. She was totally smitten by her, although it wouldn't do to say that out loud – she was fascinated by her and by her passion for wine. Zoe wished she could feel passion for something like that.

And now she couldn't settle and so she took the remains of her coffee and stood at the bay window overlooking the street. She watched her neighbours going about their business and was surprised at the amount of early morning activity on the street right outside her house.

The woman opposite who was about the same age as Zoe was returning home from doing the school run, and she wasn't the only one – a small group of women Zoe vaguely recognised were chatting and laughing on the pavement before one-by-one disappearing back into their own homes.

A couple of teenagers sloped by, students judging by their heavy backpacks probably on their way to the local college. And then Zoe heard a car door slam to her right, and peered out the window to see Trish, her next-door neighbour getting out of her car. She had a carrier bag of shopping in one hand and a newspaper in the other. Zoe pulled a querying face – did people still read newspapers these days? Everything was available online surely. Obviously, they did. She tried

119

to remember the last time she'd read a newspaper, or even listened to the news, for that matter.

She stepped back from the window in case Trish saw her, feeling both conspicuous and shamefully lazy standing there in her t-shirt nightie and scruffy cardigan. Everyone seemed to have a purpose; they were up and out and about with things to do which was making her feel distinctly uncomfortable.

She drained the last of her coffee and went back to the kitchen, putting the mug in the sink. Noticing the local paper still on the island, she opened it up, flicking through the pages, skimming over some local news articles; a fund-raising event for the local special needs school, a pub landlord who was just about to embark on a sponsored marathon cycle ride for charity and an elderly couple who were celebrating their 70th wedding anniversary.

'Blimey, seventy years,' mumbled Zoe.

She flicked over the pages of properties for sale and rent, and then a four-page wedding spread of adverts for local businesses. Towards the back of the paper there were more adverts for all sorts of things including local events – a car boot sale, belly dancing classes at a community centre, and an advert for of all things a wine tasting class.

This particularly caught Zoe's eye and she leaned in closer to read it. The heading was simply an invite to The Wine Club – commencing on 27th June for fortnightly meetings at a place in Roman Lane – she knew exactly where that was, only about a ten-minute drive away, and actually probably quicker if she walked it.

She was searching for a website address so she could look up further information but there wasn't one. Unusual, she thought. However, there was an email address and a telephone number and the person to speak to was Winnifred Mayhew.

Chapter 14

At last, it felt like summer. It had been a gloriously hot day, and even though it was now cooling into evening, it had that still balminess to it that spoke of country pub gardens and bedroom windows open all night.

The back door was open, and Gloria walked straight in, calling out to Winnie in a cheery voice.

'Hello there.'

'Come on in Glo, I'm in the kitchen.'

The first thing Gloria noticed was how wonderfully fresh and tidy the house looked. Winnie must have worn herself out cleaning. And she'd prepared the kitchen perfectly; new sparkling wine glasses were lined up on the worktop, an assortment of chairs she'd obviously collected from all over the house had been arranged casually around the large kitchen table, and she'd placed a number of candles about the room ready for lighting later in the evening. A couple of the smaller windows were open, and a light breeze gently fluttered the newly laundered pretty cotton curtains.

'This all looks very nice. You've done a brilliant job Wynne.'

Winnie was placing her typed up notes in a neat pile on the table in front of where she'd be sitting.

'Do you think so? I hope I haven't forgotten anything.'

'I'm sure you haven't. And you look nice too. Nice dress.' It was good to see Winnie out of her sloppy jeans and baggy tops for a change, but at the same time, Gloria was somewhat shocked – her friend

122

looked old. She wore a very plain navy dress which was unnecessarily loose, her soft blond hair was pulled back too severely, and she was wearing hardly any make-up.

Gloria wasn't sure what kind of look she was aiming for, but she was pretty sure it wasn't working. Although she didn't want to knock Winnie's confidence this late in the day, she drew the line at the shoes.

'What are those on your feet?'

Winnie instinctively looked down. 'These are my comfy walking sandals.'

'Sorry Wynne, they're hideous. They've got to go.'

'But I'm going to be on my feet all evening.'

'You're going to be poodling around your kitchen for a couple of hours, not doing the moonlight walk. I know you've got something prettier, go on, fetch them, and maybe put a bit of lippy on. You've got to think power dressing girl - you've got to let everyone know you're in charge.'

Winnie, suitably chastised, disappeared upstairs, mumbling something inaudible as she went. Gloria smiled. She noticed a very pretty grey scarf, with silver sparkly butterflies on it, folded neatly on the dresser, and was shaking it out just as Winnie returned.

'That's Cathy's scarf, she left it here by mistake the other day.'

'It'll go perfect with your dress, here, just drape it casually, don't tie it or anything. Oh yes, and those sandals are much better. Excellent. You look gorgeous.'

123

Winnie just smiled, somewhat in defeat. Gloria always had superb taste in style, and Winnie knew that just these couple of amendments to her outfit would have made a marked difference.

She bent, holding her scarf out of the way, and checked the nibbles in the oven. She decided they were done and removed two trays of pastries.

'They smell delicious,' said Gloria.

'Good. Come and sample one if you like.'

Gloria took a mini savoury pastry from the tray and popped it into her mouth. It was very hot. 'Mmm-mmm,' was all she could manage without burning her mouth. She smiled and gave an enthusiastic thumbs up.

While Winnie put the pastries on platters, Gloria picked up the course notes. She glanced through the pages which covered the very basics of wine tasting. A separate page provided information on handling wine and there was also a section explaining the various terminology used on wine labels.

'This is very impressive, very professional. You've done a good job here.'

'Thanks, I'm quite pleased with how it's shaping up. We'll see, I may have to tweak things.'

A loud knock at the front door had them both looking up at the kitchen clock in perfect synchronicity. Winnie looked panicked.

'I don't bloody believe it – someone's arrived early.'

'Go on, answer it, it'll be fine – I'll finish putting these on plates.'

Winnie opened the door to see three of her lifelong friends from the hospital huddled on her doorstep, all clutching a mixture of gifts – flowers, chocolates and wine.

'Hello,' they shouted in unison. 'We thought we'd come along a little earlier than everyone else,' whispered Fran. 'You know, just for some moral support. And Mary decided to come at the last minute, the more the merrier, eh?'

Winnie could have hugged them all. It was such a delight to see some familiar faces against the backdrop of the terrifying notion of having to entertain a kitchen full of complete strangers all evening.

'Bless you all. Come on in.'

'I bought a bottle,' said Mary. 'I wasn't sure whether we were supposed to bring our own or not.'

'Well actually, I'll be providing the wine, but thanks Mary, it's very kind of you.'

They stepped into the hall, all quietly thinking the same – how on earth did Mary manage to smuggle a bottle of wine out of her house without her husband sniffing it out?

Winnie took their jackets and stored them in the boot room, as everyone bustled through to the kitchen. As Gloria took the initiative and introduced herself to everyone, it took Winnie slightly by surprise to realise none of her friends had met Gloria before.

But of course, within a few seconds they were all chatting together like old friends to the point where Winnie almost felt like a spare part. And for a split-second she was convinced she was the wrong person for the job. But then, she caught Gloria pouring a short measure of gin into a wine glass – they caught each other's eye and Winnie laughed at the sight of Gloria's cheeky guilty face.

'Just a very small one,' she whispered, 'before the others arrive, and then I'll pretend to enjoy the other stuff along with everyone else.'

'You won't have to pretend - it's very nice wine.'

'I'm sure it is but you know what I mean.'

The first real guests to arrive were a married couple in their fifties – Lucinda and Clifford. Their arrival was followed soon after by two young girls Kerry and Ayisha, teenagers or maybe just into their twenties, Winnie deduced. They explained they were at catering college and had decided the wine club would enhance their culinary studies.

Everyone settled around the table and introduced themselves. It was all very easy and friendly, and Winnie breathed a tiny sigh of relief.

After a worrying few minutes without the addition of any further guests, a very loud demanding knock on the front door had them all jumping in their seats. It announced the arrival of Sheila; a tall, strongly built woman, who was rather frightening to look at. She was the sort of woman you wouldn't want to meet on your own in a dark alley. But the sort of woman you'd very much like to have with you if you found yourself on your own in a dark alley.

Winnie opened the door and tried not to look too taken aback at the sight of this woman with voluminous black hair and heavy eye makeup.

'Hello,' she smiled her friendliest smile.

'Hi, I'm Sheila. I sent an email.'

'Oh yes, that's right. Come on in.'

At that moment an elderly but sprightly man, came striding up the path. 'Ah, so are you two together?' Winnie asked.

The man looked up at Sheila. 'No, we're definitely not. I'm Peter. I don't know who she is.'

'Hello to you too! I'm Sheila and I'm here for the wine tasting evening.'

'Yes, well, me too,' he answered grumpily. Winnie stood aside as Peter entered the house, obviously keen to get away. Sheila followed him while Winnie closed the door, smiling to herself, already anticipating the colour these two would bring to the evening. By the time she returned to the kitchen, Sheila was already holding court.

'Finally! I thought I'd never get here. In fact, it's a miracle I made it at all. Roadworks everywhere, and the ridiculous diversion took me halfway across town. Insane it is. And you can't even see what they're doing.

'Anyway, I'm here now.' Sheila spoke as if everyone had been waiting exclusively for her attendance. She sat down, crossing her incredibly long legs, sheer black tights and leopard skin stilettos. She smoothed her tight black skirt with both hands and looked up expectantly, bright red lips smiling with anticipation.

After more arrivals, with one eye on the clock, Winnie decided they were pretty much a full house, and that she ought to get started. She calculated there were only two no-shows which meant there was a total of fourteen including her friends and Gloria. It was busy in her kitchen.

She gave her well-rehearsed (in front of the bathroom mirror) introduction speech, briefly outlining the content and structure of the course taking place over the next few months.

She went on to explain that this week – week one - was a simple introductory meeting for everyone to get to know each other and ask any questions they might have.

'We're not going to do any formal wine tasting this evening – we'll start with that next week when we'll be discussing English wines. But for tonight, as you can see behind me, I've provided a wide variety of wines from light-bodied whites to full-bodied reds and all from different countries. Just help yourselves, try whatever you fancy – you might see a favourite of yours here, or you might like to try something completely different.

'Take notes as you go, I've got paper and pens if anyone needs them. I'm going to open this one here, an Australian wine made from the Syrah grape, one of my favourites, so if anyone would like to join me, just say so. Otherwise, grab a glass and please go ahead and help yourselves.'

Soon the kitchen was buzzing with activity. With glasses in hand, the club members studied the variety of wines lined up on the worktop, trying to make sense of the labels to help them with their choice.

They popped corks and unscrewed bottles and tentatively sipped as they returned to their seats.

'I like this one,' said Lucinda, quietly to her husband, as if it was just the two of them in the room.

'Which one did you choose?' Winnie asked.

'The Sauvignon Blanc. It's what I usually have. I thought I'd start with something I knew I would like.'

'Ah yes, this is a light-bodied dry white wine, extremely popular, and a good wine to start learning with. The grape originates from the Bordeaux region of France but is now grown all over the world, including Chile, the USA and Australia.

'What is it that you particularly like?' asked Winnie, encouraging her to share with the group.

'Oh, I don't really know – I know this is a wine tasting class, but I always find it a little bit silly when people describe the taste of wine, you know, when they say it reminds them of chalk boards, or coal and vanilla marshmallows – I just think it's all a bit daft.'

A few of the others laughed gently.

Lucinda was relieved to see Winnie smiling.

'Yes, I know what you mean. Some descriptions, especially by some professionals, do seem rather over the top sometimes. We're going to be much more informal here, just sharing our thoughts and opinions on why we like what we do and why we don't. But do try to keep an open mind. You might be surprised by what you learn to identify.'

'Yes, OK, I see what you mean. We can be more down to earth here.' She looked over to her husband who gave her a reassuring smile.

'Exactly. Over the coming weeks, we're going to learn the 4-step wine tasting method which is a professional tasting technique. The idea is to focus your ability to separate and identify key characteristics in a wine.

'We're going to discuss the look of the wine in the glass, the smell and of course its taste before forming a conclusion. But that's all to come. This week is just for us to introduce ourselves and for me to give you an overview of the structure of the course, and for you to ask any questions or make any suggestions, all comments are welcome.'

Cliff held his glass at arm's length and cocked his head to one side as he gazed at the pale white wine in his glass. He then stuck his nose into the glass and gave a good sniff. He closed his eyes as he took a large swig, his face contorted in concentration, swishing it around his mouth before swallowing. He opened his eyes and grinned.

'Well done, Cliff,' Winnie smiled at his playfulness.

'Gooseberries!'

'Pardon?'

Cliff had a look of total astonishment on his face.

'I've got the Sauvignon too and that's what I can taste – gooseberries. Oh, wow. I can't believe it. I wasn't even trying to identify anything; it just came to my mind, out of the blue. Can you taste it Lulu?' Cliff turned to his wife who was sipping her wine and nodding in agreement, albeit a little unsure.

'Well done,' said Winnie. 'Anyone else like to add their thoughts and observations?'

'I don't really like gooseberries,' said Sheila. 'They give me an acid stomach.'

'Oh,' said Winnie, not knowing what to say to that.

'I've gone for the Sauvignon as well, and I do like this wine,' continued Sheila. 'But it doesn't taste like gooseberries to me.' She smacked her lips together several times and looked studiously into the distance as if for inspiration. 'I see what you mean,' she said, turning directly to Cliff. 'I detect a certain crispness. It's quite sharp, almost piercing.'

'Well done, Sheila.'

'But I'm thinking, more, sort of, it's on the tip of my tongue. I know – rotten crab apples!'

Kerry and Ayisha giggled aloud, and Sheila smiled at them, happy to have provided entertainment.

Mary was sipping timidly, concentrating hard. Winnie was tempted to ask for her opinion but caught her eye and picked up that she wasn't altogether confident within this group of strangers.

A couple of women who'd arrived last and were sitting over by the garden door offered a few ideas of their own; cooking apples, grapefruit and a slightly more artistic suggestion of freshly mown grass.

Time flew, and as it got to halfway through the evening, everyone seemed to be mixing and getting on well together aided greatly by Gloria who already had them all eating out of her hand, to which Winnie had somewhat mixed feelings. She'd got a huge laugh from the crowd when she confessed to not really liking wine at all and hoped they didn't mind her sipping away on her gin and tonic.

Winnie was pleased to see her friends from the hospital enjoying themselves and really getting into the swing of the evening. Even Mary seemed lighter in spirits this evening – the general attention and focus not being on home and family and drunken husbands for a change.

Everyone was finally settling in and feeling more confident to voice their opinions.

Peter, the rather odd-looking man, pale and thin, with thick rimmed glasses seemed to be taking it more seriously than most – perhaps a little too seriously. Whilst everyone was encouraged to voice their opinion, his had been consistent throughout, and rather forceful at times, grunting and guffawing at the wine descriptions of others but not suggesting any of his own.

'Did you know there are over ten thousand varieties of wine grapes that exist worldwide?' he asked generally but looking directly at Winnie.

'Yes, actually I did – fascinating statistic, isn't it?'

'Hm. And do you know how many different species of oak are available for sourcing wood for wine barrels?'

'Ah, now, you've got me on that one. How many are there?'

'Over four hundred species of oak.'

'Really? Wow, yes, that is truly amazing.' Winnie wasn't sure where this question-and-answer session was going.

Gloria was observing out of the corner of her eye.

'Did you know there are actually people who have a fear of wine. Do you know what it's called?'

Winnie took a deep breath, her lips tightly shut. It wasn't often her patience was tested in this way, and she didn't quite know how to handle it.

Thank goodness for Gloria.

'Well, I should think it's called wineophobia, isn't it?' Gloria said grinning, hoping to dissipate the tension.

'You're close actually,' said Peter, turning to Gloria, seemingly pleased she was enjoying the game. 'It's oenophobia.'

'Fascinating. Now, shall we let Winnifred continue with the evening? What's next Wynne?'

Winnie managed to focus and addressed the group around the table.

'Before the evening ends, I'd like to make sure everyone has a copy of these notes to take away with them.'

'What's this? Homework?' asked Peter. Winnie ignored him.

'I'd like our evenings together to focus on trying different wines and getting to understand the different types and the factors that effect and influence the different styles. And while I don't want this to be a classroom type situation, there is a certain amount of studying needed which will only help to enhance the whole experience for you.

'Of course, it isn't obligatory.' She pointed this comment directly at Peter, pausing for effect until he finally looked up at her, hopefully getting the point.

'But if you have a look through what I've prepared, you'll see plenty of information including the definition of wine, details on grape varieties and regions.

'There are some notes on bottle sizes and how wine is labelled, and finally of course, some notes on tasting wine. If you can find time to read through before our next meeting in a couple of weeks, it will certainly help you in understanding as we go through the course.

'So, before our session closes, I think we have about thirty minutes left, be sure to try one more wine if you like. Try to go for something completely different from what you would usually choose.'

Winnie glanced down, pleased to see Ayisha and Kerry scribbling away. They had filled a good couple of pages with notes.

'Oh yes, there are a few more pastries left – help yourselves to those. This has been a good first session, and I hope you've all enjoyed it too.'

Everyone nodded enthusiastically in agreement and exclaimed how much they were looking forward to the next session. Sheila clapped her hands, and Winnie gave a little bow, delighted to be so appreciated.

Finally, Winnie closed the door on the last person to leave who unsurprisingly was Peter. She returned to the kitchen with a heavy sigh, smiling, but totally exhausted.

'That was brilliant Wynne.'

'Oh, thanks Glo. I think it went well.'

'Yes, it went more than well. It was a triumph. Well done to you! Come on, I'll even share a glass of this bubbly stuff with you – to toast your success.'

They chinked glasses.

'And you know what, I found it rather interesting – you've really done your research.'

'Don't sound so surprised! Although actually, I am rather surprised myself.'

'At what?'

'At the fact you were listening! Anyway, you honestly think it was OK? I could hardly think straight the whole way through.'

'The opening session was bound to be the most difficult. But there were no complaints were there? And everyone went home happy – and slightly piddled!'

Winnie laughed. 'I suppose, when you put it like that, it did go OK. I'm pleased.'

'So you should be. Cheers! Here's to you and your new career.'

'And there were only two no shows. A young woman who phoned me; we had a little chat and she seemed very keen. Zoe, I think her name was. And someone else who sent an email saying they would be coming. Never mind, perhaps they'll come along next time. Do you want a top up Glo?'

Winnie turned her back and fussed with empty bottles and platters. After a few moments of suddenly noticeable silence, Gloria hugged her shoulders.

'Don't think I haven't noticed that little dark cloud hovering over you on and off throughout the evening. But come on, this isn't the time to be sad.'

Winnie gave a little smile. 'You don't get to choose the times - they just come.'

'I know. You're quite right.'

'More bubbly?'

'Actually, I can't drink any more of this stuff. Sorry Wynne, I'm going to have one small G&T, just to take the taste away.'

Winnie gave her a look of mock disapproval. 'Actually, I think I've had enough too. How about coffee?'

'Perfect. And then we'll clear this lot up, and I'll get a taxi home.'

Chapter 15

Gloria had spent a lot of time at Winnie's over the last few months, and while she was more than willing to be there for her friend, she missed her home and routine. She laid the table now for breakfast, content in the familiarity of her own space and her own way of doing things.

She opened the back door which led from the kitchen of her little cottage directly onto the garden, inviting the perfect summer day inside and then she smiled at the good timing of seeing her postman walking up the path, a small parcel in his hand.

'Morning'.

'Good morning. What a wonderful sight - a man bearing gifts at this time of the morning.'

'Well, just the one. I don't think you'll be too pleased with the other ones; they look like bills.'

'I'm hoping that package is from the wonderful eBay people with my belly dancing cymbals in it.'

The postman raised his eyebrows. 'I'm saying nothing,' he said, failing to keep his grin to himself.

'How do you feel about all the extra work from people buying things off eBay, and everyone posting here, there and everywhere?'

'Keeps me in work I suppose. On the other hand, we've lost a lot of work due to people doing their personal admin online, you know, banking, and paying their bills, and everyone wanting to be paperless these days. So, yeah, it all balances out, and as I say, keeps me in a job.'

'Well, thank the Lord for eBay then!' Gloria shook her parcel to emphasise her point and heard a faint tinkling sound from within. The postman smiled as he returned down the path, wishing all his customers were so cheerful this time in the morning.

Gloria saw her neighbour approaching the low rickety fence that divided their boundaries.

'Morning Gloria dear.'

'Good morning, Ada. How are you?'

'I'm not bad. Can't complain, you know.'

Gloria smiled. For a 92-year-old with severe arthritis and a twit of a son who hardly ever visited, she had plenty to complain about. But she never did.

Gloria could tell Ada wanted to ask something of her.

'Is there anything you need? It's shopping day tomorrow, Saturday as usual, I'll call in first and you can tell me what you need.'

'Yes, yes, I know what day it is. I haven't completely lost my marbles yet, just my ability to balance on a ladder and change a lightbulb.'

Adorable Ada – sharp as a dart, and still as quick.

'OK, I'll pop in later; I'm sure I can help with that.'

'You're a darling Gloria Fairweather or Merryweather or whatever your surname is these days.'

Yes, adorable Ada, thought Gloria as her neighbour slowly turned and shuffled back to her front door.

As she went Gloria caught her grinning – a cheeky grin.

She returned to her kitchen and made tea, a soft-boiled egg and toast, and as she ate, she opened her parcel. From the tissue paper wrapping, she took out two pairs of the cutest little metal finger cymbals with tiny leather straps to keep them in place. She'd seen a poster at the community centre advertising belly dancing classes and fancied giving it a go but planned to have a little practice first in the privacy of her own home – and with her own cymbals. She slipped a pair onto her middle finger and thumb and gently tapped them together. They were surprisingly tuneful, creating a delicate tinkling sound. She laughed to herself – she was having fun already.

Although, sure enough, the sight of the two envelopes containing bills soon stopped her fun. She opened the gas bill. It was all set up to be paid by direct debit monthly, but she still needed to check the figures. This one was a shocker, but she reasoned that it had been a bitter winter and the central heating had been on fairly constantly. And as was the norm, she offered up to whoever was listening, a little prayer of gratitude that she could afford to put her heating on without worrying about finances. She was luckier than a lot of people.

Gloria poured herself another cup of tea and took it through to the living room, thinking now of Winnie and how cold she'd been through the winter in that big old draughty house.

She lowered herself gently onto the comfy sofa, propping her feet on the antique coffee table; a souvenir brought back from one of her holidays with Bill.

Gloria glanced around her living room; small, elegant and cosy. The sweet little open fire with Edwardian surround was mostly for effect although the comfort from a log fire was unbeatable on the coldest evenings. She was surrounded by memories of her travels over the years, festival masks from Venice, and Waterford crystal from Ireland. She adored everything about her home, just as much as she did when she moved in four years before, and again she observed the contrast between this cosy space and Winnie's rambling family home.

The low ceilings and beams provided old world charm and character helped along by plenty of mod-cons in the state-of-the-art espresso machine and super-speedy broadband. She loved a bit of surfing on the internet although she wished she understood more about Instagram and Twittering – apparently, they were good resources for connecting with like-minded people. She firmly believed a person couldn't have too many friends or connections. Loneliness was the new smoking - it kills, she'd read recently.

Gloria sipped her tea, focusing on happier thoughts and closing her eyes in contentment. She was a party girl at heart, but how she loved her moments of solitude.

Thoughts returned to the previous evening and Winnie's first wine club meeting. She was so pleased for her friend that it had gone well. A good turn-out and a good bunch of people by all accounts, apart from that rather odd fellow, Peter. She wondered what exactly his story was. And how exciting for Winnie to have this new project to occupy her. Exactly what she needed. It would help to see her through this difficult time.

Gloria opened her eyes and glanced at the clock; she needed to get on, the day was escaping. She took her cup of tea and opened a narrow door to the side of the fireplace and went up the steep winding staircase leading up to the next floor. Her bedroom at the back of the cottage overlooked a serene view of farmland; fields of green, a solitary tree dotting the landscape here and there – Gloria knew them all one by one.

She stood at the window and breathed in the view, absorbing the energy from the peaceful scene. Standing here at this cottage window, she could imagine this was exactly how it would have looked one hundred years ago and more, provided she squinted and blocked out the massive superstore just on the outskirts of the village. But apart from that the place was idyllic and pretty much unspoilt.

She felt uplifted by the scene and thought to spend the morning reading in the garden, and maybe she'd take her lunch out there too. The afternoon would see her on Google, searching for websites that taught belly dancing and she'd find out exactly what to do with those little cymbals.

Later in the day, as the light was fading, Gloria suddenly remembered Ada next door – she needed a lightbulb replacing. She hurried outside and shimmied over the little fence into Ada's garden, knocking loudly on the door and calling out to reassure her who it was.

After a few moments, she saw the old woman shuffling along the hallway.

'Hello Ada, I'm so sorry, I only just remembered your lightbulb. Do you have one handy?'

'Yes, of course I do. I thought you'd forgotten all about me. That'll be old age - your memory goes.'

Gloria smiled as she followed Ada into the kitchen.

'Up in the cupboard there.' The door to a high cupboard was already open showing a stash of more than twenty or thirty 100w lightbulbs.

'Blimey Ada. You've got enough here to light Blackpool Illuminations.'

'I'm stockpiling. Bloody EU. They're banning them.'

'Are they? Banning lightbulbs?' Gloria reached up and took one down before closing the cupboard door.

'Well, something or other. They're banning bright lightbulbs or a certain type or whatever. I'm half blind as it is, I need a decent light to do my crosswords, so I'm keeping a stash of what I need.'

'Good idea. Very sensible. Where's this to go?'

'Just through in the living room there.'

Gloria led the way to the tiny room at the front of the cottage. It certainly was dark in there. She glanced around, marvelling at how a family would have huddled together in here as their main living space many years ago. Ada's cottage was hundreds of years older than hers, built in the late 1600s or thereabouts for the local farm workers, long before electricity. It was almost impossible for her to imagine living entirely by candlelight.

Ada had already placed the stepladder in position under the central ceiling light.

'Is the switch off?'

'Of course it is.'

Gloria replaced the bulb and stepped down just as Ada flicked the switch, almost blinding them both with its sudden glare.

'That's better,' smiled Ada, and Gloria immediately felt guilty for not coming over earlier.

'Anything else while I'm here?'

'No, no, that's all, thank-you very much. I'm fed and watered, and I've cleared the kitchen. Now I get to settle, finish my crossword, watch a bit of tele. And maybe a small whiskey before bed.' Ada held Gloria's arm to steady herself and laughed. She had rickety old teeth and her face was lined with deep wrinkles, but her smile was that of an old woman content with her lot.

Back in her own cottage, Gloria also prepared for the cooling evening, shutting windows and closing curtains, switching on small table lamps, grateful again she wasn't living by candlelight.

Upstairs she closed the bedroom curtains and turning back into the room, her eyes were drawn up to the collection of old suitcases gathering dust on top of the wardrobe. They'd been untouched for a while now.

She reached up and touched the old leather strap of one that had belonged to her parents – a miracle right there that it had survived so many modern airline manoeuvres. But she daren't use it now – it was far too fragile.

She thought of her neighbour, in her nineties, still independent, and hoped the same for herself if she managed to get to that age. She glanced at the suitcases again; hopefully, she had a lot of living to do before her life became just the tele, crosswords and a glass of whiskey.

Thoughts of Winnie came to mind again and her wine club project. She was suddenly envious of all that Winnie was taking on. The Wine Club – it wasn't Gloria's sort of thing at all, but she definitely needed something new for herself too, she decided – something more than just belly dancing. And as she lay in bed that night, unable to sleep, she planned and plotted - it was time for a new adventure, and she had just the thing in mind.

Chapter 16

Zoe woke with a foggy head and a blinding headache. She was used to it. And she was used to the ensuing few seconds when she tried to figure out what day it was.

Finally, she got it - it was Saturday, and she was relieved to see Lawrence was out of bed already. If things were how they should be, if she hadn't messed up yet again, Lawrence would still be in bed beside her. Their weekend would be starting in its usual wonderful way – most of the morning in bed until one of them finally lost the battle and got up to make tea which they would drink in bed in between more snuggled up snoozing.

Zoe tentatively extricated herself from the duvet, sitting on the edge of the bed and assessing the damage she'd done to herself the previous evening. It was about average.

She took her time showering and dressing – she was in no hurry to get downstairs to be swamped, once again, by Lawrence's overwhelming sense of disapproval, or was it disappointment? Probably both.

Just as she was leaving the bedroom, she caught sight of the advert she'd tore from the local newspaper – the one about The Wine Club. She pulled it out from where she'd tucked it in between some books on her bedside cupboard. Winnifred Mayhew – she sounded nice.

Zoe was inexplicably drawn to the idea of joining, although she'd already missed the first meeting. She hadn't mentioned it to Lawrence but had planned to go. He was working late, and she was going to give it a try. If it wasn't for her, she needn't go back. But then she'd downed a quick glass of white, just as a little pick-me-up, and things went predictably from there. Before she knew it, her eyes were heavy, and as she looked at the clock, she realised The Wine Club's first meeting had started half an hour ago.

Downstairs Zoe made strong coffee. The doors to the garden were open which probably meant Lawrence was doing something either in the garden or the garage.

As the coffee gurgled through its filter, she peered around outside to see if there was any clue as to what her husband was doing. She jumped on the spot as he suddenly appeared behind her, having come back in from the garage via the back hallway.

'Do you want coffee?' she asked, trying to sound friendly and casual.

Lawrence heard wooden and fake.

'No thanks.' But then he relented. 'Oh OK, go on then.'

Zoe felt uplifted. She would make him the best cup of coffee ever.

'I'll be back in a minute.'

Lawrence disappeared back outside, and it was over fifteen minutes before he returned. Zoe was still sitting at the kitchen island, looking lost, deflated, and their coffee was almost cold.

Lawrence had got caught up trying to fix the garden sprinkler system. He wasn't naturally mechanically minded but today, of all days, he was determined it wouldn't get the better of him. But now it was only adding to his bad humour.

He'd genuinely forgotten about the coffee Zoe was making for him, and he'd dashed back to the kitchen, confounded to see her exactly where he'd left her, just sitting staring into space.

Did she never have an agenda for her day? He wondered. Too irritated to speak, he gulped his lukewarm coffee as they both gazed into space – in opposite directions. He found the ever-expanding gulf between them exhausting and with a weary sigh he left the room.

Back outside, he'd lost the impetus to figure out the workings of sprinkler jargon, and he just threw the lot into a plastic storage box, slamming on the lid.

The sight of Zoe sitting in the kitchen was haunting him. She was like a ghost. He was unable to communicate with her, just didn't know how to start, or what to say. She was slipping away from him, sliding further and further out of reach.

He sat down, heavily, on the storage box and thought back to when they first met. He smirked at the idea that people would label theirs a whirlwind romance. They were living together within six months and were planning a wedding six months after that.

He couldn't wait to make her his. She was fun, childlike, silly – they'd lived the newly in love life, living minute by minute. With no pressure of long-term plans, they'd take off to Paris on a whim, go for crazy bike rides until they were too tired to cycle back and end up at a B&B for the night.

There was always someone having a party and they'd stay out drinking and dancing until the early hours. Drinking. When did it become such a habit for Zoe? He couldn't pinpoint the time. He was ashamed to admit he hadn't noticed. He had his job, he was driven, always on the look-out for the next opportunity. He'd assumed that as he provided for Zoe, putting no pressure on her to contribute an income, she would be happy.

And then in a split second, it hit him. Like a blow to the belly. He couldn't bear to lose her.

He went straight back to the kitchen. Zoe looked up. It was difficult to tell who had the saddest eyes.

'Hey.' He tried a smile, stroked her long blond hair.

She smiled back and held out her hand which he took in his.

'Do you want to do something? We could go for a ride on the bike?'

Zoe simply shrugged her shoulders. She wasn't sure she had the energy to do anything. The rollercoaster of their day was exhausting her too.

And then her mobile rang. She looked at the screen. It was her sister, but she ignored it, turning her face away.

'You not going to answer that?'

'No, it's only Tina.'

'OK, so why don't you want to speak to her?'

'Because I don't. She'll be going on about something, and I just can't handle her, or anything at the moment.'

'OK.'

'It's not my job to look after her.'

'OK, I said OK.' Lawrence suddenly laughed, a derisive snort.

'What is your job then?'

Zoe looked up at him, stunned by the directness of the question, and the implication behind it.

'You never do anything. You don't want to do anything. What's with you these days Zo?'

'I do things,' she spat back, but was unable to think of anything other than crashing the car and forgetting his passport application. That wasn't the sort of example she was racking her brain for.

'Actually, I've found something I'm very interested in getting involved in.'

'Great, what is it?'

'I'm going to join a wine club.' She chose not to mention that it had already started but she hadn't managed to get herself there.

'A what?'

'A wine tasting club.'

'You're kidding me, right?'

'No. It's only over in Roman Lane, I can easily walk there.'

'Well, yes, you'd need to – you wouldn't be able to drive it! Seriously? Is that the best thing you can think of to get into?'

'I thought you'd be pleased.'

Lawrence got up and indicated the fully stocked wine fridge.

'What is it? Isn't there enough here for you?'

He stood in front of the window, looking out onto the garden, gripping the sink and shaking his head in frustration.

Suddenly she got it. He thought she was joining a wine club simply to drink more wine. That was ridiculous. Although, she couldn't deny he was quite justified in thinking that. In her own frustration, she stormed out of the room, and hammered up the stairs, finally slamming the bedroom door.

Lawrence was left standing there with a puzzled expression on his face. Where the hell was this going?

He took Zoe's place on the stool, and sipped her cold coffee, deep in thought. He was trying to figure out when everything had started to go wrong. What had been the trigger? He had no idea.

He banged the coffee mug down – the cold dregs tasted disgusting. He looked up at the clock. It was lunchtime but he didn't fancy any food. What he did fancy was a very large glass of ice-cold wine.

Chapter 17

English Wine

Vines have been grown in England for winemaking since Roman times. The Doomsday book refers to over 42 vineyards in southern England at the end of the 11th Century.

England and Wales now have over 6000 acres of vineyards – approximately 700 vineyards – many producing world-class award winning white, red, rosé and sparkling wines.

Currently the UK produces approximately 6 million bottles of wine and two-thirds of the UK's annual production is now sparkling wine.

Winnie was carefully working on her collection of fine wine glasses. She'd washed and drained them and now for extra shine, she was holding them, one by one, over a saucepan of steaming water and then polishing with a cloth.

It was the second meeting of the wine club, but she was even more nervous than the first week, if that was possible. This was their first proper meeting where everyone would be relying on her to teach them all they wanted to know about wine tasting. Her printed notes were placed in a pile in the middle of the table, ready to be handed out.

Her nerves on edge, she jumped at the loud and tuneful knock at the back door that could only be Gloria, dutifully arriving to help out.

'Thank goodness you're here, Glo.'

'Why, has something happened?'

'Oh, nothing really. I'm just all fingers and thumbs. This isn't getting any easier.'

'Give it time – you'll get into your stride.'

'But I'm so nervous, my heart is pounding – this can't be good for a woman my age.'

'A woman your age! Just be glad your heart is pounding at all, although I could think of better ways to get all hot and bothered!'

'Gloria!'

'Oh, for goodness' sake.' Gloria couldn't help grinning. 'I brought some more tonic water; I think I drunk all yours last time. OK if I stick it in the fridge?'

'Yes of course.'

'I see you have tonight's wine chilling. So, it's all about English wine tonight? I didn't know we made any.'

'Yes, exactly, that's why I thought it was a good idea – to start with English wines. People are usually surprised we produce so much and by how good they are.'

'Mm, and some champagne too?'

'Well, sparkling wine actually, but as good as champagne in my opinion.'

'It's all Prosecco now, isn't it? That's the fashion.'

'That and fancy pink gins!'

'Don't look at me; you won't see anything pink in my glass. I'm strictly a Gordon's girl, I am.'

'OK then, Gordon's girl – try one of these mini scotch eggs. I've not made them before, let me know what you think.'

Gloria took a bite, nodding in approval. 'Devine. Make sure the platter is near me. So, how many have you got coming this week?'

'That's another thing I'm worried about. Fifteen have signed up for this week – I haven't got room for fifteen.'

'Of course you have. I see you've got some garden chairs in ready – good idea. It'll be fine. And think of the extra pennies Wynne, remember, that's what it's all about.'

'Yes, but, garden chairs, it's not ideal, is it?' She tried not to think about the electric and water bills that had arrived that morning.

Gloria simply smiled and left Winnie to faff herself out while she fetched some paper napkins and put them on the table.

The front doorbell rang, and Gloria looked over at Winnie who was still trying to arrange scotch eggs in an artistic way.

'Shall I go?' asked Gloria.

'It's a bit early.'

'Yes, but we can't leave them waiting on the doorstep. Anyway, it's probably that Peter, hoping to catch you on your own.'

'Oh, stop it! Yes, you go then.'

Gloria returned with Winnie's friends from the hospital.

'It's Mary and Fran and Sue, have I got that right?' Gloria's social skills were second to none. And they nodded, pleased to be remembered.

Winnie was delighted to see them back and touched by their support.

'Hello, it's lovely to see you back again. Thank-you all for coming.'

'We wanted to make sure we got the best seats,' said Fran. 'You said we'd be discussing English wine this week – I don't think I've ever tried one. I'm intrigued.'

The bell sounded again, and Gloria left the women chatting while she collected the next visitors, a husband and wife who she remembered from the previous meeting, although on this occasion, she had to be reminded of their names.

'Come on in, come through to the kitchen. Here you go Wynne, you remember Clifford and Lucinda from last time.'

'Ah yes, of course, hello. Lovely to see you again. Take a seat, make yourselves comfy.'

'Thank-you. A friend of ours is coming tonight,' said Lucinda. 'But she might be a little late; she commutes to London, so it'll be tight but she's going to try to make it.'

'That's fine, no problem at all,' said Winnie, racking her brain for where she might find one more chair.

Gloria smiled. Winnie was already getting extra customers through word of mouth – how wonderful.

As Winnie chatted, Gloria to-ed and fro-ed to the front door, bringing new arrivals into the kitchen. Kerry and Ayisha and Sheila all arrived together, and then a couple of minutes later Peter.

'Ah hello Peter, nice to see you again,' said Gloria, diplomatically trying to steer him to the furthest side of the table but unfortunately, he wasn't having any of it, and plonked himself down right next to where Winnie would be sitting. She and Gloria exchanged covert glances and Winnie gave a little shrug of her shoulders.

Gloria collected another visitor from the front door and led the young woman through to the kitchen.

'Winnie, this is Zoe Thomas.'

'Ah Zoe, yes I remember, we spoke on the phone. Hello, I'm Winnifred Mayhew, lovely to have you here. Find a space, squeeze yourself in.'

Zoe was momentarily overwhelmed. Winnie was so warm and welcoming; it was as if she'd been particularly waiting for her to arrive.

'Come and sit here Love,' said Lucinda, shifting her chair along a little and pulling an empty chair into the space.

'I'm Lulu and this is my husband, Cliff.'

'Thanks, I'm Zoe.' She sat down, feeling as if it were the first day at school. The others introduced themselves, they all seemed to know each other well, and she felt very much the new girl.

Everyone was chatting around her, and Zoe looked around the kitchen, noting the sharp contrast of this cosy, homely family room with her own stark, designer-inspired kitchen. She'd been determined to come tonight, especially as Lawrence hadn't taken any interest in it, hadn't even mentioned it since his scathing comments previously. He was working late again, so it was easy for her to slip out of the house without his disapproving aura descending on her.

She noticed some wine glasses on the worktop but there was no sign of any wine yet. She wondered how long it would be until they got to the actual point of the evening - as she could seriously do with a drink right now.

Winnie finally collected their attention and gave her well-practiced talk, a brief history of English winemaking and how the industry had grown to the multi million pound earning one it was today. She was relieved to observe that everyone seemed suitably interested as well as surprised by her facts and figures.

'Did you know one glass of wine consists of juice from one cluster of grapes and there are about seventy-five grapes in one cluster?' asked Peter.

Here we go again, thought Winnie.

'Thank you, Peter, that's very interesting – I should add that little snippet of information to my notes.'

She paused, wondering if there was more to come and as there didn't seem to be, she handed out the notes, showcasing three wines in particular, and then expertly popped the cork on a bottle of sparkling white, gripping the cork in one hand and twisting the base of the bottle with the other.

'This is an award-winning classic cuvée produced by a vineyard in Hampshire. And apparently it has been proved that the chalky soil of the South Downs is identical to that of the best Chardonnay vineyards in Champagne.'

At last, some wine thought Zoe, but she was immediately dismayed to see such a small amount of it swishing around the bottom of the seemingly over large glass. She was paying decent money for this – was this it? Winnie began handing out the glasses of wine.

'There's a description of this particular wine on the top page. Anyone care to read it out? Sheila?'

Pemberton English Sparkling Wine

Buttery brioche and honeycomb in a glass!

*On the nose, lemon, orange blossom
and peaches nestle among ripe
apricot and baked red apple. The*

palate intensifies, evolving into
Tarte Tatin, caramel shortbread and
lemon notes, wild honey, buttery
brioche and honeycomb.
Incredibly complex and immensely
enjoyable.

'Sounds more like a description of afternoon tea – all that brioche and caramel shortbread!' said Sheila.

There was a ripple of friendly laughter around the kitchen.

Zoe glanced at the others holding their glasses delicately by the stem, swirling the wine and dipping their noses deep into the bowl of the glass. They all looked to be expert already. Zoe just held her glass and continued to observe the others, waiting for the moment when they were allowed to taste, reminding herself that this was, after all, a wine-tasting club – not a session with her sister in the local pub.

Winnie noticed her hesitation.

'Don't worry Zoe, you didn't miss much last time. It was mostly introductions and an overview. I'll give you the notes from that session which details the structure of the course and various other information, and you can ask me anything you're not sure of at the next meeting.'

'OK, thanks' Zoe nodded, not at all sure she would be back next time.

'So, everyone, tonight we're going to start learning the four steps of wine tasting which consist of the look, the smell, the taste and then finally our conclusion. This evening we're going to think about the look of the wine in the glass.

'What are we looking for?' asked Sheila. 'How do we know just from looking at it, if it's a good one or bad one?'

'Well, that's not really what we're asking. We're observing mostly, to see what we can pick up simply from the look of the wine in the glass. And the best way to inspect it is to angle the glass preferably over a white background.'

'Ah ha, that's why you have the white tablecloth,' observed Sheila.

'Exactly. Now, generally speaking for whites, if it's pale, it's still young but if it has more colour, say a darker yellow, it may well have some age to it.

'This one would be described as deep gold, indicative of the Chardonnay grapes and showing that is has been aged.

'Now, you could give it a little swirl and then we'll be able to see the level of viscosity.'

'Viscosity? What's that?' asked Sheila.

'Anyone want to offer a definition?'

'The thickness of a liquid,' said Cliff, 'or its stickiness.'

'Yes, that's right. After swirling, watch the *tears* roll down the side of the glass. Big thick ones mean a higher alcohol content.' Winnie could see Sheila swirling her glass and peering into it, intense concentration on her face.

'It's not something to take too seriously at this stage, Sheila. It's just an observation which along with the other things we'll learn will help to build the complete picture.'

'Hm, OK,' said Sheila, looking at her glass somewhat suspiciously.

'So, what does everyone think? To start, can anyone pick up on anything in the description?'

'Lots of bubbles,' said Lulu, obviously enjoying it even though her eyes were watering. 'It's very nice.'

'It's OK,' mumbled Peter. 'I'm not a champagne man.'

Winnie sighed inwardly. Was she going to have to battle his negative comments every session?

'Well, I really like it,' said Sheila. 'I suppose I thought all Champagne tastes the same, but this is totally different from anything I've had before.'

'OK, sorry Sheila, let me just interrupt for a moment. At the risk of sounding pedantic, the only sparkling wine that can truly be referred to as Champagne is if it has actually been produced in the Champagne region of France. Otherwise, we should simply refer to it as sparkling wine which this one is as it was produced here in England, in Hampshire.'

'Oh, right, OK.'

'But carry on with what you were saying. Different to anything you've had before?'

'Yes, very different. Much softer, and more subtle to anything bubbly I've had. I think I'm getting the peachy apricot thing and a creaminess which I suppose could be the buttery shortbread.'

'Excellent Sheila, well done. And what do you think Zoe? I'm taking it you enjoyed it.'

Zoe looked down at her empty glass. A quick glance around the table and it seemed she was the only one who'd finished her drink.

'Yes, it's very nice. I really enjoyed it.' For a second, she felt like Oliver Twist, wondering if she could hold out her glass and ask very nicely for some more. And she hoped she wouldn't be asked to give a description, it had gone down so fast, she couldn't actually remember anything about it.

Another newcomer, Muriel, was sitting near the back door of the kitchen, a little apart from the group. Winnie noticed the look on her face as she sipped – staring into her glass, an intense look of concentration on her face.

'Muriel?' Is this turning out to be your cup of tea?'

Muriel swished and sipped, obviously deep in thought.

'Yes, I would say it's delicious. I agree with Sheila, I can detect fragrant peaches too. And it tastes expensive.' She looked up for confirmation.

'It's not a cheap one, just under twenty pounds a bottle.'

The group took a collective intake of breath, appreciating the golden liquid in their glasses that bit more now. And Zoe understood why they'd all got such a small measure.

'Not a cheap party plonk then?' Commented Sheila laughing. 'Normally I'd get the cheapest bubbly I can find. At my daughter's twenty-first, we had some, nothing like this of course but after a few glasses you didn't notice, especially after all the spirits we added to it to make a punch. It went down a storm. Come to think of it, a fair amount came back up, but I won't go there.'

'Ah, you have children,' said Lulu. 'How many?'

'Just the one. My daughter; she's twenty-four now. One was enough – it was a miracle I survived her birth, but that's a story for another day. You have kids?'

'Yes. We have a son. He's in his thirties. He's married and we have two grandchildren too.'

'Ah, that's lovely. I can't wait to have grandkids, although I'm not sure about being called granny – we'll have to see. But yeah, it'll be great to have some little ones running around.' Sheila was smiling dreamily.

Winnie cleared her throat, and held her notes a little higher, keen to progress the evening. But it wasn't to be.

'What about you, Pete?' continued Sheila. 'You got kids?'

'No. And I don't want to hear any stories about you giving birth either.'

A slightly awkward silence followed but Sheila smirked to the others ignoring his abruptness.

Winnie placed her notes down on the table and went to the other end of the kitchen to pour herself a glass of water. As she sipped, Gloria wandered up.

'Let them have their chat,' she whispered.

'It's supposed to be a wine club,' Winnie whispered back, thinking of all the preparation she'd done in readiness for the evening.

'It's supposed to be a fun, informal evening, sharing company over a few glasses of wine and discussion. That's what will keep them coming back.'

'But I've got two more wines to open yet. I'm trying to keep to a schedule.'

'It'll be fine. You'll fit it all in. Just relax a little, and let the evening take its own cue.' Gloria gave her a big smile and squeezed her arm affectionately.

Winnie frowned. It all suddenly felt like very hard work.

She returned to the table where everyone was animatedly getting into the spirit of swirling and sipping, and the kitchen was filled with sounds of approval as they debated more boldly now over identified flavours of scorched hay, lemon meringue pie and peanut brittle. Tasting, it seemed, was on the tongue of the beholder.

She even caught Zoe smiling at something Lulu had said – she was a pretty young thing, thought Winnie.

Zoe looked over at Kerry and Ayisha who were chatting and laughing hysterically. She was probably only a few years older than them, she reckoned, but they looked so much younger, and she felt so much older. Kerry looked up and caught her eye as she was giggling with tears in her eyes.

'We were just being silly; imagining this was a wine tasting with Harry Potter at Hogwort's – there might be undertones of dragon's breath and a high note of troll saliva.'

Zoe smiled. She'd never read the Harry Potter books. She wondered if all their giggling was because

163

they couldn't handle the alcohol. But they'd only had one glass.

'Yes, I know we're being very juvenile.' Both girls took a deep breath and sat up a little straighter, looking down at their folders of notes.

'You're working very hard,' said Zoe. 'You've made lots of notes.'

'It's for a project at college about cooking with local and seasonal produce. And we thought the whole thing tonight about English wines – well, it's great. We can use a lot of this stuff in our project.'

Zoe nodded. 'Right, I see.'

'What do you do?' asked Ayisha.

'Well, actually I'm not working at the moment. I'm not really sure what I want to do next. Just, you know, taking a career break.'

'Nice one. Lucky you.'

Zoe smiled and turned away hoping someone would rescue her from this conversation. *Career break?* Where had that come from?

Winnie managed to capture everyone's attention by bringing over the platters of scotch eggs. She'd also buttered some thin slices of baguette just in case anyone felt the need to soak up some of the alcohol. They were hardly in the realms of getting sloshed, but then again not everyone reacted in the same way.

'Please, help yourselves. I'm going to open another bottle of English sparkling. This one is a much more affordable price – see what you think between the two. This also comes from the Chardonnay grape which incidentally is the most widely planted variety in Great Britain.'

She looked across to Peter at her side. He was the only one not tucking into any food, he seemed to have gone a little quiet – lost in his thoughts.

'Here, Peter, would you like to open it for me?'

He looked up and smiled. 'Yes, of course.' He took the bottle and popped the cork effortlessly.

Everyone swirled and sipped, and generally nodded approval. There was plenty more chat as the food was finished, Winnie even managed to occasionally bring the conversation back to the subject of wine.

She felt a little flustered to discover they had less than half an hour left to discuss the final wine. She nudged Gloria and glanced up at the wall clock, indicating the time. Gloria simply shrugged.

'It doesn't matter if we go over a little, does it?' she whispered.

Winnie relaxed a little. True, ten or fifteen minutes would be fine, but she didn't want to have to start chucking people out.

'Our last wine tonight is this rather delicious dry Rosé. Rosé is generally becoming more popular the world over which is very good news for our wine industry.'

This was the most expensive bottle of wine of the evening, and Winnie was disappointed to see everyone's attention was beginning to wane and the discussion suddenly felt slightly rushed.

And it seemed, she wasn't the only one with her eye on the clock. Promptly at nine-thirty, people began fidgeting in their seats and making to leave.

165

Cliff and Lulu were the first to go. 'We have to get back.'

'What are we doing next time?' asked Sheila.

'Wines from Germany,' confirmed Winnie.

Peter mumbled something. Inappropriate no doubt, thought Winnie and didn't ask him to repeat it.

They filed out to the hallway, calling out their thanks and good-byes, and finally Winnie shut the door.

Winnie and Gloria were alone in the peaceful kitchen amidst scattered chairs, empty lipstick-stained wine glasses and not a single mini scotch egg left. Winnie was exhausted but smiled over at Gloria.

'That was a good evening, I think.'

'It was brilliant Wynne. Well done. It was very interesting.'

'Peter seemed preoccupied tonight. Maybe not quite so grouchy. I think there's more to him.'

'There usually is. He's hiding behind his grouchiness. People are usually hiding behind something. The young woman, Zoe – my god, there's something going on there.'

'What do you mean? She's incredibly pretty.'

'She is, but she's a troubled soul. Maybe we'll find out.'

'Sorry about earlier, Glo. I was getting a bit uptight there.'

'Oh, don't be daft. You're bound to get anxious now and again. But remember, you're doing a fantastic job – you should be incredibly proud of yourself. Your Doug would be.'

166

Winnie sighed. 'Thanks Glo. I mean it though; I couldn't do all this without you.'

'Of course you could, you silly!' Gloria felt a sudden twinge of guilt.

Chapter 18

It was another glorious sunny summer's day, and Gloria had a positive bounce in her step as she unloaded her mini. It was parked as close to her cottage as she could manage, but even then, she had to haul everything up the long skinny garden at the back.

She'd treated herself to a brand-new suitcase, bright red. It matched her car although she wouldn't actually be driving to her destination in a few weeks' time.

As she carried the case to the cottage, she noticed Ada's bedroom curtains were still closed. She couldn't remember if that had been the case when she'd gone out that morning. Perhaps Ada had gone up for an afternoon nap.

Gloria put the suitcase in the kitchen and returned to the car for her other purchases. She'd been quite extravagant and bought a couple of new dresses; one in floral fuchsia pink and the other in turquoise – both colours she knew suited her even though they were rather bold. And gold sandals. She couldn't possibly not buy them, and she smiled as she grabbed the bag and slammed the boot shut.

She took her time, strolling slowly up the garden, looking over at Ada's place for any sign of movement. There was none. She dumped the bag just inside the kitchen door, and stepped over the little fence into Ada's garden, knocking on the door and peering inside the frosted glass for any dreaded signs of Ada on the floor.

There was no answer and no sight of Ada either. Gloria paused, unsure for the moment what to do. She knocked one last time, and then sighed and returned to her own home.

On automatic pilot, she switched on the kettle; a cup of tea always helped her think. Ada had given her a key to her cottage years ago. Thankfully, she had never had occasion to use it, but was desperately trying to decide if maybe this was the time.

The problem was, Ada was fiercely independent, and Gloria knew if she let herself in to find the old woman simply napping in her chair having forgotten to pull the bedroom curtains – she wouldn't be best pleased.

Gloria poured water on a teabag, and dunked it up and down, hypnotically, trying to decipher where the boundary was between being a good, caring neighbour, and an overreacting meddling one.

She poured in a little milk and took a sip. And then decided. Ada was always in her cottage and if on the rare occasion someone took her out, she would always find a way of letting Gloria know about it. She was a house-proud lady, who stuck to her routines faithfully and the curtains were never left open late into the day.

Gloria set her mug of tea down. She took the old tin tea caddy from the dresser and fished out Ada's door key and then dashed back next door.

Banging on the door and calling out Ada's name, she peered through the glass. Still nothing. And so, she unlocked the door, slowly and noisily, continuing to call out, giving Ada plenty of time to appear and probably have a good rant at her for inviting herself in.

She could see straight ahead that the living room was in darkness which meant the curtains were also closed there. She looked into the kitchen to her left and saw Ada's woolly socked leg poking out at a rather awkward angle from what would have been the original pantry right at the back. At the same time, she heard a moan from Ada, and then a more reassuring, 'Come here and help me, for goodness' sake!'

Gloria rushed over and knelt down, placing her hand gently on Ada's back to reassure her and trying to work out what damage had been done and whether she should move her or not.

'Ada, are you alright? What happened?'

'No, I'm not alright. My bloody hip's gone.'

'OK, right, are you in any pain? And where does it hurt?'

'It hurts everywhere. And why did you disappear? Knocking on my door, and then leaving me. I thought I was going to be here all day. Knew you'd come when it got dark, but this is June and that's a bloody long way off.'

'Oh, I'm so sorry Ada. I didn't want to barge in, you know, and find you're just having a nap or something.'

Ada grunted in a sort of understanding way.

'I think I should call an ambulance.'

'No, no, there's no need for any of that. Just help me up. I've fallen a bit funny and got my leg stuck behind me. I couldn't pull myself up, that's all.'

170

Gloria held her under her arms and helped her to stand. She weighed hardly anything at all. There was a patch of white liquid on the floor. Ada looked down at it and frowned.

'They say "don't cry over spilt milk", and I say, don't slip on it either!' She tried to laugh at her joke but suddenly winced in pain as Gloria helped her onto a chair.

'Ada, I think we should get you checked out by a doctor.'

'I don't want any of that fuss, Dear, you know that. Just let me get my breath back. I'm just a bit stiff from sitting on the cold floor.'

'How long have you been there?'

'Since this morning. I heard you go out in your car, and I found I didn't have the puff to call out, not even when you were banging on the door.'

Despite all the chat, Gloria noticed the hint of fear in Ada's face.

'Right, how about I get you settled in the living room and get you warmed up? I'll make a cup of tea and a sandwich and then I'll check in on you later too.'

Gloria fully expected an argument from Ada and for her to tell her to stop fussing. But she was surprised that all she got was a simple nod of agreement and a little smile as Ada managed to get to her feet and she even allowed Gloria to help her through to the living room.

With Ada safely ensconced in her armchair with her legs supported on a footstool and a blanket over her, Gloria proceeded to open all the curtains. Then she mopped up the spilt milk, grinned a little at Ada's joke about not slipping on it, and made her something to eat.

Back in her place, she made herself a fresh mug of tea. All the goodies from her earlier shopping trip were around her, but the fun of the morning had disappeared somewhat. Poor Ada, for how long would she be able to continue living alone? Ada was a very private and self-reliant woman; she wouldn't want to go to any sort of care residence. It was a sobering thought.

As she stood sipping her tea and looking out the back door down the length of her cottage garden, she suddenly questioned her own plans. She was in her mid-seventies, how wise was it to be travelling alone at her age, to a remote part of France, to meet up with someone she hardly knew?

Gloria was still feeling melancholy later that evening. She'd checked in on Ada who managed to make herself some supper. Gloria helped her up the narrow steep staircase that bent round sharply near the top and couldn't help thinking it was a miracle Ada hadn't taken a tumble down it before now.

As she helped Ada into bed, it seemed that this tiny woman already in her nineties had aged another decade in the last twenty-four hours, and Gloria made the decision to check in on her every morning and every evening from now on.

Back in her own cottage, she took a luxury bath with all her favourites oils and candles. She sat on the edge of her bed, and picked up her belly dancing cymbals, giving them a little tinkle, but even they sounded joyless and flat. Nothing seemed to lift her mood.

She treated herself to a large gin and tonic and for a stupid reason that she knew would do nothing to help her feel better, she grabbed an old photo album from the shelf. It contained photos of her and Bill in their last few years together, of all their fantastic holidays, weekends away and impromptu parties.

Slowly, she turned the pages, musing over photos of them in Bali and Italy and their last holiday together in the south of France. It was beautiful, she could well understand why Winnie was so in love with the place.

By now, she'd mentioned a number of times, the idea of her and Winnie going on a little holiday together, but sadly she hadn't been interested. She needed the sanctuary of being in her own home, and sadly she was sticking to her guns in that she insisted she wouldn't be able to do the travelling she'd hoped to be able to do with Doug.

Gloria slammed the album shut and plonked it down on the sofa beside her. She sighed, long and weary, suddenly and inexplicably feeling a little sorry for herself. The evening was stretching out before her, and although she enjoyed her precious time to herself, tonight she was slightly shocked to realise she felt very much alone.

She calculated that in fact this was the longest she'd been a single woman. She'd been on her own for four years now, and she missed having a partner, to love and be loved. It didn't suit her to be single.

Her thoughts again turned to Winnie; she knew she was still struggling to deal with the sudden situation of finding herself alone.

Gloria's phone beeped beside her, and she picked it up, peering at the screen to see she had a notification thing from a dating website.

'Ooh lovely!' she muttered, opening the application to see that Lorenzo had winked at her. She took a quick look at the elderly man with pale skin and watery blue eyes.

'Hm, he doesn't look like a Lorenzo to me. More like an Eric or an Ernie! But then again, I don't suppose many of them think I look like a Jasmine either!'

Anyway, she concluded that Lorenzo looked friendly enough and she sent a wink back to him. She winked at practically anyone who took the bother to do it first.

She wished she was more savvy with this dating app thing and then laughed at the silliness of it all, taking a sip of her gin and feeling suddenly better.

She had been feeling a little guilty over her impending trip to France but as she'd reminded herself earlier, she had suggested it to Winnie several times already.

It suddenly occurred to her she ought to ask one of her other neighbours to check in on Ada while she was away. Liz, at the end of the lane, she'd be happy to do it. She and Ada had been neighbours for years, that would work fine.

And then all Gloria needed to do was pack her bags, lock up the cottage and she'd be off. She sipped the last of her G & T, feeling content at last and very much looking forward to meeting up with Bernard from Bordeaux in a few weeks' time.

Chapter 19

It was just beginning to get dark as Zoe walked along the street towards home, and as she approached their house, she smiled at the sight of welcoming light coming from the living room bay window. The windows were wide open letting in the warm summer evening.

Tonight had been her second meeting at The Wine Club and she'd thoroughly enjoyed herself. She'd studied all the notes Winnie had given her at the previous session and was able to appreciate the whole evening much more this time. She knew, without a doubt, she would stay the course which would run for the next few months.

This evening Winnie had talked about German wines and, of course, everyone had the opportunity to taste a selection. She, along with everyone else, was very impressed with the choice. And they all shared a laugh as they collectively recalled memories of Liebfraumilch being the choice wine of the day a few decades ago – the only choice in some places.

It was interesting to note how even wine came in and out of fashion, everyone pretty much in agreement it wasn't something they would choose today.

She let herself in and from the hallway she could see through to the den at the back. Lawrence was stretched out, his long legs propped on the foot stool, work papers discarded on the settee beside him. Soft music was playing, and he was staring into space, a calm and contented look on his face.

Zoe took in the moment; she hadn't seen Lawrence this relaxed in a long time and couldn't help wondering how much of the usual anxiety on his face was caused by her. He was completely absorbed in his own world, and she cleared her throat so as not to startle him by suddenly appearing in the room.

He turned his head lazily towards her, big brown eyes and long lashes looking up at her. She would have found this lazy look attractive at one time, but now she feared it must simply be disinterest.

'Hi, I'm back,' she said, throwing her handbag onto a chair.

'Hi, you're early, aren't you?'

Instinctively, Zoe looked up at the wall clock, feeling defensive. 'Er, no, the usual time. It ends at nine-thirty.'

'Oh, OK.' Lawrence picked up some work papers. He was busy, she got the message.

She picked up her handbag and went upstairs to change. She would have liked to have stayed and talked to him about her evening, about the different German wines she'd tasted and how she was beginning to notice a difference between them. She wasn't sure if Lawrence ever bought German wine for them to share – she felt her face colour as she realised with some embarrassment, she had previously been totally oblivious to whatever was in their wine fridge. It had all been the same to her.

She'd like to tell Lawrence about the lovely couple, Cliff and Lulu, the outrageously dressed Sheila, and the slightly odd older guy, Peter. There was something about him, a certain sadness maybe.

He was always a bit grumpy but even so, she liked him.

Lawrence watched as Zoe left the room. She'd just been to a wine tasting group and this was the most sober he'd seen her at nine-thirty in the evening since, well, he couldn't remember.

He didn't know what to make of her suddenly wanting to learn about wine. She'd always feigned an interest for his sake, he knew that, but she was never seriously interested.

He smiled wryly at the thought of the look on Zoe's face when she was handed a glass with only a tiny amount of wine tinkling around in the bottom of it. He wondered how she managed not to down it in one, and then he felt immediately cruel, and annoyed with himself.

He knew there was no way she was going to stick with the classes. He very much doubted she'd go for the next meeting, but time would tell. Maybe he should cut her some slack, encourage her some more, but they'd been around the block a few times already. He was fed up with being let down.

He could hear Zoe moving around upstairs, and tidied his papers away, turned off the music in the den and went through to the kitchen to find something he could rustle up for supper.

A few minutes later, Zoe followed the smell of something delicious cooking and found Lawrence stir-frying some odd vegetables he'd found at the bottom of the fridge. A jug of beaten eggs meant he was cooking a frittata.

'That smells good. I'm really starving.' Zoe sounded surprised as if not familiar with the sensation of being hungry.

Lawrence just smiled as he grated some cheddar into the egg mix, resisting the urge to say it was a pleasant side effect of not being constantly piddled – you got your appetite back. Or at least for more than a bag of cheese and onion crisps.

He suddenly turned and looked at her.

'So, do you want to choose a bottle of wine to go with it?'

Zoe looked away, suddenly self-conscious. 'No, it's OK. You choose.'

'Come on, let's pick something together. Show me what you've learnt, or is it really just a bunch of women guzzling prosecco and gossiping about new shoes and handbags?'

'No. It's nothing like that.' Zoe looked genuinely hurt, and immediately Lawrence was sorry for being so patronising.

'Sorry Babe, I was only teasing.'

'It's not like that at all. It's all very serious, but you know, not in a snobby way. It's a proper course and we're really learning this stuff. There's no pressure or anything, I mean you don't have to study the notes but if you're there to learn, you might as well get as much out of it as you can.'

Lawrence nodded, surprised but pleased to hear her so passionate about something.

'And it's not all women, there are a couple of blokes there too.' Zoe paused, pleased to see she had Lawrence's full attention now. 'And yes, we all have a chat, but no we don't talk about shoes and handbags.'

Lawrence pulled her into a big hug. 'OK, OK, I'm sorry. I take it all back, you'll be an oenology expert in no time.'

'What's one of those?' asked Zoe as she pulled open the door to the wine fridge.

Lawrence just smiled, shaking his head ever so slightly. 'OK, what shall we have tonight? What do you recommend?'

Chapter 20

Usually a tea drinker in the morning, today Winnie was in need of a very strong cup of coffee. What an awful night it had been. They'd predicted a fierce summer storm and boy had they got it right. Although it had been more like a mid-winter hurricane.

Temperatures had suddenly plummeted. Howling winds and torrential rain, like gravel being thrown against the windows, kept her awake most of the night. And as if that wasn't enough, someone's gate was banging open and shut in a hypnotic rhythm which was driving her mad. She was seriously tempted to go out in the middle of the night, in her nightclothes, and shut it. But she resorted to ear plugs instead.

The kettle boiled and switched itself off with a click that sounded unnecessarily loud to Winnie, and she tutted as she filled the cup. She felt miserable, worse than a hangover she observed, but without the half memories of having had a good time.

Cradling her cup in both hands, she looked out the kitchen window at the sad looking garden, sodden and drooping with water. She sipped her coffee, relishing its slowly reviving comfort, but was soon deflated when the rain started again.

It was the fourth meeting of The Wine Club tonight and if the weather stayed like this, no-one would come out. And she would need to take a good long nap before then. At the moment, she didn't even have the energy to think about getting everything ready for the evening.

She glanced over to the dresser just to reassure herself she had printed off all the notes ready for tonight. She was getting better organised at preparing things in plenty of time.

Her attention rested on the calendar hanging on the wall. It was eight months to the day that Doug had died. She did this every month, counting time. It just felt like something she needed to acknowledge, like a nod or a salute to him, saying she remembered, and she missed him. And another month gone by meant another marker of distance between them.

Winnie swallowed hard and finally sat down to finish her coffee. She could hear her mobile ringing upstairs but had no intention of dashing up there to retrieve it. Whoever it was could leave a message. Within seconds of it stopping, the phone in the kitchen rang. She sighed, irritated. Why did people do that? If one phone wasn't answering, surely it meant that person was, for the moment, unavailable? Why did everything have to be so urgent these days?

'Hello.' She answered, a little abrupt.

'Ooh, hello Mum. You OK?'

'Yes, I'm fine Hannah. Just tired, didn't sleep too well.'

'Yeah, that was some storm, huh? Loved it. We stayed up watching until the early hours.'

'Did you?' Winnie was tempted to comment that it would have been much more sensible not to have stayed up until the early hours when you were studying for a degree in Environmental Management and Technology. And that she would greatly improve her chances of actually graduating this time, if she was awake and alert for her classes.

'You sure you're OK, Mum? When's your next wine club thing?'

'It's tonight, provided this awful weather doesn't keep everyone away.'

'Oh, I'm sure it won't. But I just wanted to ask something. Me and Mick have got the chance of getting away for the weekend. He's got a mate with a caravan on the coast – can I borrow a little something off you, just for a couple of weeks? I'm not short or anything – I lent some to Mick and he's just struggling a bit at the moment. He will pay me back, but you know. Is that OK?'

Winnie closed her eyes and sighed. 'Hannah, we've had this conversation before. You've lent money before. Money you don't really have to lend.'

'Oh Mum, don't go over all that again.'

Winnie bit her tongue. And then she sighed noisily.

'What's wrong?'

'The blasted lights keep flickering.'

'Is it because of the storm, maybe?'

'No, it's been doing it for a few days now. It's like a disco in here at the moment.'

'Hm, you'd better get that checked out Mum. Dodgy electrics, you know, could be dodgy.'

'Yes Dear.' Yes, there was obviously a problem with the electrics in this old house. But really the last thing she needed right now was to be told the whole house needed rewiring.

'So, is it OK about the money?'

'Yes. It's OK. This time.'

'Thanks Mum. You're a saviour. I'll pop over later.'

'Alright then.' Winnie hung up. Their conversation had ended as abruptly as it had begun.

She needed more coffee. As the kettle boiled, Winnie picked up the huge electric bill and the no less huge water bill. She was cross with her youngest daughter for not managing her finances better but immediately felt humble as she reminded herself of how oblivious she had been to the cost of running this house. She'd been happy to leave everything to Doug, blissfully unaware of the true costs involved.

Finances were still very tight. She didn't need to sit down with a calculator to work it out. The money from the wine club was very useful, but it was borderline to really helping. And was it getting to the point where she would have to say no to helping her family if they needed it?

Winnie took her coffee upstairs to wash and dress. Her mobile phone showed Hannah's missed call and also informed her she had three new emails. A quick glance through showed they were all from her wine club members, all informing her they were unable to attend this evening.

The day was going from bad to worse.

Winnie rubbed her chest, tense with anxiety. At this rate, she could see the day when she would be forced to sell this house, their home, and she wouldn't be able to bear that.

After an early lunch, Winnie went back to bed to catch up on her sleep, something she never usually did.

She woke to slightly brighter skies and was relieved to see the rain had finally stopped. She spent the afternoon preparing for the evening's wine club meeting – they would be discussing French wine. She was especially looking forward to this one, it was a shame there were a few unable to make it.

She'd made some pastries and just as she was putting them in the fridge ready to pop in the oven later, she heard Cathy's car pull up on the drive.

Winnie unlocked the back door just as Cathy whizzed up the path and swept into the house.

'It's still so windy out. And it's trying to rain.'

'Not more rain.'

'I know. Hi Mum, you OK?'

'Yes, I'm fine. Well, actually I didn't sleep too good because of the storm.'

'Oh yeah. Crikey, what I'd do for a whole night of good sleep.'

Winnie smiled and followed her daughter through to the kitchen.

Cathy plonked a plastic container full of strawberries on the counter and then went over to the window to look out onto the garden, searching as if she'd lost something.

'I hate to say this Mum, but I think you've got some loose roof tiles up there. There are quite a few misplaced ones – I was expecting to see some of them landed in the garden.'

'Oh no. I don't need this right now.' Winnie stood beside her daughter and scanned the garden for any signs of fallen tiles.

Cathy pointed towards the front of the house.

'It looks worse right over the drive – I've parked a bit further back. If this wind keeps up, it could just be enough to push some of them over the edge.'

'I know the feeling,' mumbled Winnie.

'You'll need to get a professional in to have a proper look at the roof.'

'Yes I know that,' snapped Winnie.

'OK, I was just saying.'

'I know. I'm sorry Love. It just feels like one thing after the other at the moment.'

Cathy was about to agree wholeheartedly that she knew that feeling too but managed on this occasion to bite her tongue.

'Anyway, I just popped in on my way to pick the kids up from summer school to bring you those strawberries. Tom's dad, you know how he is about growing his own? Well, he's got a glut of them and insisted I bring some to you.'

'Ah, that's very sweet of him. Thank him for me. They look good.'

'Yep, will do.'

'Are you stopping for coffee?'

'No, I haven't got time.' Cathy looked up at the clock. 'In fact, I'd better be going, or I'll be late for the kids.'

Winnie checked the time too. 'Do you have to leave now? What time do they finish?'

'Not until three, but I have to get there early otherwise I'll have to park a mile away. And that's not even figuring in the traffic at this time of day. You're so lucky Mum, living minutes away from a school.'

Winnie pulled a face. 'It hardly benefits me these days, does it?'

'Oh I know but, I can really appreciate the convenience of having a school just walking distance away. Although I can remember feeling very hard done by when we were little. Some of the other kids got picked up by car but we had to walk home – it was such a hard life.'

They both laughed.

'Our old school is actually one of the very top schools in the country now. This house is in a fantastic catchment area – a lot of people would pay a fortune to buy this place. Not that you'd ever move, I know that.'

'Well, let's hope not.'

Cathy looked at her questioningly for a fleeting moment but didn't pursue it.

'Right, I'm off. Oh yes, the other thing – do you fancy coming over for dinner on Sunday? It's been a while since we've all been together. I was going to give Hannah a call, see if she's around. I don't want her to feel all neglected.'

'Well, I'd love to come, of course. But I know Hannah's away for the weekend. Going off to the coast in someone's caravan.'

'Is she?' Cathy screwed up her face, looking confused. 'I spoke to her a few days ago and she was moaning about how totally broke she was.'

Winnie gave her a look but said nothing.

'Oh Mum, you didn't! Honestly, she needs to sort herself out.'

'It's only a few pounds. She's not taking a mortgage out with me or anything.'

'Even so. She's in her late twenties, she needs to grow up.'

Winnie just smiled but she wasn't going to bite, not today. She wasn't in the mood to play piggy-in-the-middle to the many and varied differences between her two daughters.

'OK, well I won't bother calling her then. But you'll come over on Sunday?'

'Yes, of course, I'd love to. And perhaps before I do, you can explain to me why Tilly and Hugo call their aunt Hannah The Dragon Lady?'

Winnie raised her eyebrows in jest. She was trying to lighten the mood, but Cathy was getting flustered.

'Oh Mum, it was just a stupid comment I made. Just the once. About her always breathing fire about some protest or other. Tom picked it up and made something of it, the kids laughed and that was it.'

Winnie just smiled. 'She's very proud of you, you know.'

'Oh yeah, I can just see that. Look, I have to go. I'll call you before the weekend.'

'OK Dear.'

Cathy dashed out without even a kiss goodbye for her mum.

Winnie closed the door and locked it. Her daughter had gone off with a flea in her ear, but also with a few stinging tears in her eyes too, Winnie had noticed.

She returned to the kitchen and sat down heavily at the table. She still had a few things to do before this evening, but at this moment she just didn't feel like it. She got up again and stood looking out of the window. She couldn't believe it – there among the grass were three or four slate tiles having fallen off the roof.

She felt more miserable than ever. She'd managed to upset both her daughters today, her business seemed doomed to failure if any more people cried off this evening, and on top of all that, it appeared her house was falling down.

Chapter 21

French Wine

French wine is produced throughout the country in quantities of approximately 7–8 billion bottles, making France one of the largest wine producers in the world.

France is the source of many grape varieties such as Cabernet Sauvignon, Chardonnay, Pinot Noir, Sauvignon Blanc, and Syrah that are now planted throughout the world.

Although some producers have benefited in recent years from rising prices and increased demand for some of the more prestige wines from Burgundy and Bordeaux, the French wine industry has seen a decline in domestic consumption and internationally, as it now has to compete with many new world wines.

The rain had stopped, the clouds had disappeared, and the early evening sun shone warm and bright from a completely clear blue sky – Winnie felt uplifted by it.

Everything was in place, and she was pleased with herself for developing an efficient routine that was working well, avoiding any last-minute panics and leaving her feeling noticeably calmer and more relaxed.

She glanced up at the clock wondering why Gloria hadn't arrived yet, just as there was a rat-tat-tat at the back door as she let herself in.

'Hi Wynne, how are you today?'

'Not too bad. Glad this weather's brightened up anyway.'

'Yes, that was a corker of a storm, eh?'

'Tell me about it. Kept me awake half the night. And it's put a few people off coming out tonight.'

'Ah, maybe they'll change their minds now the sun's out. It's a gorgeous evening out there.'

Never one to appear miserable, Gloria seemed particularly perky today, Winnie noticed.

'I'm so looking forward to this evening Wynne – French wines, should be very interesting.'

'But you don't like wine!'

'Ah yes but French wine – it's supposed to be the best in the world, isn't it? And, you know, maybe I should take more of an interest.'

Winnie didn't say anything but gave Gloria a sideways glance, wondering what exactly she was up to.

'Does that mean we get to have real Champagne tonight?'

'Actually, yes it does. I have rather a special bottle, something of a treat tonight. And I've learnt my lesson; I'm not saving the best until last like I did before. This was an expensive bottle and we're going to kick off with it first thing.'

'I can't wait. See, would you rather I was only here for the nibbles? Speaking of which something smells delicious – what have you made this week?'

'Vol-au-vents.'

'That's a bit retro, isn't it?'

'Vol-au-vents and a selection of olives. It is French wine night after all.'

'Ah yes, of course, that's very clever.'

'Anyway, you cheeky thing – only here for the nibbles!'

The front doorbell rang. 'Thank goodness, saved by the bell as they say. I'll go,' said Gloria as she sashayed out of the kitchen, convincing Winnie all the more that she was definitely up to something.

Gloria was amused to see Peter being the first to arrive this week. He probably wanted to bag his seat near Winnie.

'Hello Peter, come on in. You're the first one here this week.'

'Well, someone has to be, don't they?' he replied huffily, stepping into the hallway.

It was a rare moment, but Gloria couldn't think of a good answer to that. She followed him through to the kitchen silently wishing Winnie good luck if she was going to attempt any sort of chit-chat with him.

'Hello Peter, how are you?' Winnie asked wondering if they would see a more amenable temper in him this week.

'Not bad.' He sat down at the kitchen table next to Winnie and picked up a set of notes for the evening and began reading. 'Ah, French wine tonight. That's good.'

Winnie wasn't sure but she thought she observed a very slight smile of approval on his face.

'You particularly like French wine, do you? We have a delicious Chablis to try later.'

Peter looked up, direct into Winnie's eyes. She was immediately taken by his sweet faraway smile. 'Ah Chablis, yes, that was my wife's favourite wine. We always saved Chablis for very special occasions.'

Winnie wanted to ask more, but she already knew from experience Peter was not a man to be pushed.

Zoe arrived next, looking pretty as ever. She appeared a little more confident each week, and sat directly next to Peter, smiling across at him. Winnie hoped he'd refrain from subjecting her to his usual gruffness but was pleasantly surprised to see him return the smile, albeit shyly and only for a second.

Lulu and Cliff arrived convinced this would be the week their elusive friend would attend. And then Sheila was one of the last, slightly out of breath having hobbled from the bus stop in her impossibly high stilettos, berating the bus driver for driving so slowly. As usual she gave her captive audience a detailed description of her journey right from her front door to finally arriving in Winnie's kitchen. Winnie caught the young girls, Kerry and Ayisha, rolling their eyes at each other, and she just managed to hide her smile.

Finally, Muriel was the last to arrive and Winnie was very pleased to see her. She was easily the most knowledgeable of the club members and was a lively addition to the group. Winnie deduced they were now a full house and made a start.

'Lovely to see you all here tonight. Especially after the awful weather we've been having.'

'A bit of rain wouldn't keep me away,' piped up Sheila. Winnie was rather touched to hear her say so.

'Thanks Sheila. As you can see, we're discussing the wines of France tonight. France is one of the largest wine producers in the world. They produce something like eight billion bottles per year. Incredible, eh?'

'Wow, blimey! Eight billion?' said Sheila. 'That says something, doesn't it?'

'What does it say?' asked Peter, looking across at her.

'It says, the world drinks a bloody lot of wine!'

Everybody laughed except Peter who put his head back down, pretending to read the notes. Sheila felt momentarily bad, as if she'd made him the butt of the joke which hadn't been her intention at all. She dismissed the thought and tried to focus on what Winnie was saying.

'We're going to start with this rather splendid bottle of Champagne.'

'Why is Champagne so expensive?' Lulu asked. 'I read somewhere you can pay over a thousand pounds for one bottle.'

'For the most expensive Champagnes in the world, you would have to pay tens of thousands for one bottle.'

There was a collective gasp in the kitchen. 'That's ridiculous!' said Sheila. 'You can buy a house for that in some parts of the world.'

'I don't think I could ever pay thousands for just one bottle, no matter how rich I was,' said Lulu shaking her head in disbelief.

'Indeed. Anyway, one of the reasons Champagne is expensive is simply because it's much more time intensive to produce compared to other wines and sparkling wines.

'True Champagne must come from the Champagne region in northern France and there they undergo a much more rigorous process than other sparkling wine producers.

'And also remember, Champagne is seen as an ultimate luxury item and therefore it can command a higher price, just for that. So, are we all ready for a taste?'

Just as Winnie was about to open the bottle, the front doorbell rang. She looked up in surprise, not expecting anyone else to come along this evening.

'Excuse me for a moment.'

A very well-dressed, well-spoken woman introduced herself as Helen, explaining that she had registered interest a few weeks ago and apologised that this was the first week she was able to make it.

'And I'm sorry I'm a little late too. I mistook the route I needed to take and got myself a little lost.'

Winnie welcomed her inside and introduced her to the others.

'A funny time to start,' commented Peter. 'You've missed most of the course already.'

Helen looked a little surprised at his comment.

'Hardly, Peter,' Winnie reassured her. 'We've got quite a few sessions to enjoy yet.'

Helen smiled, perfectly composed, as she sat at the back of the group, Cliff and Lulu just in front of her, and Muriel behind.

'Right, I was just saying to the group, Helen, this is the week for tasting French wine and to start with I'm just about to open this bottle of Champagne.'

'Proper Champagne too,' Muriel informed her. 'Not just sparkling wine, but the real stuff.'

'Well, this is absolutely perfect!' announced a beaming Helen, to which everyone turned eager to know the reason why. And she was happy to oblige.

'First of all, I'm moving to France later this year. And secondly, I've just got engaged to be married so I'm in celebratory mood. A glass of Champagne would be perfect.'

There was a murmur of congratulations around her.

'My husband-to-be has always hankered after buying a vineyard and finally he's gone and done exactly that. We're to be married in the autumn and after that we're off, moving to France. I can hardly believe it.

'I know you probably think I'm a bit long in the tooth to be a bride, but it will be a very low-key affair – simple and chic, that's what I'm aiming for.'

196

Blimey, thought Gloria, her whole life story in less than thirty seconds. She could give Sheila a run for her money. And moving to France, *buying a vineyard*? This was going to be an interesting evening.

She looked over at Winnie who appeared to be completely dumbstruck, her face had drained of colour and for a second Gloria worried she would crumble on the spot into a dead faint. And as if she hadn't heard enough, Helen was off again.

'I saw the advertisement for The Wine Club a few weeks ago, and thought, well, that is just the thing for me. I need to learn as much I can. Of course, the vineyard is already managed, and we don't plan to change anything immediately, but even so I'd like to at least show an interest so I'm not completely in the dark about the process and everything.'

A quick sideways glance confirmed to Gloria that Winnie was still in a state of shock. For a terrifying moment, she thought she would have to take over proceedings, but fortunately and to her huge relief, she was rescued by an enthusiastic barrage of congratulations aimed at Helen from the group.

Lulu swivelled in her seat. 'That's so exciting. I must say you're very brave.'

'Yeah, well done to you,' agreed Cliff.

'What part of France are you going to?' asked Muriel.

'Bordeaux. It's just beautiful, I've visited many times but to think of actually living there – I still have to pinch myself.'

'You'll be producing Merlot and Cabernet Sauvignon?'

'Er, I think so, I'm not absolutely sure. There's so much I still have to learn.'

'Highly likely. Merlot is one of the primary grapes in Bordeaux wine and it's the most widely planted grape in the region,' concluded Muriel.

Peter nodded thoughtfully, directly in front of Winnie. He was impressed. 'Knows her onions, that one.'

His comment finally snapped Winnie out of her trance. I know my onions too, thought Winnie, prickling with resentment.

Gloria picked up the pile of notes from the table. 'Shall I hand these out to everyone Wynne?'

'Oh. Yes please, thanks.'

'So, do we get to taste that Champagne or what?' Prompted Gloria.

Winnie wished the evening was over, whereas it stretched out endlessly before her with hours still to go. She really needed to focus and get on with business.

With a slightly unsteady hand, Winnie removed the cork and poured, and began handing it out.

'Remember what we've learnt about the look of the wine in the glass, and what we covered last time about the smell. Be sure to give it a good swirl first of all.'

Immediately, everyone swirled and sniffed and then sipped before exchanging glances of approval with each other. The room held a particular buzz of excitement, which was solely attributed to Helen of course.

'Hey Helen,' Sheila called out from across the table. 'Will your vineyard be producing this sort of stuff? If it does, I'll be your new best friend!'

Everyone laughed, and generally agreed with her.

'Congratulations to you then!' called out Sheila, raising her glass high in the air. Winnie looked on as everyone did the same.

Lulu observed Winnie, her eyes confirming with her husband that everything was not entirely OK with their host.

'Winnifred, shall I read the description to everyone?'

'Oh yes please, Lulu. That would be great.' She smiled, grateful, but with some effort.

Nicolas Laurent Brut Reserve NV Champagne

Smooth Champagne with a light, toasty finish!

*This celebrated Champagne
displays a wealth of toasty richness
and an abundance of tiny pin-prick
bubbles - the hallmark of the very
finest fizz.
Aromas of fruits of the forest and
pink grapefruit, individual hints of
strawberry, cherry and redcurrant
dominate and expand into delicate
scents of caramelised vanilla.*

'Lots of tiny bubbles in this,' confirmed Lulu, smiling at Winnie. I think I can taste strawberry although that might be just because you tend to think of strawberries and Champagne together.'

Cliff nodded in agreement. 'I think I can taste gooseberries again.' Cliff sipped a tiny amount. 'Maybe not. Perhaps I've just got gooseberries on the brain.'

'Anyone else like to share their observations?' Winnie looked over at her hospital friends. How she wished it was just the three of them in her kitchen at this moment. 'Fran, I know you like a glass of bubbly. How's this one for you?'

'Yes, it's lovely. Sorry I'm somewhat distracted – I keep thinking about this lady here, Helen, is it? I'm so excited for you, starting a new life in the south of France. What an adventure. I'm so sorry Wynne, I think I drunk this glass of wine without even thinking about it. I'm too easily distracted, that's my problem. Must learn to concentrate better.'

'Same with me,' piped up Sheila. 'Right back to when I was a kid. School reports; must learn to concentrate. Could do better, bla, bla, bla. Always the same. I think it's just a case of getting older; the more years you have, the more stuff is going on inside your head, it's hard to keep track of it all.'

Everyone smiled in general agreement.

'And what do you think of the Champagne Sheila?' asked Winnie, desperate for some wine conversation.

'It's very nice indeed,' said Sheila, but I think I'm actually in agreement with Fran – my mind is on Helen's vineyard. I wish I was there right now. Hey, Helen, you could run a B&B, have you thought about that? Or those little self-catering places, what are they called?'

'Gites. They're called gites. Yes, we might look into that. There's still so much to take into consideration, so many options.'

The rest of the evening continued in the same vein with Winnie constantly trying to bring the conversation back to her chosen wines and the story of their production. She'd been particularly looking forward to this evening; discussing her very favourite wines of all and it had simply turned into a disaster.

As Winnie showed the last guests to the front door, Gloria collected dirty glasses and stacked them by the sink for handwashing. She heard the door close with a bang, a final full stop on a tricky chapter of the wine club story.

Winnie returned to the kitchen, stony faced, silently helping Gloria clear things away.

'That was an interesting evening,' said Gloria, aware of the immense understatement of her words.

'Hm. Very interesting.'

'You're annoyed.'

'No. Not really.'

'Come on, out with it.'

'Well, you saw for yourself. It was just a bit frustrating that's all. I've put a lot of effort into this and it's difficult when it all goes off the rails.'

'Don't be daft. It didn't go off the rails. Everyone enjoyed themselves, that was obvious. And shouldn't that be what it's all about? Isn't that exactly the thing that's going to get people coming back each week? And paying you for the pleasure of it.'

Winnie just sniffed as she collected her notes and shuffled them into a neat pile.

'Anyway, that's not it. What are you annoyed at? Surely not just because Helen got so much attention. Or is it the fact she's off to live in France?'

Winnie sighed. 'Yes, OK, both of those things. Both of those bloody things.'

'Well, don't be taken in.'

'What do you mean?'

'Something's not right there.'

'Oh, what are you wittering about now?'

'I don't witter.'

'Well, you're doing your medicine woman act. Pretending you can see through to the souls of everyone.'

Gloria smiled. 'I never quite saw myself like that. But, yes, sometimes, I do pick up things. And as you know, I'm often right.'

'I just can't believe it. Someone turning up like that, announcing all of their everything and rubbing my nose in it.'

'That's hardly fair Wynne – she knows nothing about you or what you were planning, she wasn't rubbing your nose in it.'

'Well, she was so full of herself. She'd only just walked in the door and suddenly everyone's gushing all over her.'

'Exactly. That's what I was trying to say. Something's not sitting right. She was too much. Just think about it this way. Who exactly was she trying so hard to impress or convince? A room full of strangers, or maybe herself?'

Winnie looked away. 'She's still moving to a vineyard. In France. With her husband. Whereas all of my dreams are well and truly over.'

'They don't need to be Wynne. There's nothing to stop you doing whatever you put your mind to.'

'At my age? On my own? I don't think so.'

Gloria sighed. She was beginning to despair now.

'First of all, that woman isn't much younger than you.' Gloria lowered her voice as if she knew this was going to hurt. 'And second, you don't need to have a husband to be someone.'

'But you always seem to have someone in tow,' snapped Winnie, regretting her comment immediately. She looked at Gloria who simply looked back, a tolerant, half smile brushing her lips.

'Careful Wynne. Don't let yourself slip into being bitter. This isn't like you; back in the day, you'd be the first to encourage someone to be brave and do their own thing.'

'Thing were different back in the day. I'm different now.'

Chapter 22

Middle of August and, of course, it was raining. They hadn't had much of a summer at all thought Winnie as she drank her coffee while looking out the kitchen window. She allowed herself a few seconds to fantasise about sunnier climes – blindingly bright turquoise skies and the warmth of the sun on her bare skin.

Her attention back on the garden, dripping with rain, she scanned the lawn to make sure no more roof tiles had come off. The fallen tiles had been replaced and the bill for it hadn't been too enormous but even so, it was one she hadn't been anticipating. She was increasingly anxious these days, worrying what else around the house would need attention next.

She checked the time and quickly finished her coffee. She would need to leave soon to get to Cathy's house. She was looking forward to spending the day with her family, especially the children – they were growing up too fast.

Winnie went from room to room checking windows were shut and everything was as it should be before leaving the house for the day. From the living room window, she noticed a young couple, hand in hand, strolling down the street. They were smiling at each other, they looked happy, and Winnie couldn't help smiling too.

But then her thoughts turned to her youngest daughter. Poor Hannah, she thought. Earlier in the week she'd received a phone call from Hannah, near to tears, as she explained she'd finished with her boyfriend of nearly ten years.

Winnie had persuaded her to come to the house where little by little Hannah explained how she'd finally come to her decision. She talked a lot throughout the evening, Winnie listened and tried to avoid giving advice – this wasn't the time. Hannah also cried a lot, and her mother provided the cuddles.

Despite promising to be miserable forever, Hannah was finally persuaded to come to Cathy's today. Winnie checked the time again, hopefully she would be here soon. She looked out the window hoping to see her walking up the path but instead she saw the couple from earlier walking back down the street. They were looking up at the houses as they went, studying them almost as if they were looking for something. She wondered if she should pop out to help.

But just at that moment, she heard Hannah at the back door and rushed to unlock it.

'Hi Mum, sorry I'm a bit late. I stopped off to get the kids some chocolate. I haven't seen them for ages – don't want them bad-mouthing me for being a bad aunty.'

'That's nice.' Winnie smiled, hoping there wouldn't be any dragon comments today. 'OK, I'll just get my cardigan and then we can go.'

As Hannah reversed off the drive and set off, Winnie noticed the young couple again walking back down the street towards them. She turned in her seat to look at them as they drove past.

'Everything alright Mum?'

'It's just that couple there. This is the third time I've seen them walking up and down the street this morning.'

'Mm, I wonder what they're doing.' Hannah straightened in her seat and looked in her rear-view mirror. 'They're going up to the house.' Hannah slowed down a little, and Winnie tried to turn around in her seat. 'Oh, it's OK, they're leaving again. They just put something through the letter box, that's all.'

Winnie looked across at her, puzzled.

'Do you want to go back? And see what it is?'

'No, no, let's carry on. It'll be nothing. Cathy will be expecting us, and the kids will be driving her crazy. Let's get there and take them off her hands for a while.'

Hannah parked her battered old banger of a car next to Cathy's huge shiny black one. 'Sorry Cath, I'll be lowering the tone of the neighbourhood for a while!' She laughed but her mother simply gave her one of her looks. 'Play nicely today.'

'I will.'

Cathy was already waiting at the open door and Hugo and Tilly were milling around excitedly. They all piled into the kitchen, greeted by wondrous smells of a lavish roast dinner cooking. The kettle had boiled, and Cathy set down three mugs to make tea.

'Tom not around?' asked Winnie. She assumed he must be somewhere nearby. Tom always cooked their Sunday dinner - as a treat for Cathy to have a day off from family cooking.

'No,' she replied with a weary sigh. 'He had to go in to work this morning.'

'On a Sunday?' piped up Hannah.

'Some emergency. He should be back for dinner later. Anyway, Hannah, he doesn't have a choice. It's his own business so if something needs doing, he has to do it. Doesn't matter what day of the week it is.'

Hannah nodded sullenly in agreement, then suggested to her niece and nephew that they play a game. They needed no persuading as they each took a hand and led her through to the living room.

Winnie stood at the kitchen island as Cathy finished making the tea. She looked completely exhausted. Both her daughters seemed to be going through it at the moment.

'Go a bit easy on her. She's had a rough few days.'

Cathy frowned. 'It's about time she finished with him. Total waste of space. She'll be better off without him.'

'I hope so. But it's easy for us to say that but they were together a long time. I think she was expecting more. And she was sobbing her heart out just a few days ago.'

'Was she?' Cathy looked up in surprise.

'Yes. And it took a lot of effort for her to come here and do the family thing. Just don't be too hard on her.'

Cathy nodded.

'Now, there must be something I can do as Tom's abandoned you and left you with all the cooking.'

'I know, I was so looking forward to him taking care of all of that today. I've bought all the stuff to make a good old-fashioned trifle and I haven't had time to do anything with it yet.'

'Oh, don't worry about that.' Winnie noticed a big glass bowl of strawberries on the side. 'There you go, we can have strawberries and cream for dessert. Easy peasy.'

Cathy smiled. 'OK, there's nothing that needs doing just yet. You can help with the vegetables a bit later. Let's take our tea in with Hannah. It's horribly quiet in there, I wonder what the kids have done with her.'

Hannah and Hugo and Tilly were out in the garden. Winnie and Cathy watched through the open glass doors that almost spanned the entire wall. Hannah was chasing the two little children all over the place, round the trees, the playhouse, the swing and climbing frame, pretending to very nearly catch them as they made an extra dash to escape. Their high-pitched squeals made Cathy and Winnie glad they were inside.

'Where does she get her energy?' asked Cathy as she sat down heavily in an armchair. 'I feel like I'm a hundred years old lately.'

'You do look a little tired. Everything OK?'

Cathy just nodded. Winnie could sense the emotion building and decided this wasn't the time to push any further. She sat down on the settee and they both watched the mad goings on in the garden.

Winnie smiled. 'Anyway, I know what you mean about feeling old but if I dare happen to mention anything like that to Gloria, she gives me such a lecture.'

Cathy smiled back. 'Gloria. She is amazing, you have to admit.'

'Yes, she is. And she's a very good friend. I'd have been lost without her these last few months.'

Again, Cathy nodded, staring down into her mug of tea, momentarily lost in her thoughts.

'I meant to say the other day – it's eight months, isn't it? Since Dad went.'

Winnie nodded. There was nothing else she needed to say.

Cathy checked on the roast in the oven and came back into the living room, looking as though she had the troubles of the world on her shoulders.

'That was Tom. He's stuck at the bloody office.' She instinctively looked over at the children to see if they'd caught her swearing, but they were engrossed sitting on the floor playing a board game with Hannah. 'He won't be back in time for dinner.'

'Ah, that's a shame,' said Winnie lightly, picking up on Cathy's generally stressed-out appearance.

Whatever they were playing, Hugo had obviously just won judging by the way he sprung up off the floor, waving his arms and cheering. Unfortunately, as he jumped, he knocked a framed photo off the wall which fell to the wooden floor with a crash.

'Hugo!' shouted Cathy. 'Be careful. For goodness' sake.' She dashed over to retrieve the photo which Hannah had already picked up.

'It's OK, it hasn't broken,' she said gently as she handed it up. Cathy attempted to replace it on its hook, but her hands were shaking so much, it took her several attempts.

The room was silent as she left to return to the kitchen. The children were finishing their game, but they were whispering now, their mood suddenly deflated. Hannah looked over to her mum questioningly, but in this instant Winne didn't know what to do for the best and shrugged her shoulders.

'Shall I go and see if she's OK?' Hannah asked quietly, very aware of the very good hearing of very small ears.

Winnie nodded.

Hannah returned barely a minute later and sat on the settee next to Winnie.

'She's making a trifle. Doesn't want any help. Isn't happy, she's got lumps in her custard. And I think she's been crying.'

Winnie grimaced, raised her eyebrows and sighed. 'She wants everything to be perfect. All the time.'

'That's a recipe for disaster.'

'It certainly is.'

Hannah gazed out into the garden, frowning. She looked worried. 'I've never seen her like this. It's like, I don't know, like she's on the edge.'

Winnie was just about to get up and go to Cathy herself when they heard an almighty crash from the kitchen followed by a piercing squeal. They all looked up, and then immediately all got up. Hannah turned to see the frightened look on the children's faces as they prepared to instinctively run to their mum.

'Stay with the kids,' she said to Winne, as she ran to the kitchen.

She found Cathy on her knees on the kitchen floor, a pool of hot custard in front of her, the saucepan on

210

its side and a china bowl smashed in pieces. She had one hand resting in the custard and the other covering her face as she sobbed.

Hannah was at her side in an instant, kneeling in the custard herself. She tried to hug her sister to her, but she was rigid, tension armouring her entire body. Hannah pulled away slightly, her hand still on her sister's back.

'It's OK, it's OK Cath.'

'I can't do this,' she cried, still sobbing. 'I can't do this anymore.'

Hannah didn't know what she was referring to. Not the ruined trifle, surely? What could she say to help?

'You missing Dad? Me too.'

Cathy nodded. 'I just can't cope with any of it anymore. Putting on a brave face. I feel like I'm broken. I'm broken into a million pieces. And I'm scared I'll never be mended.'

'I know Cath,' she said, rubbing her back, suddenly painfully aware she didn't have a clue how Cathy was feeling. Of course, she was grieving her dad too, but she realised she didn't have a fraction of the commitments and responsibilities that Cathy had.

'It'll be alright. You'll be alright, Cath. You will. I promise. It'll just take time.'

Cathy was shaking her head, whispering now. 'Sometimes, I get scared, I think I'll never be mended. I'll never be me again. Sometimes I don't even know who me is.'

Hannah was about to remind her sister that she was a wife and a mother, but she managed to stop herself spewing these clichés. This isn't what her sister needed to hear.

Hannah took her sister's hands away from her face and held them in her own, custard squelching between them. She smiled and Cathy managed a smile back, some tiny semblance of relief on her face.

'You're right about one thing – you make lousy custard. Completely full of lumps.' Hannah grinned as she swirled the custard with her fingers on the floor, and then flicked some at Cathy who laughed and flicked some back.

At that moment, Winnie stuck her head around the door to see both her daughters kneeling in custard, laughing as they flicked the yellow goo at each other.

'I used to tell you off for throwing food.'

Hannah held up her arm in command. 'Don't worry Mum, as unlikely as it seems, I have it all under control. Nothing for you to do here.'

'OK, if you say so. I'll leave you to it.' And she disappeared as suddenly as she'd appeared.

Cathy looked about her. 'Oh god, look at this mess. And I think the joint is burnt as well – I was trying to hang on for Tom getting home. Where am I going to start?'

'You're not going to start anywhere. You're going to go upstairs and have a long nap, so that at least you'll look better and stop scaring the children.' Cathy looked suitably ashamed.

'I'm only joking. But you do look frightfully tired – and frightful too, to be honest! I'll clear this lot up.' Cathy gave her a questioning look.

'OK, I'll ask Mum to come and clear this lot up. And then I will take your gorgeous monster of a car, because at this moment in time, you're weak and won't deny me anything – and I'll pick up a disgusting takeaway of some sort which means your children will love me forever. I'll put some of it in the oven to congeal and go soggy and you can eat that later when you're rested. See, told you I had it all under control.'

Cathy looked down at her hands in her lap. She didn't know what to say. Hannah leaned in for another hug and this time it was reciprocated, and she was delighted to feel Cathy's sticky custardy hand on her back holding her tight.

They helped each other up from the mess on the floor. Hannah picked up the saucepan and a couple of the bigger chunks of broken china.

'I loved that mixing bowl,' said Cathy, looking as if she was about to start crying again.

'You can get another,' soothed Hannah. 'Go on, shoo now! I'll wake you in a couple of hours.'

Winnie cleaned the kitchen while Hannah went out to collect a takeaway. Having eaten most of the pizza and then the mini doughnuts, the children were getting sleepy. Just as Hannah was thinking about waking Cathy, Tom arrived home. He sensed something wasn't quite right, confirmed by the four of them watching tele and the takeaway boxes still on the coffee table.

'Everything OK? Where's Cath?'

Hannah got up and led Tom back to the kitchen where she explained the events of the afternoon. He

213

nodded and sighed, rubbing the back of his neck wearily.

'I knew this was coming. She's been bottling everything up and overdoing it. I should have done more to help. I need to be here more.'

Hannah smiled. She'd built some bridges with her sister today, but she wasn't about to start offering her brother-in-law relationship advice. And anyway, she knew they'd work it out.

'OK if me and Mum get off? Sorry, the kids are full of pizza and sugar – they're sleepy now but they'll probably be hyper-active in the early hours!'

'Thanks.' Tom was used to her dry humour. 'Yeah sure, you get off home. I'll take Cath up a cup of tea and start getting the kids ready for bed.'

They drove home in comfortable silence, each with a busy mind going over the day. Hannah parked on the drive.

'You coming in for a tea or coffee?'

'Yeah, of course.'

'Why don't you stay over? I could do with the company – unless you've got plans for this evening.'

'Nope, no plans, and I'd love to stay over. I could do with the company too. And I know you have a good stash of drink.'

'Yes, good idea, let's open a bottle of something nice.'

Winnie unlocked the back door, and they went through to the kitchen, and she left Hannah there choosing a bottle of wine while she went around closing curtains and putting little lamps on. In the hallway she saw an envelope on the doormat. It must be what the young couple had posted earlier, she'd forgotten all about it.

Hannah had opened a bottle of wine and poured a couple of glasses and was already enjoying hers as Winnie returned to the kitchen, reading the letter.

'Oh, I'd forgotten all about that. Ooh, it looks like a posh letter. It's nothing serious, is it?'

Winnie was completely engrossed in the contents of the letter, but her face was unreadable.

'Mum? Is everything OK?' Hannah put down her glass and moved towards her.

Winnie had finished reading and looked across at her daughter, a stupefied look on her face.

'That couple who put this through the door – they want to buy this house.'

Hannah frowned, not sure whether to feel offended or complemented on behalf of her mother. Winnie handed her the letter to read. Hannah's eyebrows shot up and she clasped her hand over her mouth in shock.

'Blimey Mum! This house can't possibly be worth that – they're offering you an absolute fortune for it.'

Chapter 23

Lawrence was away on a business trip, just for the one night and Zoe had plans for her evening. She was going to study her wine club notes from the last session and prepare for the next one. Thursday's meeting was on Italian wine, and she intended to spend the evening on the internet for some extra studying.

She had already set up various folders on her laptop to organise all the material she'd been given as well as her own studies. Lawrence had even commented on how much time she spent huddled over the screen. At times she allowed herself to think that maybe he was a little impressed she was sticking with it and taking her studies seriously.

Zoe, warm and relaxed after a hot shower deliberated over whether to cook first or treat herself to a small glass of cold wine. The wine won.

As she poured a small measure, then a little more followed by a little more still, she took stock of the fact that she'd been very well behaved lately. In front of Lawrence, she was very careful to monitor the amount she drank and was succeeding very well in keeping pace with him, constantly keeping an eye on his glass. It was a little game she was playing – in trying to never have an empty glass before him. Silly really, but it helped.

As she sipped at the kitchen island, she realised how nice it felt for a change, not to have that pressure on her. Tonight, she could relax a little and treat herself for all her previous good behaviour.

216

She took the glass though to the living room. Her studies on the Italian wine industry could wait a while. For now, she wanted to look at some images of cosy country kitchens. She clicked Instagram open – she was a whizz with this platform.

She'd got it in her mind to adapt their kitchen somehow. Every time she stepped inside Winnifred Mayhew's gorgeous home, it reminded her of how cold and stark her own home was.

She cringed guiltily when she remembered the enormous price tag that was the result of what she always thought of as her dream kitchen. Lawrence would not be pleased to know that her taste had completely changed. Maybe she could somehow incorporate some softer touches that would lessen the harshness of it. She needed to seriously start thinking about getting a job, that would undoubtedly help her cause.

Lounging on the sofa with her glass of wine in one hand and the computer mouse in the other, the next half hour flew past, and then she saw her glass was empty.

Back out in the kitchen for a top up, she noticed the mushrooms and eggs and fresh herbs she'd bought to make a frittata for her supper this evening. She was going with the Italian theme. She filled her glass halfway and promised herself she would cook after this one.

Her mobile phone was ringing, and she dashed back into the living room thinking it would be Lawrence. He'd better not be checking up on her, she thought. She saw it was her sister ringing, and plonked herself down, feeling irritated for some reason. She didn't feel like speaking to her and let it go to voicemail, although Tina never did leave a message and that irritated her too.

Zoe placed her glass on the coffee table, noticing it was already nearly empty again. She felt a little woozy, realising she wasn't used to drinking this quickly anymore.

'I'm becoming a light weight,' she giggled to herself.

The laptop screen had gone blank, and she slammed it shut, not in the mood now for kitchen pictures or wine studies. She picked up the remote and flicked through the channels finally settling on a long-running soap opera – a not too cheerful scene with a well-worn looking mother shouting at her teenage daughters while they gave back just as forcefully.

Zoe grimaced. This kind of thing brought back memories. Bad memories. Her mother used to shout.

'Bad tempered old baggage,' she muttered.

She wondered where she was and what she was doing right now, trying to convince herself she didn't give a damn although the painful knot in her stomach always twisted harder when she thought like that - as if to contradict her.

'Why should I care?' Zoe snatched her glass up and drank the remains. 'You abandoned us. How could you? Why did you leave us?' She felt tears prick the back of her eyes, annoyed that thoughts of her mum could still do this to her.

She flew to the kitchen and grabbed the wine bottle from the fridge, taking it back to the living room and filling her glass full to the top.

She sat there, glass in hand, going through her mind, all the relations of her rotten family. The only really good one was Aunty Wendy, her mother's sister. She was always sweet to her and Tina. Although she had the terribly annoying habit of saying how alike her mother she was. From that day to this, she denied she was, or would ever be, anything like her mother.

It was dark outside, but Zoe hadn't pulled the curtains, and couldn't remember if she'd locked the back door. She'd check later. Her phone rang and her lazy eyes glanced sideways not caring who it was. And then she focused to see it was Lawrence calling. It was late, she didn't think he'd ring now.

'Hi! Hi Honey. How are you doing there? How's it all going? Are you having fun?'

There was a pause, and a quietly spoken Lawrence confirmed he was fine, and the conference was OK.

'What are you up to there, Zo? You're not having a wild party there without me, are you?'

'No, no, nothing like that. Silly. Just, you know, sitting here with my laptop. Keeping myself busy. Off the streets. Out of trouble. You know me.'

'OK. Now listen, have you locked the back door? Don't forget, will you?'

'Yes, yes, I've done that. All locked, safe and sound.'

'OK, that's good. Right, I'd better get back. I'll see you tomorrow.'

They said their goodbyes and hung up. Zoe flung her phone down beside her. She knew that Lawrence knew she'd had a lot to drink. She smiled sardonically – she'd deal with that flack tomorrow. She'd dealt with worse.

'Lock the door, lock the door,' she sang sarcastically, and got up to do just that, fetching another bottle of white on her way back.

The following morning Zoe awoke with a dry scratchy throat and her head was pulsing, ready to explode. She stretched her eyes open, surprised to realise she had a hangover. She hadn't had one of those for a while.

Various questions bombarded her fuddled brain. What time was Lawrence getting home? Was he going straight to the office or coming home after his flight? What was the state of the house downstairs, and did she need to do any desperate cleaning and tidying? She couldn't remember and decided she'd better get out of bed sooner rather than later to investigate.

Down in the kitchen she made strong black coffee. Her stomach was too queasy for even a dash of milk. She hadn't got around to cooking anything the previous evening and quickly put the mushrooms and eggs in the fridge. She felt ill and couldn't bear the sight of food.

But the overriding feeling she had, as she sat on a kitchen stool with her hurting head resting in her hands, was of total and utter disappointment in herself. Lawrence had been away for just one night and she'd had to hit the bottle like an immature teenager.

She remembered opening at least two bottles. They were still in the living room, probably both empty. And now what, should she hide them in the kitchen bin or take them out to the recycling? What was the point? She vaguely remembered chatting to Lawrence late last night. She was babbling, like she always did when she was trying to be coherent.

Lawrence would know she'd overdone it again. And this evening would be another one with a stony silence between them probably making her feel like doing it all over again.

Oh well, she thought, at least I have the wine club tomorrow. It was fast becoming her sanctuary. She didn't chat much, but she liked everyone there. She liked being among them. It was comfortable and she even felt they liked her too.

And now that another person had joined, Helen, it meant Zoe wasn't the new girl anymore. She thought about Helen for a minute, with all her exciting plans of starting a new life in another country with her new husband. Did Zoe envy her? No. Definitely not. She liked living in this country with her husband. She'd just like to make more of a success of it than she had to date.

Chapter 24

With a perfectly manicured hand, Helen closed the dishwasher door, wiped the already clean worktop and neatly folded the cloth placing it tidily next to the tap.

It had been a long day at the office. She was a legal secretary for a top global company and had been there for most of her working life. It had been a good job, she'd been well looked after, and it would be a wrench to leave the place - she'd miss her friends terribly.

She made herself a cup of peppermint tea, bone china cup and saucer, and took it through to the lounge where she sat on the little two-seater settee, tucking her legs underneath her. She sighed contentedly. It was good to be home, how she loved her little modern flat. And she knew this was one thing she definitely would be sad to leave.

Helen reached across for her diary, checking the pages over the next few days, making sure she hadn't missed anyone's upcoming birthday or anniversary. Everything went in here, coffee with girlfriends, dates with Seth, hairdressing appointments. And tomorrow The Wine Club. Wines of Italy she'd scribbled on the page.

Tonight she was meeting up with some friends from her swimming club. She looked at her watch, she had less than an hour. It was a birthday celebration, and they were going for cocktails at a bar nearby.

Helen thought back to her first attendance at the wine club a couple of weeks ago. She still wasn't sure what to make of it. Winnifred was a lovely lady of course. The other woman, Gloria, she wasn't too sure about her. And everyone else had been pleasant enough, and suitably impressed as everyone always was when she spoke of going to live in France.

Although, on this occasion she hadn't got the same kick out of telling her story. The oohs and aahs didn't have the same uplifting effect on her. It was as if everyone else that evening had been more excited for her than she was for herself.

She sniffed and sipped her tea, determined to pull herself together. Through Seth, she was being offered the opportunity of a lifetime. For goodness' sake, soon she'd be living in the south of France on a vineyard. It was the perfect lifestyle people dreamed about.

She twisted in her seat and pulled a pile of wedding brochures onto her lap. This would cheer her up. She hadn't expected to have to wait until her late forties to get married but now it was finally here, she was determined it would be the perfect day, regardless of her age.

Flicking through the pages and pages of wedding dresses, she had to acknowledge, with just a tinge of sadness, that the huge extravagant ones with endless layers of netting and lace would not be appropriate.

She came across a full-page photo of the wedding cake she wanted and tore out the page to show her friends later. There was so much wedding-associated paraphernalia, it would be easy to get completely carried away. She didn't want to go over the top, but her day would be perfect.

At the bottom of the pile of magazines was some literature Seth had given her to read through – details about the house and surrounding land and the vineyard they would be moving to later in the year. She hadn't got around to looking at it yet, but she put it next to her handbag to show everyone later, knowing how impressed her friends would be.

Chapter 25

Italian Wine

Etruscans and Greek settlers produced wine in Italy before the Romans planted their own vineyards in the 2nd century BC. The Romans greatly increased Italy's vineyard area by using efficient viticultural and winemaking methods and by pioneering large-scale production and storage techniques such as barrel-making and bottling.

Today, Italy is the world's largest producer of wine and is home to some of the oldest wine-producing regions, representing approximately a quarter of global production.

Grapes are grown in every region of the country and there are more than one million vineyards under cultivation.

Winnie went about her usual preparations for the evening, confident and comfortable with what she was doing. This evening was all about Italian wine and she was particularly looking forward to this one, not least because she'd included one of her favourite red wines.

Instead of cooking today, she'd bought some cold meats and olives to put out halfway through the evening and as she arranged them on platters to put in the fridge, she glanced at the clock, wondering why Gloria hadn't arrived yet. She was usually here well before any of the others.

Everything was ready and Winnie felt a bit lost. She and Gloria would usually be chatting away by now, a calming few moments before everyone arrived. She checked her mobile phone to see if she'd missed a message but there was nothing.

She decided to give her a quick call; check everything was OK. Gloria's phone rang and then switched to voicemail. Winnie frowned but didn't leave a message, reassuring herself she was probably on her way. She was most likely in the taxi right now and didn't hear her phone ringing in her bag. That would be it.

A few quiet moments to herself had Winnie taking stock of the last few months. She looked about her kitchen, cosy, warm and inviting, very pleased to note that all of her club members were coming back week after week, no-one had dropped out. Although, she had to admit, she wouldn't mind in the least if Helen didn't return this week, and then immediately felt the slap of Gloria's words about not becoming bitter.

She looked up at the clock yet again. 'Gloria, where are you?'

A knock at the front door had her dashing to answer it, hoping she'd finally arrived, but it was Peter. She was sure he came earlier each time.

'Hello Peter, how are you? Come on in.'

'I'm not too bad.'

They went through to the kitchen where Peter took his usual seat next to Winnie.

'How are you?' he suddenly asked, for the first time. Winnie hoped the surprise she felt wasn't showing too obviously on her face.

'I'm very well thanks, Peter.'

'It's nice and warm in here. Very nice.' Pleasantries and a compliment, observed Winnie.

After that, everyone seemed to arrive at once. No sooner had she closed the door on the chilly late summer evening, then the doorbell rang again. Within a few minutes the kitchen was full. Everyone bustled to their place, hanging jackets and coats on the back of their chairs. It was amusing to Winnie to see they each had their favourite place to sit which they aimed for each week. Even Helen, had taken her allotted seat near the back of the room, obviously not wanting to tread on anyone's toes.

Just as Winnie was about to start, she heard a knock at the back door as it opened. Thank goodness, she knew it would be Gloria. She could stop worrying now.

Gloria poked her head around the kitchen door.

'Hello everyone. Sorry I'm late Wynne. I'll just hang my jacket up and I'll be in.'

Something was wrong. Gloria was pale faced and nothing like her usual jolly self. Instinctively Winnie wanted to follow her to the boot room, but she had a room full of people. She dithered for a second and shuffled some papers in front of her.

'Help yourselves to the notes here for this week, have a glance through. I won't be a minute.'

She dashed to the boot room. 'Gloria, are you OK? No, you're not. What's happened?'

'Sorry I'm late Wynne. I'm fine. I'll tell you about it later, but get back to your guests now, come on, they're waiting for you.'

With that, Gloria led the way back into the kitchen, not giving Winnie a chance to keep her there any longer. She stood in her usual place over by the worktop, just to the side of Winnie who was now completely distracted by whatever it was Gloria had to tell. It had to be something awful judging by her ashen face which was usually so animated and yet now remained almost expressionless.

She looked across the room, which was now somewhat subdued as if everyone had picked up on Gloria's sadness. This was going to be another challenging evening, she thought grimly, as she looked over at Helen, who thankfully, at this moment was also very quiet.

Even Zoe, sitting next to Peter had lost the little spark that had very slowly been developing week on week.

Winnie attempted a smile. 'Right. I reckon we could all do with a drink.'

Everyone murmured their agreement.

'So, the first wine of the evening is a full-bodied red from Italy made from the Nero D'avola. This is one of my absolute favourites, and I hope you all like it too. It's a wine which likes to be decanted so I opened this a couple of hours ago.'

'Shall I read the description?' asked Cliff.

'Yes, good idea Cliff. Go ahead.'

Terredora Di Paolo Algianico

This is a tremendously complex and intense example of one of the region's most celebrated grapes, Aglianico.

Blackberries, dark cherries, tar and violets characterise the nose, while the palate offers black cherry, liquorice, smoke and sweet spiced plum.

There's a rich fully body, smooth tannins, a fresh acidity, and a long lingering finish.

'Thanks Cliff.' Winnie began handing the glasses out.

Lulu rolled her eyes to the ceiling. 'Tar and smoke? Who wants to taste that in their wine?'

Everyone laughed, finally relieving some of the tension that had spread through the room.

'Each to their own,' declared Sheila. 'I reckon if tar and smoke is your thing. You know, go for it.'

'I'm just about to find out,' said Cliff as he gently swirled his wine and put his nose to the glass.

Everyone swirled and sipped and looked to each other to see if they agreed in opinion, all having fun trying to detect the elusive aromas of tar and smoke.

Winnie left them to it while she turned and checked on Gloria. At some point she'd poured herself a very large measure of gin and was standing there, glass in hand, staring into the middle distance.

'You OK?'

'I'm fine Love. You carry on.'

Winnie turned back to the room to see Kerry and Ayisha both wrinkling their noses at each other – this wine obviously wasn't to their liking. Whereas at the back of the room, Muriel seemed to be in her own heaven, eyes closed, savouring the flavours before swallowing. Winnie stood there watching her little crowd practising all the things she'd taught them over the last few weeks. It was a little oasis of enjoyment in that moment.

And then she noticed Zoe, holding her glass which was virtually untouched on the table. She was deep in thought, miles away.

'Zoe, what do you think of this one?'

It took Zoe a moment to realise Winnie was speaking to her. She turned slowly to look up at her as if she were in a daze. After a couple of thoughtful seconds, she spoke.

'My husband thinks I drink too much. He thinks I'm an alcoholic.'

The room was hit with sudden silence. Everyone had heard despite her tiny voice. But, of course, no-one knew how to respond.

Finally, Muriel came into her own, and Zoe turned around to face her.

'Do you fall out of bed in the morning, wanting a drink?' asked Muriel, very direct and matter of fact.

'No. I never want a drink in the morning. And I don't fall out of bed either.'

'Do you ever fall over because of drink?'

'No!'

'Do you ever wet yourself, or poop the bed?'

'That's gross. No I don't!'

'Right, well you're not an alcoholic then. My husband is an alcoholic, and he does all the above and worse.'

The silence grew, if that was possible.

Zoe continued, still facing Muriel, as if it were just the two of them in the room.

'But, maybe I drink too much.'

'Maybe we all drink too much. I drink too much, it's the only way I can cope with my husband's alcoholism.'

Mary's ears pricked up. Was there really another woman in the room who had an alcoholic husband?

'Come on, lighten up everyone,' continued Muriel. 'It's a serious subject, but you've got to laugh at that.'

They weren't quite ready to laugh at the previous conversation but at least they smiled and seemed to relax a little.

Zoe turned around again. Peter placed his gnarled old hand over hers on the table.

'Do you think you drink too much?' he asked quietly.

Zoe nodded her head. 'Sometimes,' she whispered.

'And why do you think that is?'

'I don't know.' She shrugged.

'Have a think. What makes you want more?'

Zoe closed her eyes and sighed, thinking back to the evening when Lawrence had been away.

'I start thinking about things, sad things. Like when I was growing up, my parents arguing, my mum walking out and never coming back. A bit of wine, I don't know, it stops the feeling.'

'Stops the pain?'

Zoe nodded again.

'I think most people would need some help with that kind of pain.'

Zoe looked up at him questioningly.

'Have you ever talked to anyone about it all?'

'No, not really. Sometimes, a bit with my sister, but she's a lot younger than me. I don't like to say too much.'

'You'd be surprised how tough young ones can be.'

Winnie sat down. 'What about your husband? Would he listen?'

'Oh yeah, he would. He knows I didn't have a great childhood, but I've never really talked about it. I just try to shut it out.'

'You can't shut stuff like that out. It'll rear its ugly head some way,' said Peter, very knowledgeably, thought Winnie.

She looked directly at him, the question in the air.

'I've been through my own stuff,' he said, a little defensively but not angrily. He closed his eyes and nodded. 'I went through a time when this was my saviour.' He pointed to his glass. 'Not this, not wine, that wasn't enough for me. Whisky. That became my friend every evening. Too much of a friend. I can't touch a drop of it now though.' Peter shuddered, and smiled, squeezed Zoe's hand before letting go.

'You talk it out. And like Winnie says, your husband, he'll be your best friend. I'll bet he doesn't like seeing you unhappy.'

'No,' whispered Zoe. 'And thank-you.' She looked up at Winnie. 'Thank-you.'

Winnie smiled and stood up again. How was she ever going to continue after that? Food. That was the answer. She'd bring the snacks out, let everyone have a little chat. She turned to see poor Gloria topping up her glass with another large gin and tonic. Crikey, she thought, everyone is an alcoholic tonight.

'Gloria, do you want something to eat?' Gloria shook her head smiling weakly.

Winnie fetched the platters from the fridge, took a side plate and loaded it with cold meats, olives and salad and placed the plate next to Gloria. 'Just in case you get a little peckish later.'

The next wine was a Soave – a light bodied white which was very popular with everyone, and finally they finished the evening with a bit of a twist, in that she provided a dessert wine - a Marsala made in Sicily.

Apart from what appeared to be merely polite conversation, hardly any reference was made to

Helen's impending wedding or her emigration to France. She seemed to be very much the active listener tonight, offering the odd comment here and there on the various tastings but other than that Winnie was almost able to forget she was there.

For obvious reasons, Winnie wanted to wrap things up promptly and everyone seemed to understand. As it was getting towards nine-thirty Sheila took it upon herself to clear away people's food plates and empty glasses, stacking them on the kitchen worktop.

'Thanks Sheila.'

They pretty much left all together. Winnie closed the front door and returned to the silence of the kitchen where she found Gloria tidying the rest of the things.

'Leave that, I'll do it later. Bring your drink, let's go and get comfortable.'

Gloria didn't need any persuading and followed her through to the living room where she closed the curtains and switched on some table lamps.

'Is it cold enough for a fire do you think?'

'I'm OK, Wynne. Don't bother just for me.'

'You're not OK. Tell me what's happened.'

'I'm OK, honestly.' Gloria smiled, properly for the first time in a couple of hours, looking a little more like her old self.

'I'm in a bit of shock, that's all. You know my lovely neighbour, Ada?'

'Yes, I've met her a few times, at your place.'

'Well, she died today.'

'Oh Gloria, I'm so sorry to hear that. She was lovely, wasn't she? How did you find out?'

234

'I've been checking in on her for a while now. A few weeks ago, she had a fall, was on the floor for a few hours. So, I've been sticking my head in at least once a day.

'But today, for some crazy reason, I woke this morning full of energy, and thought I'd give my whole place a bit of a spring clean.'

'A spring clean in August?'

'I did say it was crazy. But anyway, I'd been in the house all day doing that, intending to pop into Ada's early evening. I took some rubbish out mid-afternoon and noticed all her curtains were still shut. That's how I knew something was wrong before.

'So, I let myself in straightaway, and that was it. I found her dead in her bed.'

'Oh, Gloria that's awful. You poor thing.'

'No not really, it wasn't awful. She was in her own bed in her own home after all. And she was in her nineties too. I don't know, just the shock of it I suppose. And I had to call her wretched son. He'll probably knock the place down and build a five-bedroom executive home on it, or whatever they're called.'

'He won't be able to do that, will he? Her place must be a listed building, surely?'

'I don't know. It probably is. I know, he won't do that, he'll just sell up as fast as he can. I'm just being miserable.'

'You're never miserable. But you are beginning to slur your words. Will you let me cook you some supper? I can do soup, or I've got a pizza in the freezer.'

'Oh, let's have the pizza – let's live a little.' The words were out before she could stop them. She gave a little grimace and they both laughed.

Chapter 26

Winnie couldn't persuade Gloria to stay the night last night. She insisted she wanted to get back to her own home, and Winnie helped a tearful Gloria into a taxi just before midnight.

And today, right now this morning, she was going to go and make sure she was alright. Gloria had been a total rock over the last few months, the best of friends to Winnie, and she didn't want to hear any words of bravado, she was going to be looked after today whether she thought she needed it or not.

She took a taxi to Gloria's, thinking not for the first time lately, how useful it would be if she could drive. She thought of Doug's huge car still sitting in the garage. Maybe it was time to think of selling it and learning to drive – maybe buy something smaller and more economical to run.

As the taxi pulled up outside Gloria's cottage, she realised it was an absolute age since she'd been there. Feeling somewhat guilty, she let herself in through the little garden gate at the back, looking across at Ada's now empty cottage as she walked the length of the long garden path. Whoever bought it would need to have a lot of work done on it. But it was very cute, she observed, and very old with heaps of character, and as it was the last cottage in the row, it had the largest garden to the side of the property.

Seeing Gloria making tea in her kitchen, she tapped lightly on the door.

'Hello Wynne Love, what are you doing here? Not checking up on me, are you?'

'Yep. I am. You look tired Glo.'

'Mm, I was up late last night. I didn't leave yours until midnight, was it? And then I sat up a bit longer, a bit thoughtful you know.'

'I certainly do.'

Gloria made the tea. 'Let's take this through to the other room.'

'Are you feeling a little better today?'

'Yes, I'm fine really. Although it will feel strange knowing she's not pottering around in there. I've been of some help to her over recent years, but I realise now, the comfort I got from having her there. A friendly old woman, never had a cross word with her.'

'Hopefully, you'll get another nice neighbour.'

'Hm, it does concern me a little – who will buy the place and what plans they might have. Imagine if they do want to knock it about a bit. Think of the noise all day, every day. It'll be a nightmare.'

'Or they might not. Come on Glo, it's not like you to think the worst. Hey, you never know, you might get a nice young man in there?'

'What use would that be? It's not a pretty sight seeing an old woman drooling at the window. Or pathetically popping around every other day to borrow a cup of sugar.'

'OK, you might get an old, wrinkly man move in next door then.'

'Now, that could be much more beneficial.' Gloria looked away, trying not to look guilty.

'What was that look for? What are you up to?'

'Nothing. Why?'

'Because I know you are. I've known it for a while. Come on, out with it. Ah, I know, all this talk about men next door....'

'You started that. I never mentioned anything about men next door.'

'You're seeing someone. Aren't you?'

Gloria smiled, stupidly, pretending to be shy.

'Might be.' She grinned. 'Well not exactly. But I will be soon.'

Winnie looked puzzled. 'Why didn't you tell me?'

'I don't tell you everything!'

Gloria took a deep breath, and sat up straight, putting her cup of tea on the table.

'I'm going off on a little holiday soon. To France actually, and before you make a fuss – I have suggested to you a number of times that we could scoot off somewhere for a few days.'

'I know you have. I've just never really felt up to it.'

'Yes, I know, and that's fine. I just don't want you to get upset now, at me going.'

'No, I'm not upset, really. I'm pleased for you. Especially now, after what's just happened.'

'OK, good. So, I got myself on one of those dating websites, you know?'

'No. Why would I?'

'I don't mean have you been on them. But you've heard of them, right?'

'Yes, of course.'

'So, I got chatting with a nice French chap. We've been chatting for a few months, first online, and then on the phone. And we've even done a few Skype calls. He's rather lovely actually.'

Gloria was actually blushing. Winnie smiled.

'Mm, so what's his name?'

'Bernard. Bernard from Bordeaux. He has a restaurant there.'

Winnie giggled.

'What's funny?'

'Oh nothing – it's just that, you hear of these scams. Bernard from Bordeaux might turn out to be Benny from Billericay with a fish and chip van.'

Gloria gave her a look of disapproval. 'Thanks for that.'

'Actually seriously, you have checked all this out properly. Don't take any silly risks, will you?'

'Don't worry. I've been perfectly sensible. I've rented a little gite on a holiday farm – so plenty of other people around. I'll hire a car when I'm there so I'll be completely independent and we'll meet in public places. I'll be careful to watch for him putting drugs in my drink and I'll make sure I'm in bed by ten o'clock every night. Or maybe earlier, if he is as gorgeous as he looks.'

'Gloria, you're terrible!'

Gloria laughed out loud, realising how much she was looking forward to this trip.

'You mind keeping an eye on this place while I'm away? I'm conscious of all the comings and goings next door and this being empty for a couple of weeks.'

'Yes of course I will.'

'Just tidy the post away and switch some lights on and off, things like that.'

240

'Yep, no problem.'

Gloria sighed. 'I know it's still very soon, but do you ever think of meeting someone?'

'No. I don't even think about it.'

Gloria nodded. Enough said.

Chapter 27

Winnie had planned to spend the day indulging herself with a good book, and tea and biscuits on tap. But so far, on this Saturday morning, all she'd done was potter about putting various things away.

That was the known problem with big houses, she thought, there was more room to accumulate things, more room to leave things lying around, and then always more tidying to do.

Plus, her mind was too busy to concentrate on reading. She was thinking about poor Gloria losing her friend and neighbour like that, which led to thoughts about not so poor Gloria and her fancy French boyfriend.

Winnie laughed as she went upstairs into the bathroom. Gloria was such a colourful character. She was truly amazing; heading off to France to meet up with Bernard from Bordeaux. Winnie shook her head, still smiling as she gathered clothes from the laundry bin. Talking of colourful characters, she noticed that most of her clothes ready for the wash were either black, grey or navy blue. Perhaps she should follow Gloria's example and liven herself up a bit.

Surely her own wardrobe held some colour in it. She felt obliged to go immediately and check, pulling open the doors and rummaging inside. Sadly, she didn't find much, and what she did hadn't been worn for years. Perhaps she and Cathy could plan a day of shopping, a bit of retail therapy would do them both good. Or maybe she should take Hannah – take her for a treat to pick her up; she'd had a tough time lately. Although maybe she wasn't quite ready for Hannah's stylistic recommendations just yet.

She glanced over to Doug's side of the wardrobe. She hadn't touched any of his things yet. They would need to be sorted at some point, and things would have to be cleared out. She smoothed her hand over his favourite blue cashmere jumper. She didn't think she'd ever be able to part with that, and then she smiled at his pile of t-shirts all with funny slogans on them. It would be too much of a wrench to get rid of them. Hanging up were all his work shirts, mostly white, a couple of pale blue. He didn't particularly like wearing office wear and only did so when he was meeting with clients or the like.

She lifted half a dozen shirts down and lay them on the bed. This lot could go, there was nothing sentimental here. She took out the hangers and folded the shirts. She'd take them to the charity shop next week.

As she loaded the washing machine and shut the door, she likened it to the state of her own mind at that moment. So many thoughts were swishing around in her head, tumbling and tangling themselves up into a terrible mess.

She didn't know what to make of Gloria going off on her adventure, which was nothing compared to what Helen was doing – upping and offing to live in a different country altogether. Both women were very brave.

And here she was rattling around on her own in this big old house. What should she do with the house? And if she sold it, what then? She just couldn't decide.

Zoe hung some washing out in the garden. Usually, she would simply shove it in the tumble dryer, but she decided it was just lazy and wasteful on a bright sunny blowy day like today.

It was Lawrence's birthday in a few days, and she knew exactly what she was going to do. She had her laptop open and was preparing to spend some time trawling through the travel websites to make sure she got the best deal. But first she had a call to make.

It only rung a couple of times before her sister answered.

'Hi.'

'Hi Tina, how are you? Sorry I haven't answered your calls. I've been a bit, well a bit down, lately.'

'Me too actually, that's why I wanted to talk.'

'Look I'm really sorry. I haven't been much of a big sister lately, have I?'

'What do you mean? You make it sound like it's your responsibility to look after me. I think you always have.'

'Well, Mum wasn't around that much was she?'

'So? It doesn't mean it's your job. Anyway, I don't even think of you as my big sister anymore. I just think of you as, I don't know, a friend. Well, more than a friend, obviously. And anyway, if anyone needs looking after, it's you.'

'No I don't.'

'Don't get snappy. I get that you're not in a very good place at the moment. You never come out anymore, and you don't answer any of my calls.'

'OK, true, but I'm ringing now, aren't I?'

'Yes. Good. So, what do you want?'

'I was going to ask, little sister, if you would like to do something together – the pictures and pizza? Abseiling down The Shard, skydiving, bungee jumping, afternoon tea at The Ritz?'

'Ooh yeah, that last one.'

'Really? Or are you joking?

'I'm not joking. What not? Let's do it.'

'OK, I'll check it out, and let you know.'

Zoe was laughing as they finished their call. She scribbled a note 'book the Ritz' to remind herself to book something later.

'And now for other important business,' she announced to herself as she sat at the kitchen island, pouring over her laptop. She was looking for a good last-minute deal for a perfect weekend away.

Helen flicked through glossy holiday brochures of glamourous destinations, unable to make her mind up of where they should go on honeymoon. In truth, she was unable to muster any enthusiasm. Just last-minute nerves, she concluded - even though the wedding was still months away.

Gloria hoisted her new bright red suitcase onto the bed in the spare room and made a start on her packing. She still had a couple of weeks before setting off, but it was good to be organised. She placed her new dresses inside; fuchsia pink and turquoise, with either matching or clashing accessories, ready for whatever mood she was in.

This was her first break of the year. She'd suggested it to Winnie several times, but she hadn't wanted to go, and at the time Gloria didn't like to leave her. But now, she was looking forward immensely to spending some time with Bernard.

She was always a little anxious at leaving her home, but comforted knowing Winnie would be keeping an eye on the place.

Later in the evening, just before it got dark, she took a stroll around her garden, removing the odd dead flowerhead and generally checking everything over. As she returned to her cottage, cosy looking with warm lights shining out from the windows, she looked over to Ada's place – dark and empty looking, and once again the sadness overtook her. She would be very glad to get to the bright warm sunshine of France.

Chapter 28

Australian Wine

Australia is the world's fifth largest exporter of wine with approximately 780 million litres a year to the international export market with only about 40% of production consumed domestically.

Hot and sunny vineyards produce ripe, juicy, approachable and affordable wines, while cooler regions in the hills or next to the sea produce lighter, more elegant and restrained ones. In between, countless micro-climates offer a huge range of styles, quality and value.

Wine is produced in every single state in Australia. There are over 100 grape varieties planted - major grape types include Shiraz, Cabernet Sauvignon, Merlot, Chardonnay and Sauvignon Blanc.

'Hello everyone, wonderful to see you as always. We're a slightly smaller group this week. We have Gloria away for a couple of weeks – she set off this morning. And Zoe emailed me to say she also is away – she's taken her husband on a surprise getaway for a long weekend for his birthday.

'Good girl,' chuckled Peter, a satisfied smile on his normally grouchy face.

'And Ayisha and Kerry have taken themselves off for a few days as part of their college project, would you believe it, on a wine tasting weekend. So, we can look forward to hearing all about that next time.'

Because of the absentees, everyone managed to squeeze in around the table, sitting a little snugger together than usual. Winnie's friends continued to return – Fran, Sue and Mary, all sitting together. But as Winnie looked around the table, she felt that, actually, she was surrounded by friends.

She got off to a prompt start, smoothly easing into her opening introduction.

'As you can see, this week we're going to be tasting some Australian wines. I'm sure you've all enjoyed a bottle of Syrah - also known as Shiraz.'

Pretty much everyone nodded in agreement.

'Lulu's not so keen on the more full-bodied reds, are you Love?' said Cliff.

'I tend to prefer the lighter reds. I know you like Syrah, but I find it a bit heavy.'

Winnie continued. 'Australia is most famous for its Shiraz although the Syrah grape actually originates in France. And we're going to enjoy some a little later in the evening.'

Lulu was in a chatty mood which Winnie attributed to it being a smaller group this evening.

'It's interesting how, you know, the same grapes that grow in France are also grown to produce wine on the other side of the world.'

'Ah yes, but depending where they're grown, the climate and the landscape produce vast differences in the flavour of the wine. I find it fascinating that the same grape variety produces such different results depending on all these variables.'

Sheila was listening with interest as always. 'And just think how big Australia is.'

Winnie knew what was coming next. It just wouldn't be the same without the tradition of Peter offering some interesting statistic.

'Australia has a land mass of more than 7.5 million square kilometres - you could fit England, Scotland, Wales and Northern Ireland into Australia 30 times, and still have a bit left over.'

'There you go,' said Winnie. 'It's not surprising then that the climate and topography are so varied. Although having said that, the best wine-producing regions are located on the southern side of the country.

'OK, despite all this talk about the Syrah grape, we're actually going to start with something very different.

'This is a full-bodied white wine from the Semillon grape. Sheila, care to read the description?'

Coonawarra Oyster Bay Estate Semillon

Luscious, with flavours of peach and vanilla

*Wine made from very sweet and
concentrated Semillon grapes, the
use of which results in a luscious
wine with a thrilling array of ripe
fruit flavours of juicy pineapple,
peach and vanilla, and a slightly
nutty character, balanced with
lovely zesty lemon and lime hints.*

'Thanks Sheila.' Winnie placed glasses of wine on the table as everyone helped themselves, and without waiting for instruction, got on with the job of swirling, smelling and tasting.

'Ooh yes, the peach definitely, I can taste that. This is lovely,' said Lulu. 'What's it called again?'

Winnie showed her the label on the bottle and Lulu wrote down the details.

'Mm,' murmured Muriel, studying the liquid in her glass as she held the wine in her mouth. 'I don't usually go for anything like this, but it is delicious.'

Mary leaned slightly across the table in Muriel's direction. 'I think so too, it is delicious. And I think I can really taste the juicy pineapple.'

This was turning into a very interesting evening, thought Winnie. She was sure that was the first time Mary had spoken out loud – to everyone, even though her comments were directed at Muriel. Mary looked up at Winnie and smiled. Perhaps there was something to be said about having a slightly smaller group. Even Helen had stopped vying for attention.

'How about you Helen, sorry you were deep in thought there.'

'Yes, sorry I was. But I am listening, I agree Mary and Muriel, the wine is gorgeous. Very moreish. No, I was miles away thinking about the others. I was thinking about Zoe, just hoping she's having a nice time away with her husband. She was very brave speaking up last time.'

'Yes, she was,' agreed Winnie.

'Where have they gone, for their weekend away?'

'Italy, Tuscany. Yes, I hope they're having a good time too.'

Peter smiled next to her, obviously recalling some memory.

'You been to Italy Peter?'

At first, he just nodded, as if the words wouldn't come. 'For my honeymoon. Beautiful place. Long time ago now.'

'You never went back?'

Peter was gazing into his wine glass, but Winnie could see his eyes were red and watering, as he shook his head.

'What was your wife's name?' she asked gently.

'Roseanna. She died.'

He looked up at Winnie. The sadness on his face would melt anyone's heart. She smiled and took a breath.

'I lost my husband too, not long ago. Last Christmas. You?'

'Thirty-five years ago.' Peter looked down into his glass as if seeing the past right there in it. He drummed his fingers on the table. 'She died in childbirth. I lost my wife and my son on the same day.'

Utter silence enveloped the room. Eyes met eyes, no-one moved.

A soft, husky voice spoke, and everyone was surprised to realise it belonged to Sheila. First, she placed her hand gently over Peter's.

'And don't let anyone tell you it gets any easier.' Peter smiled knowingly, nodding in agreement.

'I lost my Dave. Three years ago. In a car crash. They like to call it a road traffic accident. Sounds less personal, doesn't it. Actually, I take it very personally that I lost my lovely David in a bloody car crash because some lunatic was driving too fast.'

Peter turned his hand and held her fingers, giving them a brief squeeze before letting go. He looked her directly in the eye.

'You're an attractive woman, in your own way.' They both grinned. 'There'll be someone else out there for you.'

'You think I do all this to attract another man?' Sheila flapped her hands at her heavily made-up face, and wild black hair. 'Oh no. This little get up is to keep them away. And so far, it's working well. No, no-one could ever replace my Dave.'

'It's not about replacing him.'

'No, I'll never want anyone else.'

'Ah, never say never.'

'OK, Peter, so you've been putting yourself out there, have you?'

Peter looked down into his glass again. 'OK, touché,' he whispered, smiling.

Everyone looked on, mesmerised but at the same time feeling they were intruding on something very personal and private. All they could do was to keep very still and very quiet.

Winnie brought out some food, a little earlier this week, but this seemed a good time for a bit of a break. She particularly enjoyed baking for the group and for tonight she'd cooked some mini salmon and asparagus quiches and laid out some bowls of various dips and bread.

Intuitively, she made a snap decision not to bring the food to the table but to lay it out on the worktop, encouraging everyone to get up and move around and help themselves. Hopefully, it would help break the slightly heavy atmosphere. It was the right decision, and immediately the noise increased as friendly chatter filled the room as they left their seats and headed for the food.

Winnie couldn't help noticing how Mary made an obvious beeline for Muriel. And she could guess why.

'Hello, Muriel, isn't it?'

'It certainly is. And you're Mary?'

'Yes. I've been thinking about what you said the other week – about your husband being an alcoholic. Is that true? Or were you just making a joke?' Mary looked down at her food, thinking she was just about to find out she was barking up the wrong tree.

'I wouldn't joke like that, about something like that.'

Mary took a deep breath. 'My husband is an alcoholic.'

Muriel nodded, understanding. 'Actually, mine is a recovering alcoholic. Which means we can't have a drop in the house. But, you know how it is – he's *recovered* before.'

'No, mine's never even tried.'

Again, Muriel simply nodded and smiled, and Mary continued.

'It's nice to talk to someone who really understands.'

'There are support groups out there.'

'Oh, I know, but, I'm not that good around strangers. My friends are all lovely.' Mary nodded over at Winnie and the others. 'But I think they feel sorry for me, which isn't really what I want. I don't think anyone can really understand, if they've not been there.'

'No, absolutely not. That's why the professional groups can be useful.'

'Yes, I suppose you're right.' Mary made to go back to her seat.

'Wait Mary, if you like, we could meet up, away from here. Have a good moan, about all our woes. And maybe get sloshed into the bargain!'

'Yes. Yes, I'd really like that. Thank-you.'

As everyone gradually returned to their seats, the atmosphere noticeably lighter now, Winnie made an effort to keep it that way.

'Peter, you can open the next bottle. But first read the description for everyone.'

Peter read aloud, a shy grin spreading across his face.

The Hedonist Shiraz

*Voluptuous, silky red with bold
tones of rich blackberry fruitiness
with tempestuous flavours of
indulgent dark chocolate – a wicked
little spicy number!*

'Yes, very funny Winnifred. Where did you get that description from?'

'OK, maybe I got a little carried away there – a bit of poetic licence. Each to their own and all that.'

Peter was blushing from ear to ear, and Winnie together with the others were laughing to see how he was revelling in the attention. She'd have to remember this.

The wine choice went down well with everyone except for Lulu who sipped bravely but couldn't help pulling a face at the intense flavours, which were proving too much for her palate.

'Don't worry Lulu, you'll enjoy the final wine of tonight. It's a Sauvignon Blanc – that's your favourite, isn't it?'

'Yes, it is.' Lulu was impressed she'd remembered right from the first meeting.

'Good, this one has delicious passion fruit aromas and a fresh citrus spritz to it.'

'Lovely, that sounds much more like my kind of thing. Here Cliff, you can finish this Shiraz.'

The evening naturally wound up a little earlier than usual, and no-one seemed to mind. Winnie closed the front door as Peter and Sheila left together – there was something she didn't think she would see from week one. As she headed back to the kitchen, she realised with a little discomfort that there was only Helen left.

'Would you like some help in clearing this away?'

'Oh no, not at all – it won't take me long, but thanks anyway. You get going.'

'Yes, I will. It was a good evening. I enjoy coming here.'

'Thank-you. So, er, how are the wedding plans, and everything, coming along? Lots to organise I expect.'

'Oh, you know, getting there slowly. It'll be fine.'

Winnie showed her to the door and while she was glad to have her house back to herself, she couldn't help feeling Helen had been lingering for a reason – as if she wanted to talk. But she'd never really felt drawn to the woman. Apart from the fact she was living her dream or at least taking off and planning all sorts of adventures with her partner – it wasn't that. There was something aloof and distant about her, something not real.

'Damn Gloria!' she said aloud, as she cleared glasses and plates, finishing the last of the bread and dips. Gloria had said there was something odd about Helen the first time they'd met, and as always, she was right.

Winnie continued clearing the kitchen and stacking the dishwasher. She missed Gloria. It was usually just the two of them by now, cleaning things up and chatting about the evening, and then sharing a coffee together before Gloria left for home.

Her mind was buzzing with the revelations of the evening. Poor Peter, to think what he'd gone through, was still going through by the look of things. And whoever would have thought it would be Sheila to offer comfort and for him to return the sentiment. Such bravery to survive what they had, and to talk about it like that.

Gloria would never believe it all. She wondered how she was getting on in Bordeaux with Bernard on their first evening together. She smiled and shook her head as she poured the last of the Shiraz into her glass, taking it through to the living room. She was brave too – it seemed Winnie was surrounded by brave people.

Chapter 29

Sunday morning and Winnie enjoyed a long lie-in, making tea and bringing the papers back to read in bed. She could hear the rain outside making her self-indulgence all the more cosy.

Finally, feeling stiff and achy, she got up. As she made more tea, she pondered the day ahead, not quite sure what to do with it. It sometimes happened like this, where she had no immediate chores to do and, while that should be a good thing, leaving her the whole day to herself – she just felt lost, and didn't know what to do with herself.

Mug of tea in hand, she stood in her usual place at the worktop looking out the window into the garden. The rain had eased, and the sun was doing its best to fight its way through the thinning clouds. Suddenly inspired, she decided to take a long walk to Gloria's cottage and check in on the place. She reckoned it was a good half hour walk, but after her long laze in bed, she felt the need to stretch her limbs.

She set off well prepared in good walking boots, a hooded jacket and an umbrella just in case. Gloria had only been away for a few days, but she was seriously missing her friend. They had texted each other the first day, Gloria confirmed she had arrived safely and the farmhouse where she was staying was totally charming.

Winnie couldn't help feeling more than a little envious – not because of Bernard – she just wished she'd taken Gloria up on her offer of getting away together. Right now, she felt she'd like nothing better than to take off for a nice long holiday somewhere in the sunshine.

As she came into the village, she was charmed at its chocolate box prettiness. She'd never walked here before. It was always Gloria driving or Doug dropping her off or occasionally a taxi ride. She slowed her pace to a leisurely stroll and passed cottage after pretty cottage; some thatched, some with lattice lead windows, perfectly kept front gardens with hanging baskets, some with their geraniums and fuchsias still in full bloom.

She arrived at the back garden of Gloria's cottage and let herself in through the little gate, looking over at Ada's dark and empty home. The curtains had been taken down, and without having to peer through the windows, she could see the furniture had been taken away. She sighed, a mixture of thoughts running around her mind.

The sun was shining strong now. It was the sort of early autumn weather that could catch you out. Windy and rainy one moment, clear skies and warm sunshine the next.

Winnie unlocked the door and immediately threw off her jacket and took off her muddy boots. It felt very chilly in the cottage, having been shut up for a few days, but the chill was cooling and welcome at this moment. She filled the kettle and began making herself a cup of tea, and then picked up the little pile of post that had landed on the doormat which turned out to be mostly junk mail. For some reason the letter boxes in this row of cottages were all at the back.

While the kettle boiled, Winnie checked the other rooms of the cottage, opening closed curtains and closing open ones, and switching various lights on and off. Everything was as it should be, and she returned to the kitchen. The sun was at its autumn angle, beaming into the kitchen and beginning to warm it from its earlier chill.

Winnie loved this place. It had such character and Gloria's design skills had made it a cosy, stylish haven. She thought of her own huge home. Winter would be here soon, and she would be back to the never-ending battle of trying to keep it warm. It had been their family home, but it wasn't that anymore; her daughters had their own homes, life moved on, things changed. Winnie shivered and finished her tea. She was getting maudlin and decided to lock up and walk a loop of the village before heading home.

Out through the garden gate, she turned left into the village. A narrow pathway led down into the main high street where there were a few shops including a florist, a general grocery shop, a separate bakers with coffee shop attached and a little further down she thought she could see a pub. But she didn't go down that far, instead she turned left again and up the roadside passing more pretty cottages. It was an idyllic little village.

Eventually, she found she was walking along the road that would bring her to the front of Gloria's cottage and finally Ada's place which was the last one on the end. She couldn't recall ever seeing it from this angle. The pathway dipped down steeply, and these cottages on her right all had a steep flight of steps up to their front doors. Perhaps this was why some postman, in the deep distant past had elected to have their post delivered at the back.

She looked up at the windows of Gloria's cottage seeing the curtains she'd just closed, and the landing light just about shining through. And then on the end was Ada's cottage – all the windows bare of furnishings and the empty rooms, dark and eerie. As she came level with it, she saw the 'For Sale' sign that had been erected on the far corner – obviously to gain maximum exposure to cars or walkers in all directions. Crikey, she thought, Ada's son certainly hadn't wasted any time in putting it on the market. She decided to take a walk all around the perimeter, and as she did, she could see the true size of the plot of land adjacent to the cottage that was currently overgrown with wild grass and weeds.

Winnie turned for home, carrying her jacket and the superfluous umbrella, strong sunshine warming her back. As she walked, there was a definite lightness in her step, and she felt more cheerier than when she'd arrived.

She perfectly understood Gloria's concern. A developer could snap up this place, possibly at a steal of a price, depending on how desperate her son was to sell, and they could potentially put something huge here.

Chapter 30

Helen arrived home late after an exhausting day at work. She closed the front door and immediately slipped her shoes off, leaving them on the mat, simply too tired to put them away just now.

Her boss, Richard, had just taken on a new case, a big one, and she reckoned there would be many more late nights over the coming months.

She smiled, remembering the moment when Richard had brought a huge box of cakes into the main admin office – everyone had groaned. It was a well-known code, his way of explaining that the company had just taken on a mass of work and there would be overtime. He literally tried to sweeten them up. He was funny, and he always bought totally scrumptious cakes. Despite the hard work of the day, she'd had a good laugh with her colleagues.

In the kitchen, Helen took off her jacket and hung it carefully on the back of a chair. She'd bought a few groceries on her way home and had also bought a bottle of that Australian Semillon they'd all enjoyed at Winnifred's wine club. She was tempted to open it now, it had been a heck of a day, but she was good and put it in the fridge to chill. She'd enjoy a glass later, after a hot bath and something to eat.

She made a coffee and while the kettle boiled, she switched on the heating and then whizzed around the flat closing curtains on the dark evening.

In the living room, she refrained from switching on the television, preferring some silence after her day in the busy, noisy office. This was a favourite time of day, retreating to her own space, tidy and ordered, with its simple but stylish décor. She sighed, contented and rested her head back on the settee cushion. And then a memory from earlier in the day, not a good one, invaded her tranquillity.

Her fiancée was currently visiting their future home in Bordeaux, and he'd sent her a video via email which she'd watched during her lunch hour, over her Tupperware container of sprouted bean salad. It made shocking viewing, and she still wasn't quite over it.

She'd accepted there would be a period of time spent getting the place to their liking, but the video showed the main house was just about liveable. It was in an appalling state. Whatever could Seth be thinking about? Her heart sank at the thought of it.

He'd been to her flat numerous times; he knew how she liked to live. In fact, he'd teased her endlessly on her fastidiousness, and her liking of things to be just so. How, on earth, could he think she would want to live in that dilapidated building? It would take years to put right.

The only way it could work in her mind was if they were to rent a small place nearby, something much more habitable until the main house on the vineyard was complete. Seth would be phoning her later this evening, when she would put the suggestion to him.

She finished her coffee and went to run a bath. Having consumed too many cakes in the office, she'd already decided on a light meal for dinner, to balance out the calories. She would whisk up a cheese and mushroom omelette with a mixed salad, chat with

263

Seth and then an early night ready for another long day tomorrow.

The alarm was set for earlier than usual. Helen wanted to get to the office promptly. Tonight was wine club night and she didn't intend to work late this evening but she'd get a bit extra done first thing before anyone else arrived.

She struggled to get out of her cosy bed, luxury crisp cotton bedlinen cocooned her in comfy-ness. Immediately she recalled her conversation with Seth which hadn't gone too well, and she'd had a fitful night's sleep. She'd hit the snooze button too many times already, one more and she'd have to miss breakfast.

Dressed and make up on, she only had time for coffee, and stood drinking it in the living room, standing at the French doors that opened up onto a tiny Juliette balcony. She looked back into the room – the place was becoming a mess and it was beginning to irritate her. There were samples everywhere. Samples of wedding dress fabric, of fabric swatches for her maid of honour, and examples of wedding favours she'd picked up at various exhibitions over the last couple of months. And that was without the countless magazines she'd bought and the brochures she'd sent off for. They were littered everywhere.

She'd even sent off for dozens of wedding cake samples, on the hunt for the perfect recipe. She sighed, wishing she hadn't done that now.

Suddenly she couldn't wait to be out of there. She poured the remains of her coffee down the sink, grabbed her jacket from the back of the chair, slipped her shoes on by the door and slammed it shut.

Chapter 31

Argentinian Wine

Argentine wine, as with some aspects of Argentine cuisine has its roots in Spain. During the Spanish colonisation of the Americas, vine cuttings were brought to Santiago del Estero in 1557.

Not only is Argentina one of the most beautiful and diverse nations in South America, it's also the fifth-largest wine-producing country in the world and becoming increasingly well-known for the outstanding quality - and incredible affordability - of its premium wines.

Argentine wines are currently growing in popularity, making Argentina the largest wine exporter in South America.

Winnie had perfected her preparation routine, and everything was ready for tonight, but still she fidgeted and tweaked things into place. There was an air of anticipation in her kitchen – she was looking forward to this evening and seeing everyone back. It seemed an age since she'd had a full house of wine club members.

She glanced at the clock, hoping Gloria would arrive soon. She'd only got home from Bordeaux in the early hours that morning, so Winnie had left her to sleep. A quick text to each other confirmed they would catch up on all the news tonight. But she wanted, at least, a quick debrief before everyone else arrived.

Right on cue, Gloria knocked on the back door before letting herself in.

She came bearing gifts which she left on the worktop before giving Winnie a big hug.

'Gloria, you look fantastic. Wow, you've got an amazing tan.'

'Thank-you, thank-you. You look well yourself, in fact you look very well. What have you been up to?'

'Wouldn't you like to know?'

Gloria did a double take. Did Winnie have a sparkle in her eye?

'Winnie, tell me everything.'

'No, nothing like that. I'll update you on my news later. Are you limping Glo? What have you done?'

'Oh nothing. I think I put my hip out a little – my belly dancing.'

Winnie said nothing. She didn't want to know.

Gloria smiled. 'Hm, it looks different in here, I noticed as soon as I walked in. You've moved things.'

'I've been clearing out a bit, that's all. I missed you. I was bored. I had to find something to do with myself.'

'Always good to have a clear out – good for the mind and soul, I think. And usually the charity shop too!'

'Yes, exactly. Anyway, enough about charity shops, how was your holiday? And Bernard? I'm guessing from the smile on your face, it went well?'

'It went very well. He's a delightful man.'

Winnie smiled encouragingly.

'Gorgeous actually. And don't look at me like that – yes, it's not unheard of that two people in their seventies can find each other gorgeous.'

'I'm very glad to hear it. And before you start down that road, we're talking about you, so carry on.'

'Well, what can I say? It was two weeks of absolute bliss. We toured around a bit, went to some totally divine restaurants, not to mention he's a very good cook.'

'And you're seeing each other again?'

'Oh yes, I'm not going to let this one go easily. He's looking into coming over here in a few weeks.'

'It doesn't sound like he wants to go; he sounds equally keen.'

'I hope so.' Gloria smiled a faraway smile, obviously recalling fond memories.

A loud knock at the front door had them both looking up at the clock.

'Crikey, I didn't realise the time.' Winnie took a quick glance around the kitchen, good thing everything was in place.

'Oh, I wanted to hear all the news before everyone arrived. Is there much to tell?'

'Like you wouldn't believe! I'll fill you in later.'

Winnie hurried to the door to find Zoe, Ayisha and Kerry all arrived together.

'Come on in, lovely to see you all back.'

The three girls chatted together as they piled into the kitchen, where they were pleased to see a very healthy-looking Gloria. Winnie left them regaling their various holiday stories as she hurried back to greet more club members.

This time it was Lulu and Cliff together with a woman Winnie didn't recognise.

'Hello Winnie, this is our friend Rita. I hope it's OK for her to come along this week?'

'Yes, of course. Hello Rita, you're very welcome.'

Back in the kitchen, Winnie left everyone to themselves for a few minutes while they caught up with each other. She fussed with plates and napkins and checked on some nibbles cooking in the oven.

Gloria was looking at the food with an eager eye, just as the doorbell rang again.

'You're slacking there! Go and answer the door and stop drooling over your fancy man.'

Gloria just grinned and went to do as she was told.

Finally, judging from the noise, Winnie assumed she had a full house and as she turned to address everyone, she was taken by surprise to see all her guests were, for some reason, sitting in different places. It took her a moment or two to acclimatise.

The first thing she noticed was that Zoe was sitting in Peter's seat. How had that gone down? Kerry and Ayisha were seated next to her, and they were all giggling together about something or other.

Mary was sitting with Muriel, both chatting away.

Helen, who always kept herself somewhat apart even when speaking, was now ensconced between Winnie's other friends from her midwifery days, Fran and Sue, looking as if they'd know each other all their lives.

And the most amazing thing of all was that Peter obviously wasn't bothered that his usual spot next to Winnie, the spot he'd bagged every week, was taken by Zoe. He was now happily on the other side of the table near Cliff and Lulu, sitting right next to their friend Rita. What on earth was going on?

Only Sheila was in her usual spot, and as always, she chatted with anyone and everyone. Winnie caught Sheila looking at her, then over at Peter and back again with one very raised eyebrow. Winnie gave a tiny shrug of her shoulders in response.

The room was noisy with chatter and laughter, and Winnie was momentarily flummoxed as to how to get everyone's attention. She felt like a schoolteacher at the head of an assembly.

There was a buzz of energy in the room – a lot had happened since their last meeting. And there seemed to be a new camaraderie between them this evening, something more than their usual polite friendliness. All keen to know and tell their news. Winnie herself was itching to sit down with Gloria and hear in more detail about her time away, and she had her own news too, but she might decide to hold off on that a while, until things were more definite.

She picked up her notes and looked out at her audience, a little unsure of whether she would be able to hold their attention this evening.

'Are we ready to begin?'

Everyone looked up, some with surprised expressions as if they'd forgotten this was a Wine Club meeting. They shuffled in their seats to face Winnie and finally give her their full attention.

'So, this week is all about Argentinian wine.' She was finding it difficult to concentrate and had to read from her notes.

'At one time it was said that the Argentinian wine producers focused more on quantity than on quality, and that most of their wine was unexportable. But thankfully that's not the case now due to an influx of passionate producers who have elevated Argentina from the domestic stage to the truly worldwide. So, the obvious choice to start with is a Malbec this evening.

'Apologies to you Lulu, this is another rich red.'

'It's OK, I'd still like to try it.'

'Malbec, a favourite of mine,' said Peter.

Winnie looked across to answer, only to see that his comment was addressed to Rita who was nodding enthusiastically in agreement.

'Shall I read the description?' offered Sheila.

Good ol' Sheila, thought Winnie, she was as reliable as ever.

'Yes please Sheila, that'd be great.'

Argentinian Malbec

This wine is a powerful, intense and richly fruited red with fine structure and a satisfying finish.
Bold, dark and concentrated, this wine has incredible herbaceous notes of thyme and black pepper, bright bramble fruit and a dark chocolate finish.

'Thanks Sheila. What do you think Peter, is it up to standard for you?'

Peter sipped and considered, swirling the wine expertly around his mouth.

'Definitely up to standard. Yes, I'm very pleased with that.'

Was it Winnie's imagination or was he being a little pompous, showing off to the lady on his right perhaps? Good for him, thought Winnie.

'Anyone else like to comment?'

'This isn't too bad,' said Lulu, sounding more than a little surprised to which everyone laughed – after all, it was rather an odd comment to be made at a wine tasting club.

Poor Lulu blushed a little. 'Oh, you all know what I mean.'

Cliff gave her a big smile and a little wink.

The evening continued in its by now well-established pattern. Everyone was in high spirits resulting in light-hearted teasing and much laughter.

The second wine, a Cabernet Franc, generally went down well, but poor Lulu was having a hard time of it tonight with another full-bodied red, almost savoury wine. Thank goodness Winnie had the forethought to finish the evening with something completely different.

She opened the final bottle of the evening, a Chardonnay sparkling wine.

'This is produced in the Uco Valley, one of the most remote winemaking regions in Argentina. Lulu, I'm hoping this will hit the spot for you. Here you are, you'd better have the first glass.'

Lulu sipped, and it was as if someone had switched the fairy lights on. Her eyes positively lit up and were watering from the hit of fizz and after just a few sips, she held the glass aloft with a big happy smile on her face.

'Yes, this is the one for me! I know what I like, and this is it.' Everyone gave a little cheer.

'Trust you,' said Cliff, 'To prefer the expensive sparkly stuff.'

'This one's not too bad Cliff,' said Winnie. 'It's about ten pounds.' After calculating some time ago, the cost of the wines against what she was taking for each wine club session, she tried to mostly avoid the more expensive wines. She just hoped no-one had noticed.

'So, our next session in a couple of weeks' time is to be our last one.' As she spoke, Winnie realised how sad she was.

And likewise, everyone in the room groaned in unison.

'Does it have to be? asked Peter.

Winnie was caught off guard. Originally, she had designed an eight-session course, done her research on the wines of seven different countries and prepared all the handout notes. She hadn't thought much further than that. If it turned out to be a success, she thought maybe she could run the course again for a different group of people. She hadn't reckoned on this group simply wanting to continue on.

'Why stop? We're all enjoying ourselves, aren't we?' continued Peter, encouragingly, as Winnie paused for thought.

A loud cheer resounded from everyone.

'Well, I hadn't really thought about it. I thought you might have had enough by now.'

'You can never have enough of wine,' said Lulu, cheekily, her empty glass on the table in front of her.

Winnie was trying to calm her mind. Thinking frantically on her feet wasn't her forte. This was a turn up she hadn't figured in her plans. They were right, there wasn't any reason The Wine Club couldn't continue. She would need some time to prepare more material and she had a few other things in the pipeline that would take time, but really, it was a rather wonderful idea.

'I must say I'm flattered that you all want to continue, and actually, I can't think of a good reason why we shouldn't.'

Another loud cheer went up, and Winnie couldn't help laughing.

'But as I said, I've only planned for these eight sessions, so I will need some time to prepare some more material.'

'Ah, let's just get together for a chat over some wine,' said Cliff. 'We could all bring our own.'

'Well, that's an idea,' said Winnie, wondering whether that would work.

'No, I like it the way it is. It's interesting to learn,' said Sheila, and others confirmed that they too liked the present format. 'And anyway, if we all brought a bottle, we'd be too sloshed to find our way home.'

Winnie had made up her mind. 'OK, our last meeting will be at the beginning of October. How about we have a small break after that? Let's say a couple of months. I'll send out invites – I must make sure I've got all your contact addresses or emails or whatever. Yes, in two- or three-months' time, I'll send out invites and details and everything of the next meeting. How would that suit everyone?'

Much to Winnie's delight, everyone seemed perfectly happy with that, and so it was suddenly arranged that her wine club was to continue.

She collected the last platter of pastries from the worktop where Gloria was perched in her usual spot, glass of gin and tonic to her side. She noticed Winnie's serene Mona Lisa smile, and gave her a crafty scrutinising look, to which Winnie simply put her nose in the air, blinked innocently in her direction and held out the platter to her. 'Sausage roll?'

Everyone had left except for Helen who seemed to be holding back like the last time. She was helping clear things from the table and Winnie decided to let her, wondering where this was going. Gloria was stacking the dishwasher.

Winnie left them to it while she went upstairs to the bathroom.

'You had a good time in Bordeaux?' Helen asked.

'Yes, I did, thanks. It's a beautiful place, but of course you know that.'

'Mm. Yes. It is. I must say your tan suits you. You are perfectly glowing. And you look very happy.'

The response that came to mind was for Gloria to tell Helen she didn't look very happy at all.

'How do you feel about going to live there? It's quite a different thing from being on holiday.'

Helen paused, thinking. 'I have mixed feelings. It's a big decision.'

Gloria said nothing. She knew what was coming, if not now, later.

'But it's what I've always wanted – to be married, you know, the perfect dream, live happily ever after, and all that.'

Gloria smiled.

'If you don't mind me asking, have you ever been married?'

'Yep, three times.'

'Oh.'

'All very happy marriages. And not one divorce. They all died. Nothing to do with me, in case you're wondering.' Gloria was grinning but Helen was totally serious.

'I wasn't thinking that. I was thinking you have an amazing capacity for happiness.'

'I like to believe we all have that.'

'Do we? I suppose, sometimes you just have to be brave, don't you? Take a chance, take a leap into the unknown.'

'Maybe. But I don't believe bravery is always about taking a chance. Sometimes bravery can be in the form of recognising the truth and honouring it and yourself. Sometimes bravery can be in not taking that leap.'

'You're very lucky to have had three happy marriages.'

They could hear Winnie coming back down the stairs.'

'Helen, we make our own luck – that, I definitely believe.'

Chapter 32

Winnie was deep inside a cupboard in the bedroom that used to belong to Hannah. It had been a dumping ground ever since Hannah left home over ten years ago. She thought she heard a noise, perhaps a knock at the back door and leant back on her heels poking out her head to hear better.

Yes, there it was again. Winnie dashed down the stairs to find Cathy walking back down the garden path. She unlocked the door quickly and called out to her daughter.

'Oh Mum, I thought you must have gone out. I've just dropped the kids off; thought I'd pop in for a quick cuppa.'

Cathy followed her through to the kitchen.

'No, I was just sorting some things out upstairs in Hannah's old room.'

'Oh? What sort of things?'

'I just felt like attacking that big cupboard up there. Haven't touched anything in there for years.'

'What's in there?'

'Nothing very interesting. You know, things you keep because you think they are too good to throw away at the time and you might need them some day. Light shades, piles of curtains, a couple of rugs.'

'Curtains? I was thinking of decorating Hugo's bedroom. Anything in there for that?'

'Only if he likes psychedelic green from the seventies.'

Cathy pulled a face. 'No, it's OK, you can keep them.'

Winnie switched the kettle on, aware of Cathy looking around the room, taking in the absence of things.

'Are you getting rid of things down here too?'

'Yes, actually, I'm having a bit of a clear out.'

Winnie was sensitive to her daughter's sensitivity, but she wasn't a child anymore. They were a family, but they all had their own lives to lead. And Winnie was entering a new chapter.

'Can I have a look upstairs? At Hannah's room? I bet there are some of our old toys in that cupboard.'

'Yes, of course, go on up. I'll bring the tea in a minute.'

Cathy hurried upstairs and Winnie took her time making the tea, knowing what Cathy would find up there, and giving her some time to process it.

Over the last week, Winnie had been systematically working her way through the contents of the three bedrooms. She was leaving her and Doug's room until last. The whole of the upstairs was littered with big black sacks and cardboard boxes, some full and some ready to fill.

After a few minutes, she went upstairs carrying their mugs of tea. She found Cathy in her old bedroom which had been decorated as the main guest bedroom in pretty blue and white a number of years ago.

Cathy was standing by the window staring out at the view, something she would have done many times as a teenager.

Winnie set the mugs down on the dressing table and joined her daughter at the window.

'You're selling up?'

Winnie nodded. 'Yes. Actually, I've sold.'

'Oh Mum.'

'Someone approached me, a couple with a young family. They're paying a fantastic price.'

'Yeah, Hannah mentioned it to me. I told you someone would pay a premium for it.'

'Yes, you were right.'

'I still wish you weren't leaving.'

'Cathy, I can't afford this place. At first, I wished I could. I thought I would do almost anything not to have to leave. That's how the idea of The Wine Club came about – to make a little extra, to enable me to stay here.'

'It's a success, isn't it? Your wine club?'

'Yes, it is. It's a great success. And I'm going to continue with it. But it's not enough – the little extra. It doesn't anywhere near cover what I need to pay the enormous heating bills and the rest.'

'But what if you found another job? A proper job back into midwifery?'

'I really don't know. Maybe I could manage. But actually, I really enjoy not working those hours. And if we've learnt only one thing this year, it should be not to take anything for granted because we don't know what's just around the corner.

'What about Dad's business? The sale's going through, and Tom said it should all be finalised soon.'

'That's right. I'm expecting the money into my bank any day now. But even then, it just doesn't make sense for me to stay here. This is a family home – it should have a family in it.'

'But where are you going to go? You know you can stay with us for a while if you need to.'

'Ah, that's lovely, thank-you. I might have to hold you to that. But I think I've found somewhere, close by. I'll keep you posted.'

Cathy was lost for words. She knew her mum was right, but it was so difficult to accept.

There was a pause, and silence.

'Do you understand, Cathy?'

Cathy nodded. 'Yeah, I think so. I'm sorry to be such a wimp. I just wish everything was as it used to be.'

Winnie gave her a big hug. 'That doesn't make you a wimp. And that's a big compliment for me, as a mum. Thank-you.'

Cathy sighed and wiped her watering eyes. 'Let's take our tea back down.'

Back in the kitchen, Winnie managed to shove some paperwork in a drawer, valuations from various estate agents. They'd talked enough about all of that today.

'Have you spoken to Hannah lately?' asked Winnie, determined to lighten the conversation.

'Yes, she phoned me yesterday. She had an exam and passed with top marks, one of the top in her group. She was so full of herself.'

'Fantastic. Good for her.'

'Yeah, cheeky cow. She bet me lunch she could do it, and now I owe her. The bet was for lunch of mine or her choice. And you know she'll choose the most expensive place she can find.'

Winnie laughed. It was warming to see her daughters getting along despite their different lifestyles.

'Right, I'd better get off. I've got some work to do before picking the kids up again. I've off-loaded some of my clients, had a good chat with my boss, lightened my workload for a while at least.'

'Good. That makes sense. You're no good to anyone unless you look after yourself.'

'Yes, I know. You always say that.'

And, I'm right, aren't I?'

'Yes. You're right.'

They got to the back door and hugged. Cathy kissed her mother on the cheek.

'It's nearly ten months, isn't it? I can hardly believe it.'

'Yes, that's right. I know.'

Cathy nodded. Of course, she knew. 'I miss him so much, Mum.'

Winnie kissed her daughter's forehead, closing the door after watching her walk up the path. She sighed and went back upstairs to resume her packing.

Chapter 33

Zoe heard Lawrence's motorbike pull up outside. He'd phoned from the local station to say he'd finished work a little early and would be home soon. She was unloading the dishwasher as he came into the kitchen.

'Hello, this is nice for a change.' She leaned up for a kiss.

'Yeah, things were a little quiet today, so I thought why not? I've put in enough overtime lately. It's nice to be home.'

Zoe nodded, and Lawrence stood close behind her, pulling her to him for a hug. He spotted a small liqueur glass beside her on the worktop.

'What was in that glass?' he asked, a little too aggressively for Zoe's liking.

Zoe looked at the glass then slowly turned, pulling away to look at Lawrence. 'It had blackberry juice in it.'

'Blackberry juice?'

Zoe placed the glass in the dishwasher, and closed the door, standing up to face Lawrence directly.

'Yes. Blackberry juice. I was making blackberry frozen yoghurt this afternoon. I had to heat the blackberries in a little water and sugar. Before adding the fruit to the yoghurt, I decided there was too much liquid which would make it all sloppy, so I tasted a little and it was delicious. So then I poured some into this glass so I could drink it.'

Lawrence didn't say anything. He went to the cupboard and took a couple of mugs out. But Zoe wasn't going to let it go. She turned to face his back.

'You're talking to me like I'm a raging alcoholic.'

He turned to look at her, still not speaking, but his look spoke volumes – if the cap fits, it said.

'Honestly, do you really think if I was having sneaky drinks on my own in the afternoon, I would be stupid enough to leave the bloody glass out?' She was shouting now. And then a little quieter. 'Anyway, I thought we'd talked this through. Things are better now.'

'Well, I don't know. You could be doing a double-whammy bluffy thing. Just to try to catch me out.'

'A double-whammy bluffy thing? Followed by a double somersault backflip, you mean?'

'Yeah, one of them.' Lawrence had turned away slightly, but she could see him smirking, and looking a little sheepish.

'You asshole!' She said, and he turned back to her to see her grinning.

'Yep, I'm an asshole. And I'm sorry. And anyway, whenever did you start making blackberry frozen yoghurt?'

'Ever since I started having more energy, kinda ever since I stopped hitting two bottles of wine a night! Maybe.'

Lawrence smiled affectionately and winked at her.

'I was thinking,' said Zoe. 'I have an idea and I want to know what you think.'

'Oh dear. Should I be worried?'

284

'No. I think it's quite a good idea actually. Some of the people at the wine club, well most of them actually, they're quite a bit older than me. And a few of them have said they'd like to learn more about using Facebook and Instagram and things like that.'

'Yeah?'

'Well, as I've spent pretty much the last two years sitting on my butt playing around with these applications, I'm now a bit of an expert. And I've offered to help someone at the group.'

'OK.'

'And I was thinking there are probably more, let's say more mature people, who'd like help with this sort of thing. I could set up a little advisory business. I could even do it online. I could set up an Instagram account to teach people how to use Instagram. What do you think?'

Lawrence was nodding thoughtfully. 'Yeah, you might have something there. Give it a go. It won't even cost much will it, to set things up?'

'No, hardly anything. I thought it'd be nice to get some business cards made and take them along to the wine club next week, hand a couple out.'

'Good idea. It's your last one next week, isn't it?'

'No, we were all talking about it and it's going to continue. Winnie wants a break for a few weeks, and then it's going to start up again. You could come along? It'd be nice for us to go together.'

'No, it's your thing. They're your friends. There are loads of other things we can do together.'

Chapter 34

Californian Wine

The US state of California accounts for nearly 90 percent of American wine production. If California were a separate country, it would be the world's fourth largest wine producer.

The state's viticultural history dates back to the 18th century when Spanish missionaries planted the first vineyards to produce wine for Mass.

Today there are more than 1,200 wineries in the state, ranging from small boutique wineries to large corporations with distribution around the globe.

Gloria was helping Winnie prepare the kitchen for the last Wine Club meeting, until it restarted in a couple of months' time.

It was only a few weeks away from Halloween and Winnie had bought half a dozen pumpkins as decoration. She soon regretted buying so many after spending ages trying to hollow them out to make Jack-O-Lanterns. It was hard work and she called it a day after four pumpkins, supplementing her display with lots of little tea lights in pretty dishes dotted around.

Gloria was clearing the main worktop area ready to lay out the buffet. It had been agreed that everyone would bring a contribution to the evening, something either sweet or savoury.

She noticed a sturdy cardboard box over by the wall. 'What's this? Shall I move it out of the way?'

'No, it's OK, leave it there. That's Doug's whiskey collection – I thought of giving it to Cliff. Do you think that'll be OK, to offer it to him?'

Gloria was surprised. 'Yes, I'm sure he'll be delighted. You're giving it all away?'

'Most of it. There were a couple of very special bottles, I'm hanging on to those.'

It was dark outside, and Winnie had just finished lighting the candles as they heard the first knock at the door.

'I'll go,' said Gloria, leaving Winnie to take a last look around the room pleased with the result of their hard work.

Lulu and Cliff together with Rita arrived first which gave Winnie the ideal opportunity to ask Cliff if he'd like to take the whiskey off her hands. There were some half bottles in the box, and she wasn't sure if he'd want to take those. She needn't have worried; he was visibly moved that Winnie had thought of him. He sensed that she was offering to give them to him, but even so.

'I'd like to pay you something for them Wynne – they're worth a small fortune, that lot.'

'No.' Winnie flapped her hands at him. 'I don't want anything for them. I'll be glad they're out of the way, and I can't ask for more than to know you'll enjoy them.'

'I certainly will.' Cliff picked up a few of the bottles to look at the labels, recognising most of them. 'There are some excellent bottles here, I wouldn't dream of allowing myself to buy. I'll savour these, and they'll be a real treat. Thank-you.'

Cliff and Lulu went over to their seats. Cliff was somewhat overwhelmed. He was thinking what a shame it was that this was their last week – he could have bought a present back as a thank you. And then he had an idea and whispered across to Lulu.

'We could send a bouquet of flowers, couldn't we, to say thanks?'

'Yes, that's a lovely idea. And as a thank-you for the last few months, it's been great, hasn't it?'

Cliff sat down and Lulu and Rita went to place their contributions over on the side. Lulu had made a blackberry cheesecake and Rita had bought a selection of oriental snacks.

Peter arrived next and removed a large pork pie from a carrier bag handing it over bashfully to Winnie, before sitting down next to Rita.

Among the last to arrive were Kerry and Ayisha and their contribution undoubtedly outshone all the others. They had prepared a large platter of seafood, which they'd arranged so beautifully, it was almost a shame to disturb it. Rows of plump pink prawns complemented the wee yellow yolks of halved quails' eggs, cherry tomatoes filled with bright green pesto added more colour. And the ultimate luxury was the addition of a tiny dish of caviar on each corner of the platter, and beside each was a small mound of mini blinis.

'Wow, girls, this is splendid. Thank-you both so much,' said Winnie, taking the platter.

'It might be best to put it in the fridge for a while,' said Kerry.

'Yes, I will.' Winnie was thinking how she could have drawn more on Kerry and Ayisha's catering knowledge. She could have asked them to recommend what foods best accompanied the various wines of the evening. She was already thinking ahead, and contemplating incorporating something along those lines for the next wine club meeting towards the end of the year.

There was a warm buzz of a party atmosphere in the kitchen as Winnie noticed the only person missing was Helen, and she was surprised to realise she really wanted her to turn up tonight. She'd seen a different side to her over the last couple of meetings. It would be a shame if she wasn't here to enjoy the evening.

'No Helen tonight?' said likeminded Gloria. 'That's a shame.'

As if by magic, the front doorbell rang, and Winnie hurried to answer it, delighted to see Helen on the doorstep. They went through to the kitchen where she was greeted warmly by the others.

'My goodness, what a spread. This is some party tonight. I feel a little bad now.' Helen opened her shopping bag and lifted out several small packages, putting them on the table. 'I haven't actually made anything myself.'

'Don't worry Helen,' said Peter. 'My pork pie contribution came via Sainsbury's.'

Helen smiled. 'Well, my little contributions have mostly come via Bride Magazine. They're wedding cake samples – I'm sure they're all delicious.'

Helen was faced with a crowd of puzzled faces. 'You've brought leftovers?' asked Sheila.

'No, they're not leftovers. They are samples I sent off for to help me and Seth choose what we'd like for our wedding cake.'

'Am I being dim here?' asked Sheila. 'If we're eating your samples, how will you and Seth know which you like best for your wedding cake?'

'It doesn't matter.' Helen focused her attention on meticulously folding her carrier bag. 'There isn't going to be a wedding, so there's no need for a wedding cake.' She looked over at Gloria who was looking straight at her. Helen smiled a grateful smile.

'Oh,' said Sheila, not often lost for words.

'Don't feel sorry for me. It's my decision and I know it's the right one.'

Winnie was reminded of the time Helen had breezed into the wine club announcing her plans of marriage and of starting a new life on a French vineyard – she'd been dumbstruck then, as she was now.

'The first wine Winnie?' prompted Gloria.

For a moment Winnie looked as if she had no idea what Gloria was talking about. It was already well into the evening, but she hadn't even opened the first wine of the evening.

'Yes, we ought to start.' Winnie addressed the room. 'Who's for a glass of wine?'

Within a few seconds everyone was comfortably seated, with their full attention on her even though they were thinking about Helen and what had happened to bring her to this decision.

'Lovely.' Winnie took a deep breath. 'This week then, we're looking at Californian wine. America's golden state, California, is famed for its rich, ripe, fruit-laden wines, its hot sunny weather and big personality.

'The state's best wine-growing areas are located just north of San Francisco, and include the prestigious Napa Valley, Carneros, Sonoma and Mendocino.

'Allow me,' said Sheila, going ahead and reading the description.

Majestic Vines Chardonnay

*From a beloved Chardonnay vine
that produces brilliant fruit with
rich, mouth-watering flavours*

*This Chardonnay exhibits appealing
aromas of ripe pear, pineapple and
melon. Medium-bodied with a
creamy mid-palate, this delightful
wine offers flavours of peach and
coconut, with hints of lemon and
toasty vanilla spice.*

Rather than prompting and encouraging everyone to speak, this week Winnie stood back and merely observed her friends as, almost without thinking, and certainly without any sense of self-consciousness, they swirled and sniffed and sipped, commenting to each other – agreeing or disagreeing on whether the dominant aroma was pear or pineapple.

She smiled and mumbled. 'My work here is done.' Gloria overheard her.

'I think you'll find it's only just beginning. They want more, how wonderful is that?'

'I know. I didn't expect it.'

'Look at them all, they're having a ball.'

Winnie and Gloria looked about the room. Peter was engrossed in conversation with Rita, and Cliff and Lulu were laughing together like young lovers.

She saw Zoe leaning over and handing out what looked like business cards to all of them, and then Muriel catching the thread of the conversation asked for one too.

Peter said something, sadly inaudible, that made them all laugh, and Zoe put her arm around his shoulder and gave him a hug. Winnie could hardly believe what she was seeing.

'I've still got two wines to get through yet,' said Winnie. 'And we haven't even started on the food yet.'

'I'd give up, just for tonight,' suggested Gloria. 'Declare it an open evening and put some music on.'

'Actually, that's not a bad idea.'

'Yes, let's party. I think we all deserve it.'

Winnie captured everyone's attention and suggested they abandon their usual structure tonight. She suggested they help themselves to food and wine and enjoy themselves.

'And go ahead, if you feel like a boogie. But not on the table please.'

'Yeah,' shouted Sheila. 'Helen, no dancing on the table with your knickers on your head!'

Helen blushed bright red, but managed a smile, secretly thinking – if only I had the guts.

Chapter 35

The following morning had Winnie up almost with the light of day. She had lots to do, and lying there awake in the early hours, thinking about the mess left from last night, she had no choice but to get up and get on with it.

Last night's wine club meeting had run over quite considerably. Cliff and Lulu were the last to leave at about eleven o'clock. Rita had made a move to leave a little while earlier, and Peter offered to walk her home. They left amidst a crowd of raised eyebrows and knowing looks.

After quickly washing and dressing and settling for just a mug of strong coffee for breakfast, Winnie grabbed a rubbish sack and began clearing away the left-over food and napkins, and there were plenty of empty bottles too.

With the dishwasher finally churning away, she was now able to start on the real work. Out in the garage there was a huge stack of cardboard packing boxes which she now began bringing into the house. And her next job would be to figure out how to assemble them. The first one took her over five minutes and although she was pleased to have mastered it, she couldn't remember how she'd done it and the next one took just as long. This was extreme origami. Finally, by the fourth box, she'd got it and had got assembly down to a few seconds.

She had already sorted through cupboards, storage drawers under beds and even the attic, but now that she'd been given a definite date to be out of the house by, the whole process had an increased sense of urgency.

There was a little more to be done in the attic, but she needed to keep an ear out for someone calling around late morning, and so she decided to start on the huge linen cupboard.

A beautiful old wardrobe stood in Cathy's old room. It had been Winnie's linen store for years and she began pulling out piles of sheets and pillowcases, single duvet covers with fairy patterns and cartoon characters – why had she held on to these for so long? She started throwing everything onto the bed but quickly realised all she was doing was making a mess. So, she started again, arranging a keep pile, a throw-out pile and another pile for undecided-as-yet.

It was late morning before Winnie had finished clearing out the wardrobe. She'd seriously misjudged the task – she had hoped to have done a lot more by now. As she decided it was time for a tea-break, there was a knock on the back door, and she hurried downstairs.

Before stepping outside, she lifted the car keys off their hook and went out to join the nice-looking young man and together they went into the garage.

He was all smiles, nodding, as he looked over Doug's car, as if to acknowledge to himself, he'd made a good decision in making this purchase. He'd come to look at it only yesterday morning and had paid a small deposit there and then.

He handed over an envelope full of cash. 'This is for you. You might want to count it, but I promise you it's all there.'

'Oh, I trust you,' said Winnie, at the same time, wondering if she should, and then managing to convince herself that he looked to be very trustworthy. 'And these are for you.' She handed over the keys to Doug's car, swallowing down the lump in her throat as she did so. She was very gradually getting better at dealing with these sentimental moments.

She opened the garage doors. The new owner of Doug's car wasted no time in climbing into it and starting it up.

'Cheers, I'll look after it,' he called through the open window, as he very carefully drove the big black car out of the garage, and away down the road.

'Yes, please do,' whispered Winnie as she watched her husband's car disappear into the distance.

For some reason, Winnie had been very elusive over the last couple of weeks. She always seemed to be busy with something or other. Gloria had popped in a couple of times to find her either clearing things out or in the middle of endless cleaning. She never seemed to want any help, and so she'd left her to get on with it.

Feeling a little lost today, she'd sent Bernard a text message to see if he fancied a chat. Good old Bernard, he always fancied a chat and they'd just had a very lively one in which he confirmed he was planning to visit in a few weeks' time.

She was now all smiles and switched the kettle on to boil, and while it was boiling, she slipped on her jacket and decided to take a stroll around her garden. Gloria took many strolls around her garden lately, ostensibly to check on the roses and any other shrubbery that might need a little prune.

But really, she was planning to have a peek over at next door to see if there was any activity. Gloria walked the length of her long thin garden and then turned and strolled back, very slowly. She knew that Ada's son would sell up quickly, but even so she was astonished to return from France to see the 'For Sale' sign replaced with a 'Sold' one – that was incredibly quick work. Someone must have got the place for a steal.

She had no idea who'd bought it and was still anxious in case she awoke one morning to find the diggers had arrived.

She heard the gate click open and turned to see her friendly postman coming down the path towards her. He nodded towards Ada's cottage.

'Found out who's moving in yet?'

'No, haven't found out anything. All a bit too mysterious for my liking.'

'It's been empty for a good few weeks now, eh?'

'Yes. I've seen the odd person mooching around, measuring up maybe. But I don't like to go and ask anything; it would seem like I'm being nosey. I mean, I'm being nosey now, but this is covert nosing.'

'Don't worry I won't tell anyone.'

'Please don't. Or I will have to kill you.'

'Now you're scaring me. Here's your post, I'm off.'

They both laughed, and Gloria's postman waved as he went back up the path. She had a letter or maybe a card, her address had been handwritten and she thought she recognised the writing.

Back in her warm kitchen, she re-boiled the kettle and tore open the envelope. It was an invite, and she was right; it was from Winnie. It was an invitation to the next Wine Club meeting. It was some way off yet, not until early December, on Thursday as usual and at seventy-thirty as usual. But there was a special notice in bold type asking the invitee to take note of the different address.

17 Meadowsweet Lane, Ducks Folly

Gloria was confused – that was her address. What was Winnifred doing holding the wine club at her home and without even speaking to her about it? And on top of that, she hadn't even written the address correct, Gloria's cottage was number 15. She looked at the envelope, even more confused, Winnie had managed to get it right there.

Number 17 was Ada's place. And then the penny dropped.

'Oh my goodness. I don't believe it. The sneaky thing.' Gloria laughed out loud, delighted and not a little relieved. Winnie had bought Ada's cottage – she was to be her new neighbour.

Chapter 36

It was bonfire night and Winnie and Gloria were on their way back from the village pub. They'd enjoyed a couple of glasses of hot port punch and watched the slightly disappointing firework display. Fortunately, the impressive bonfire more than made up for it as they stood beside it warming their faces in the heat.

They'd finished their drinks and as a light drizzle had started to fall, they decided to head back. Inside Gloria's cottage, she put the kettle on for coffee. It was chilly inside, and Gloria switched the heating on.

'How about lighting a fire Wynne? You're the expert – the logs are in the basket there.'

Winnie smiled and set to. She soon had a good fire blazing away throwing out heat into the small room. She was thinking how much she was looking forward to building a fire in her own place soon. Gloria brought in the coffees, and they sat next to each other on the sofa.

'Thanks for taking me in, Glo. I know I've said it before, but I do appreciate it.'

'Yes, I know. You've said so a hundred times. It's no problem. It's nice having you here. I'm going to miss you when you go next door.'

'Hm, you'll be glad to have me out the way by the time Bernard gets here.'

Gloria just smiled.

'Anyway, next weekend hopefully, I'll be moving in. The electrics and heating should both be finished

299

by then. And the windows too, they've made a good start on them.'

'They have. They're looking very smart.'

'And the conservatory people should be here on Monday. It's all happening.'

'I'm chuffed to bits for you Wynne. It's all very exciting.'

'Yes, it is,' agreed Winnie. It was all very exciting, and she was looking forward to moving into her new home.

Chapter 37

Cathy and Hannah arrived at the same time and parked next to each other on their mother's newly gravelled drive.

'Good timing,' said Hannah, carrying a bottle of Winnie's favourite red wine.

'Yes, couldn't have timed it better. How are you?' Cathy gave her sister a kiss on the cheek. She'd brought an arrangement of flowers – winter reds and berries and lots of dark green foliage - as a home-warming present.

'I'm OK. Come on let's get inside, it's freezing.'

They navigated their way carefully down the rickety path, avoiding oddments of building rubble and slippery patches of mud.

Winnie was standing at the open door waiting for them.

'Come on in, it's bitter out there, isn't it?'

The girls went in and were immediately swathed in warmth.

'Oh, it's so cosy in here Mum,' said Hannah, peeking into the kitchen to see Gloria making coffee.

Winnie planned to have a small extension built on the back of the cottage which would provide her with a much bigger kitchen and dining area. At the moment it was very snug with just the four of them in there.

The area to the side of the cottage had been cleared of weeds and the base for the conservatory had been laid. Eventually, it would lead off direct from the kitchen. It was a large structure and apart from being a comfortable summer room, it could also double as a more formal dining room, but its main purpose was where she would hold the wine club meetings.

'It's going to be a huge room, Mum,' said Hannah looking out the window.

'Yes, well, I'm hoping it looks bigger than it will be, at this stage.'

'That doesn't make much sense.'

'You know I mean – it won't look so big once it's properly finished with windows and everything.'

'I suppose it needs to be big. You need somewhere to put all your stuff.'

Winnie's furniture and boxes had been stored at Cathy's in her huge garage, and this morning a removal van had collected the lot and transported them to Winnie's new home. Gloria had been helping her since first thing but there were still dozens of packing boxes they hadn't even opened yet.

'Come on, I'll give you the tour.'

Cathy and Hannah had only seen the cottage once before, just after Winnie had bought it. Hannah could see its potential, but Cathy had been horrified at the pokey rooms, dark and cold.

'I've had quite a bit of work done while I've been staying at Gloria's. There's still lots more to do but you'll see it's quite different now with a lick of fresh paint – even that makes a huge difference.'

She was right. The entire cottage, walls and ceilings, had been painted white which made the whole place look fresh and clean and bright.

'It's a blank canvas now, and I can take my time deciding exactly how I want it. I'd love to put down new carpets, but I'll be patient and wait until the worst of the building work is done.'

Cathy was very quiet as they went around, and Winnie understood it would take a while for her to get used to it. She'd wandered off into the smallest bedroom and stood at the window looking out at the beautiful landscape.

Winnie and Hannah gave her a minute while they took a look at the other rooms, all meeting back on the little landing.

Cathy sniffed. Winnie knew the emotion of it all was getting to her.

'It's nearly one year, isn't it? I can't believe a whole year has gone by.'

Winnie put her arm around her daughter's shoulder and gave a squeeze.

'Come on, let's get back downstairs.'

They congregated back in the kitchen where Gloria had set out their cups of tea and some mince pies.

'Ah, this is pretty Glo. And where did you get those from?' Winnie asked, pointing at the pies.

'They're in all the shops Wynne – it is nearly Christmas.'

'No, I mean – you've been with me all morning. Where did you magic them up from?'

Gloria placed her hand gently on Winnie's arm as she sat down. 'Winnie, I only live next door!'

A few weeks later and Winnie was getting ready for her first wine club meeting in her new home. There was a great deal to do – it was to be more of a home-warming party and Christmas party rolled into one rather than a structured wine club meeting, and accordingly, it was a non-fee-paying week.

She'd been busy all morning, baking and tidying and trying to clear the garden. She was surprised Gloria hadn't appeared yet to help out. Soon remedy that, she thought, and slipped out the back door and across to Gloria's garden. Winne and Gloria had agreed to remove the old rickety fence that divided their gardens, deciding instead to mark the boundary with a row of small lavender bushes, leaving the area directly next to each of their doors clear, giving them both easy access.

Winnie had previously had the odd doubt about moving next door to a friend, but they were soon dismissed. It was an absolute delight having Gloria next door.

Gloria was in her kitchen, sitting at the table with her feet propped up on a chair and reading a magazine. She looked up and smiled as she saw Winnie approach, and got up to let her in.

'Good timing, I was just making tea. Are you stopping for a cup?'

'No, and nor are you. We haven't got time for that. Get your boots on and come and help me – there's stacks to do before tonight.'

'My goodness, you can be such a bully! I'm not sure about having you for a neighbour.'

'Shut up, or I won't invite you to my party.'

'You have to invite me otherwise I'll complain about the noise.'

Winnie had been shopping for new Christmas decorations. She threw most of the old stuff away that they'd brought out year after year for nostalgic reasons. Of course, there were a few things she couldn't bear to part with – Christmas tree decorations the girls had made at school and a collection of very old baubles that held so many special memories.

The two women decorated the kitchen and the new conservatory. Strings of fairy lights were hung at every window. She had picked up lots of fresh greenery from the village florist and together they hung it across the mantlepieces in the kitchen and the living room. Winnie had already arranged several vases of Christmas coloured flowers and placed them about the rooms. By the time everyone arrived, it was dark outside, but the inside of Winnie's new home was a fairy-lit cottage of magic.

Cliff and Lulu arrived first. They had become particularly good friends with Winnie and had kept in touch over the last few months. They had also kept her up to date regarding Peter and Rita, and so neither she nor Gloria was surprised to see them arrive together.

For this week only, partners were invited, and Zoe arrived with her husband Lawrence. Zoe was wearing a stunning silky dress in Christmas berry red. She and her husband looked very happy together. Shortly after, Muriel and Mary arrived together – a united force against their difficult home situations, and the fact they could never invite their husbands to a party like this. Lawrence smiled and nodded, he recognised them both as being Zoe's first paying customers to her social media advisory service. She'd helped set them up on Facebook and join some appropriate support groups for their needs.

Winnie had taken the brave step of inviting more of her friends from her hospital days – lovely people she'd lost touch with over the last year. She was delighted to see Fran and Sue heading up the small crowd making their way up the garden path. There would be lots of catching up to do this evening.

Kerry and Ayisha arrived with their boyfriends, dressed as if they were attending The Oscars. Winnie was flattered but then reasoned they probably weren't planning to stay long and were going on to another Christmas party.

Peter and Rita finally arrived, arm in arm, Peter as always, the perfect gentleman. He gave Winnie a kiss on the cheek and gave her a rather clumsily wrapped gift.

'It's a decanter,' he informed her. 'Might come in handy next year,' he said with an almost cheeky grin. 'Oh yes, and another thing – coffee beans.'

'Sorry Peter?' Winne was laughing. 'You'll have to explain.'

'I just read something, in a wine magazine. Apparently, a small sniff of coffee beans is an effective way to cleanse your palate when wine tasting. It resets the button on your nose!'

'OK, I'll remember that, and I'll get some coffee beans in just for you.'

Peter wandered off looking very pleased with himself, to get himself and Rita a drink.

Helen arrived alone, calm and collected as ever, she was still enveloped in a little cloud of sadness.

Winnie watched her as Peter saw to pouring a drink for her.

'Don't worry,' whispered Gloria following her thoughts. 'She'll find her happy ever after.'

'I hope so,' said Winnie.

'And then she'll realise she's made another terrible mistake and back out at the last minute.'

Winnie slapped her playfully on the shoulder. 'Oh you! You can be rotten sometimes.'

'I'm not being rotten. She just needs to discover exactly what it is she wants.'

'Come on, let's get a drink.' Winnie led her to the drinks table set out in the conservatory. She'd stocked it with what she hoped she remembered was everyone's favourite wine. Sauvignon Blanc for Lulu and Shiraz for Cliff and Muriel. But there was plenty of other Christmas booze too.

'No Sheila tonight?' Gloria asked.

'She replied to say she was coming.' She's probably on her way, having a treacherous journey, we'll no doubt hear all about it when she gets here.' They both smiled, and at that moment they looked out the conservatory windows to see Sheila coming down the garden path, both wondering who the man was accompanying her.

As Sheila came into the conservatory, it was obvious that she and her man were together, and everyone was smiling around her.

The party was soon in full swing. Kerry had checked with Winnie if it was OK for her boyfriend to play some music on his phone. Winnie had agreed but was a little concerned – what did twenty-somethings like to listen to at Christmas parties? She needn't have worried; Christmas classics were soon filling the room and later as things were finally winding down, the melancholy sounds of Christmas carols brought an emotional glow to the party.

Everyone had left and it was just Winnie and Gloria sitting in the fairy-lit conservatory.

'That was a superb party. Well done to you Winnie.'

'And to you too. You did as much to help.'

'It was a brave thing to do – at this time of year.' Gloria placed her hand over Winnie's and gave a little well-meaning squeeze. 'And how about Sheila? How lovely to see her with someone.'

'Yes, it is. That was a great surprise.'

'And talking of surprises.' Gloria leant across and retrieved a gift-wrapped package that she'd hidden behind the drinks table earlier. 'I have a surprise for you. This is just a little early Christmas present.'

Winnie tore the wrapping off and laughed as she took out a beautifully soft cashmere sweater, in a soft coral red. 'OK, I do like the colour.'

'Good. It's about time you started wearing red.'

Winnie smiled. 'OK, you win. Now I have a surprise for you too.' Winnie got up and went out to the kitchen, returning with two envelopes in her hand – a small one and a large one. She handed the small one to Gloria who opened it to find an invitation inside. She took a moment to read it and looked up, puzzled.

'You're inviting me to France, next month?'

'Yep, an all-expenses paid trip, as a thank-you for being such a good friend over this last year. You've invited me away enough times, and so I thought I'd better get in before Bernard snaps up all your spare time.'

'I'll always have time for my friends, don't you worry about that.'

'Good because I want your help with this.' Winnie opened the large envelope and took out some paperwork and spread it out on the table.

Gloria looked through the papers, still not understanding. At first, she thought she was looking at details of the place they would be staying.

'But these properties are all for sale.'

'Exactly. And I'm going to buy one. Just a small place – right in the middle of the Loire Valley. My own little bolt hole in the middle of one of the biggest wine regions in France.'

Gloria was beaming. 'Oh Winnie, that's fantastic. Congratulations. You deserve it.'

'Thanks Glo. Hey, maybe sometime next year, we could organise a Wine Club trip over there. Do a tour of the vineyards all together. Wouldn't that be wonderful? Shall we drink a toast – I think there's some Champagne left in the fridge.'

'Actually, Cliff persuaded me to try some of that French Syrah earlier. And, I don't believe I'm really saying this, but it's really very nice. How about we forget the bubbly, and have a nice glass of red.'

I hope you enjoyed reading A Nice Glass of Red and if you did, I would be very grateful if you would leave me a review on Amazon, letting me and other readers know what you think.

www.JennieAlexander.biz

JennieAlexander@hotmail.co.uk

Other books by Jennie Alexander

The Beach Hut

Ella Peters used to enjoy her good life, including the little things like the first buds on a newly planted rose. But when her husband leaves her, she struggles to find pleasure in anything. However, Ella is determined to rebuild her life and makes plans for a fresh start. But she is soon to realise that no matter how far you run, you can't escape yourself.

Libby Pinkney thinks she has life under control; with two well-behaved teenagers, the biggest house with the best sea view and an increasingly impressive presence within the local community. But when a new neighbour moves into the old cottage next door, her well–ordered life threatens to tumble around her like a house of cards.

The beach hut, on England's beautiful Hampshire coast stands bravely against the elements. Inside, it is as individual as its owner; a cosy home from home, a love nest and a place to shelter from the sun or rain. It plays witness to events that bring joy and tragedy and provides a little retreat for those who seek solace there.

Winnifred Cottage

Abigail Morgan's world has fallen apart; she returns from work to find her home ablaze. The cause is a mystery, but her partner Jack is suspiciously involved somehow.

A welcome escape route presents itself in the form of Winnifred Cottage situated in the heart of The Lake District – a summer holiday paradise. It has recently been left to Abbie in her grandmother's will, but her sister Jilly is not at all happy about her decision to make it her home.

Abbie has grand plans for the cottage, but they are not to be. It bears no resemblance to her memories of the place, and she is left wondering if she has made the worst mistake of her life.

Great aunts Eva and Lilleth hoard their own secrets, and both are suspicious as to why Winnifred Cottage has been left to Abigail. Their wise and charismatic friend Jed Tobin appears to know more than he's letting on, but everyone has to wait until he's good and ready to reveal all.

Abbie's sister Jilly descends for a summer holiday with her family, and with her visit comes a storm of another sort – the worst weather for years. Torrential rain causes chaos in the village of Kirkby Bridge and people are forced to evaluate what's really important to them.

Tied with a Ribbon – A Christmas Story

It's only four weeks until Christmas but Alice has had a tough year and is struggling to get into the Christmas spirit. As the owner of a gift-wrapping shop 'Ribbons and Bows', this is her busiest time of year and as much as she'd like to, Alice cannot possibly escape all the seasonal festivities.

Dena has worries of her own, not least of all, financial ones which are threatening to put a dampener on Christmas for her and her family.

These two life-long friends do their best to help each other out at this particularly poignant time of year when it's all too easy to feel alone.

Or maybe it will take some festive magic to help things along. A guardian angel perhaps or maybe the loving, helping hand of a certain ghost from Christmas past.

The Reunion Party

Five young women become good friends at The Ashford Chefs Academy where they've signed up for three years intensive training.

Talented and passionate, they are also wildly ambitious - determined to succeed in their chosen profession.

Imogen Ravenscroft is not included in their little group. She's the one born with a silver spoon in her mouth; the girl who has everything. But a decade after graduation it's Imogen who's holding the Reunion Party.

Ellen and Janey, Alicia, Fran and Mel reflect on the last ten years, reconciling their hopes and dreams of the past with what has become their reality. Inevitably, they contemplate how they might compare to their former friends. Who might be found lacking?

The Reunion Party is a huge success. Good friends reunite and inspirational stories bounce round the room like champagne corks. True to form, Imogen has spared no expense; her generosity and kindness still a mystery, but soon to be revealed.

Live Laugh Love

In a pretty village in the Surrey countryside, life is good for neighbours Hope Clements and Josie Bell. Both are happily married and working hard on their hopes and dreams for the future.

Hope has prepared meticulously for six months and is ready to set off for her dream holiday – six weeks at a well-being retreat in Bali.

But something happens the night before departure which threatens not only her long-awaited holiday but everything she's worked for in life.

Josie is on hand to provide comfort and support. But what starts out as a seemingly harmless favour soon forces her to reassess her own life, threatening to destroy her own happiness in the process.

It seems to Hope that every way she turns, she is met with lies and deceit, even from her daughter who is supposedly away studying at university.

How will she manage to maintain the roles of wife and mother and carer in the face of such dishonesty? And will she ever find the courage to challenge those in question?

The Coco Club Series

A four-book series set in 1920s London with plenty of fun and frivolity.

Genevieve (Book 1)

A year to the day on her first wedding anniversary, Lady Genevieve Pilkington-Hugh finally conceded, after too many gin fizzes, that her marriage to Howard was an unutterable sham.

But what can she do? In 1923, options were limited.

And then...

Genevieve's racy Parisienne friend introduces her to The Coco Club, and life begins to improve in rather surprising ways.

Blue-Bell (Book 2)

Delphine (Book 3)

Lily (Book 4)

Gift Wrapped (Non-fiction)

Basic Techniques and Exquisite Gift Wrapping

Creative gift-wrapping adds to the joy of both giving and receiving.

You may be surprised to learn that this form of paperwork craft is easy and many of the elaborate effects shown in this book are actually very simple.

It provides step-by-step photo instructions showing how to wrap a gift to make it look both impressive and stylish.

There's advice on the best type of wrapping paper to use for each project and finally a chapter on ribbons and bows to add the final finishing touches to your gift.

The Owl who made Friends with the Moon

Oswald the Owl may be a nocturnal bird, but he keeps getting lost in the wood.

Luckily, he soon makes a friend who helps him find his way back home.

Enjoy the rhyming story in this children's picture book, ideal bedtime reading for young ones.

Made in the USA
Middletown, DE
23 February 2024